"Claire MacLeary has, with little fuss or fanfare, written a crime series that subverts and rejuvenates the crime genre, and that is as welcome as it is admirable." SCOTS WHAY HAE

"Gripping." GOOD HOUSEKEEPING

"A terrific writer." KIRSTY GUNN, SCOTSMAN

"Dynamite ... The author loves to smash gender and age stereotypes." SHARON BAIRDEN, CHAPTER IN MY LIFE

"Absorbing. This is a thoroughly entertaining series that could run and run." SUNDAY HERALD

"You should make time to get to know Maggie and Wilma." LOUISE FAIRBAIRN, SCOTSMAN

"A great crime novel [featuring] two of Scottish fiction's most engaging characters." SCOTS WHAY HAE

"An utterly riveting and often unexpected read, absolutely brilliantly done." LIZ LOVES BOOKS BLOG

"Strong advocacy of and for women ... that's what makes this such an engrossing read." LIVE AND DEADLY

"Incredibly gritty and compelling ... absolutely superb writing." THE QUIET KNITTER

"A brilliant new talent for the lover of crime ... a vibrant crime partnership and sound forensic expertise." SUE BLACK, DBE, FORENSIC ANTHROPOLOGIST

"A refreshingly different approach to the private investigator genre ... a fast-paced tale." SHIRLEY WHITESIDE, *HERALD*

"MacLeary's prose is assured and engaging, bursting with the liveliness of the Aberdonian vernacular ... an impressive debut." RAVEN CRIME READS

DEATH
DROP

Claire MacLeary

CONTRABAND 🔒

Contraband is an imprint of Saraband

Published by Saraband,
3 Clairmont Gardens
Glasgow, G3 7LW

Copyright © Claire MacLeary 2022

ISBN: 9781913393618

10 9 8 7 6 5 4 3 2 1

Printed and bound in Great Britain by Clays Ltd, Elcograf S.p.A.

Supported by
The National Lottery®
through Creative Scotland

CREATIVE SCOT LAND
ALBA | CHRUTHACHAIL

MIX
Paper from
responsible sources
FSC® C018072
FSC
www.fsc.org

For Ged

I

Vinnie

The body swung from a crossbeam.

Police Constable Ian Souter dashed forward. 'Give us a hand,' he panted, shouldering the weight.

'Bit late for that.' Fellow PC Dave Miller clocked the bulging eyes, the clenched jaw. Stepping gingerly around the puddle that pooled the concrete floor, he wrapped his arms around the woman's legs and heaved.

She was tall: five ten at a guess. Slight, but toned. Souter groped at the throat for a pulse. None. The length of nylon rope was knotted at the side of the neck. Not a cry for help then. This wasn't Souter's first death by hanging. Nor would it be the last.

He took in the figure-hugging frock, the perfectly groomed blonde hair, the scarlet-painted lips.

Classic.

Wanting to look her best, even in death.

Especially in death.

The drip-drip of escaping urine drew his gaze downwards. In the pool of piss, a white stiletto shoe lay on its side.

'Can I let go now?' Miller huffed. 'This is minging.'

'Give us a mo.'

Souter's eyes flicked back to the body. White shoes? He wouldn't have thought. And that hair? Perfect. Too perfect. His instincts sharpened. Might be a wig.

His mind whirred. Cancer? Could that be the reason—?

'Big feet.' Miller broke his train of thought. Holding grimly on, he jerked a gelled head at the shoe's twin, which still shod one stockinged foot.

'For God's sake,' Souter spat. Trust Dave to say something puerile.

Except … He looked more closely. His partner had a point, right enough.

It was only then he spotted the telltale bulge between the corpse's legs.

Harcus & Laird

'Glad that's out the way,' Maggie said, biting into her toastie.

Mouth turned down, Wilma groaned, 'You and me, both. If I have to spend another minute on admin, I'll go off my head.'

They'd spent most of the morning wrangling over billing hours, and had agreed a ten-minute break for a piece and a fly cup before Wilma went back next door. A divorcee, she'd moved into the adjoining bungalow in Aberdeen's west end suburb of Mannofield on her re-marriage.

'It's part and parcel of being private investigators,' Maggie soothed. 'We've broken the back of it. You'll feel better when you've had your lunch.'

'Private investigators my arse. I'm sick to death sitting at that computer: online telephone directory, electoral roll, I could recite them in my sleep. When I took on this job, I thought I'd be out there doing exciting stuff: covert surveillance, high-speed car chases—'

Running an exasperated hand through a mass of titian curls, Maggie shot back, 'I've had enough car chases to last me a lifetime. And you are out there. Most days, anyhow.'

'Doing what?' Wilma demanded, spitting toast crumbs. 'Process serving. Taking precognitions. Sitting through court proceedings.' She took a thirsty swallow. 'Where's the fun in that?'

'We've had enough excitement: drug running, money laundering, people trafficking, prostitution. And that's only two of the major cases we've been involved in since George died and you talked me into taking on the business.'

'Not forgetting that dead student in St Machar kirkyard.'

'Would I ever?'

Fishing a blob of cheese and pickle out of her cleavage, Wilma popped it in her mouth. 'Give me an outside job any day.' With a grimace, she added, 'I'd even settle for a marital.'

'We should be so lucky.' Marital surveillance cases had dwindled with the easing of divorce legislation, and infidelity was as likely to be picked up on a mobile phone or social media.

With a sly sideways glance, Wilma added, 'Now, if we were to happen on another body.'

'Don't even go there.'

'Seriously. 'I was watching CSI last night, and...'

'You're letting your imagination run away with you again,' Maggie remonstrated, pink-faced. 'How often do I have to tell you this isn't a game?'

Flapping her hands in the air, Wilma said, 'Calm down.'

'I'm perfectly calm. But I repeat, we've had enough excitement to last a lifetime. What the business needs is a period of consolidation.'

'More bloody desk work, is that what you're saying?'

Maggie buried her nose in her mug of tea.

She was saved by her mobile's insistent ringtone.

Reaching for her phone, she scanned the caller display. Then, putting a finger to her lips, threw Wilma a warning look.

'Harcus & Laird,' she announced confidently. 'How may I help?'

Jean

'Can we run through this again?' Souter asked, one eye on the woman who sat opposite, the other on Miller, whose fingertips were drumming on his trouser leg like a demented concert pianist.

Jean Sellars raised a tear-streaked face. 'Alright.'

After they'd contacted the deceased's wife at her place of work and run through the formalities of every copper's nightmare – the death intimation – the pair were installed in the pin-neat living room of her end-terrace in Heathryfold, north of the city.

Souter looked down at his notebook. 'You last saw your husband, Vincent—'

'Vinnie. That's what I call...' With a shudder, she corrected herself, 'Called him.' She broke down in tortured sobs.

'Vinnie,' Souter repeated, with a sideways look at Miller, whose fingers were now tracing patterns on the sofa. They'd agreed Souter would lead, but a bit of back-up wouldn't have gone amiss. 'You last saw him at breakfast time. That would be around 7 a.m., is that right?'

Jean nodded. 'Before we left for work.'

'You work as a care assistant?' Souter asked with a small nod of encouragement. If he could get the woman to open up, they'd get another couple of actions under their belts before dinner time.

'Yes. It was all I could get when the bairns were wee. And after they left home, well...' She gave a hopeless shrug. 'I'd been doing it that long, it wasn't worth the bother of looking for something better.'

'You've a son and daughter, is that right? We've been trying to con-tact them.'

'Harvey's away. Travels with his job. Lauren works at Foresterhill. Her phone's maybe switched off.'

'And Vinnie?' Souter ventured. 'You said he was in the building trade?'

'That's right. Man and boy. Left school at sixteen. Worked his way up to site manager. He built our extension.' She waved a hand towards the rear of the house, face brightening for an instant.

'Did he have problems at work?'

'No more than usual. Building sites can get a bit mad, sometimes.'

'What about financial worries?'

'The house is paid for. We don't get out much, not working full-time, and the kids are well set up, so, no.'

'Had he shown any signs of depression lately? Been to the doctor, maybe?'

'Nothing like that.'

'And your relationship, there hadn't been a row?'

Jean Sellars' face twisted into a sneer. 'You wouldn't understand, young loon like you, but when you've been married as long as me and Vinnie there's not much worth rowing about.'

'I'll remember that,' said Souter, his expression dubious. Didn't take much to set his Shirley off. 'Can you think of anything he's done recently that seemed out of character?'

She shook her head.

'In short,' Miller piped up. 'You're saying there were no prior indications your husband intended to take his life.'

'None that I can think of.'

'If it's okay,' Souter said, coming back in. 'I'd like to ask you something more personal.'

Jean looked back at him, empty-eyed.

'I have to tell you that when your husband's body was found...' He hesitated, reluctant to inflict further misery. 'He was dressed in women's clothing.'

'No.' The word spoken with such vehemence Souter jolted upright. He darted a glance at Miller, who was equally straight-backed, all of a sudden.

Gathering himself, Souter asked, 'Do you have any idea why?'

Jean Sellars looked from Souter to Miller and back again, a tumult of expressions flitting across her face. 'No,' she said, again. Quietly,

7

this time, as if she were talking to herself. Hugging thin arms to her chest she rocked back and forth. 'No.'

You Should Be So Lucky

'Did you hear that?' Wilma said, catching a clip of the news on the car radio.

'What?' Maggie asked, absent-mindedly. They were heading to the Forties Industrial Estate at Altens to meet a corporate client, and she'd been rehearsing bullet points in her head.

'Heathryfold man. Hung himself in his garage.'

'Poor soul. You'd have to be desperate to do a thing like that.'

'What they're not telling you,' Wilma said archly, 'Fella was in fancy dress.'

Maggie reached to switch off the radio. 'Meaning what?'

'Full drag, suspenders an' all.'

'How do you know? No, don't tell me. They brought him up to ARI.'

Wilma turned an injured face. 'Don't mock. My wee hospital job has come in handy before now.'

'I'm not saying any different. And keep your eyes on the road.'

'Don't get your knickers in a twist.'

'There's no need to be vulgar.'

'There's no call for you to be so snooty,' said Wilma. 'An' me thinking I was telling you something.'

'A suicide? How sad.'

'Is that all you've got to say? Nae wonder the emergency services are struggling: putting taxpayers' money out on stuff like that.'

Maggie was tempted to pass comment. Her neighbour's views were frequently ill-informed. Plus, she was a walking advert for the black economy. She bit her tongue.

'The NHS especially,' Wilma ran on. 'Ye canna get near a doctors' surgery nowadays, far less a hospital. As for the wee bitties extra...' Hoiking up one leg of her trouser suit, she inspected a well-developed calf. 'I could fair do with getting my veins stripped. Nae chance. Not unless I'm willing to...'

Maggie yelled, 'You just jumped a red light.'

'Oops!' said Wilma, stepping on the gas.

'How did you come by this information, anyhow?'

'Texted one of the paramedics.'

'Don't you think that's...?'

With a flick of her blonde ponytail, Wilma finished the sentence. '...a welcome diversion from feckin deskwork. And there's more. My pal told me high-end underwear you wouldn't believe: Coco-something-or-other.' Turning, she gave Maggie a dunt in the ribs.

'Don't start,' Maggie snapped, smarting from the allusion. Not long before, she'd splurged on expensive underpinnings in anticipation of a hot date.

'All I'm trying to say is, suicide was that well turned out you would never have known. Not until...'

'I get the picture.'

They lapsed into an uncomfortable silence. Then, 'Last cross-dresser I came on was at the bingo.'

Maggie did a double-take. 'Really?'

'Mecca in Berryden Road. Me and my pal Savannah used to go. Every Wednesday, regular as clockwork. One teatime, this quine rolls up. Near on six foot must have been. Dressed to the nines – sequins the lot – and us in our leggings.' She blasted the horn at a white van driver, giving him the finger. 'Finer-looking woman you never saw. "Meet Gloria", sez my mate. Well, Gloria stuck out her mitt. False nails. I stuck out mine. She gripped me that hard I could hear my knuckles crack. And the palm of her hand. Real navvie's hand. Calloused to hell. "Pleased to meet you", sez Gloria. "You, too," sez I, bare able to speak for the pain.' She sniffed. 'It was then I clocked the fake tits.'

Maggie stifled a giggle. Then, remembering what had occasioned Wilma's story, she cautioned, 'You shouldn't be so quick to pass judgement.'

'Thought that was your department.'

'Was,' Maggie retorted, with heavy emphasis. 'This detecting business has taught me things are rarely black and white. Besides, you can't use that sort of language.'

'Sez who?'

'Hate Crime Bill.' After protests from bodies as disparate as publishers and police over its implications for free speech, the heavily amended legislation had passed into law in 2021. 'We get a bad enough press in our line of business without breaking the law.'

'Huh.' Wilma pulled a sulky face. Changing down, she overtook a line of lorries.

'Wilma,' Maggie urged. 'Try not to write us off. My blood pressure's already sky-high.'

Cutting in, Wilma grinned. 'You should be so lucky.'

Chisolm

In North East Division's Queen Street HQ Detective Inspector Allan Chisolm wasted no time. 'Heathryfold incident. Who'll fill me in?'

'I will,' DS Brian Burnett offered, straining forward in his seat. 'IC-1 male. Vincent Sellars. Age 47. Suspected suicide.'

'Who called it in?'

'Neighbour. Noticed Sellars' van hadn't moved from the drive. Wondered if he needed help. Went to investigate. Found him hanging in the garage.'

'First responders?'

'Souter and Miller. I've their report here.'

With a sigh, Chisolm said, 'Not the brightest in the box. What have they got to say?'

'Put all the routine questions: medical, money problems, marital strife. Wife ruled out all of them.'

'No secrets, then: second family, drink/drug addiction, gambling habit?'

'Seems not. The Sellars appear to have been a regular couple.'

'So regular the husband took a notion to top himself,' fellow sergeant, Bob Duffy observed with grim irony. 'Begs the question, why?'

'Married twenty-plus years,' Brian read. 'Two grown kids. Own their home. Nothing untoward there, or on the deceased's mobile or laptop.'

'The kids, have they been notified?'

'Lauren, the daughter, works at ARI. She's been notified and taken to her mother's address. The son is out of town. We're still trying to contact him.'

'Any evidence of involvement by an outside party?'

'No, boss. There is just one thing,' Brian ventured, turning a page. 'It says here Vincent Sellars was in full drag.'

'And you didn't think to mention at the outset?'

'Sorry,' he answered from beneath lowered lids. 'I've not long got the report, and the way things are—'

'You don't need to tell me,' Chisolm snapped. His job was a daily balancing act between escalating crime and diminished resources.

'Might not be that significant,' volunteered Douglas Dunn, a graduate entrant never slow to venture an opinion. 'Loads of guys like to dress up.'

'Present company included?' Susan Strachan joshed.

Colour crept from the nape of her fellow DC's neck to the roots of his carefully mussed hair.

Chisolm silenced her with a stern look. Eyeballing Brian he said, 'The hanging. Give me the details.'

'Rope secured on a crossbeam of the garage.'

'Victim climbed up how?'

'A-frame aluminium stepladder.'

'Where was it when the body was found?'

'Pretty close.'

'Still upright?'

'Yes.'

Brow furrowed, Chisolm asked, 'Are you familiar with the term "erotic asphyxiation"?'

Miserably, Brian nodded.

'Does the name Gareth Williams ring any bells?' Getting no response, he expanded, 'MI6 spy.'

Susan said, 'I remember, now. Wasn't he locked inside a zipped sports bag?'

'He was, indeed. After conducting experiments, the investigation concluded he died as the result of a sex game gone wrong.'

'You thinking Vinnie Sellars was doing the same?' asked Duffy.

'I'm saying it's an unexplained death. We have to treat it as suspicious until we determine otherwise.'

Consulting the report in front of him, Brian protested, 'The way the rope was knotted, Sellars had obviously read up on the subject.

Knew its position would determine whether the effects of traction were unilateral or bilateral. Calculated how long the noose would take to do its work. So...'

Douglas picked up. '...it's not unreasonable to assume.'

'You've been in the job long enough,' said Chisolm, 'I shouldn't have to remind you: assume nothing, question everything.'

Cheeks aflame, Douglas stole a sideways glance at Susan, who was struggling to suppress her mirth.

'This puts a different complexion on the incident. Get back out there, you two. Have another word with Mrs Sellars. Speak to the neighbours. Visit his place of work. Establish the full facts. Got that?' Chisolm turned the force of his glare on Douglas, who was fixated with the double cuffs of his button-down shirt.

'Boss.'

Turning to Brian, 'We've wasted enough time. What else have you got for me?'

Brian cleared his throat. 'Same old: drugs, gangs, muggings. But before I start, is there any word on Dave's replacement?' Following a much-extended sickie, DS Wood had finally made it over the line to full pension. 'It's just, undermanned as we are, we can't do justice to...'

'I know, I know.' Running a distracted hand through his hair, Chisolm replied, 'Chance would be a fine thing.'

Colin

Colin charged through the back door. 'What's for tea?' His backpack hit the floor with a thwack. 'I'm starving.'

Maggie looked up from her laptop. 'Hadn't thought about it.'

'Ooh,' Colin groaned, sticking his head in the fridge. He rummaged for a few moments, then backed out, holding aloft a pot of mango yoghurt, 'Can I have this?'

'I suppose.' Maggie had planned to have it for lunch but got caught up. Stomach growling, she watched Colin tear off the foil cover. Pulling a spoon from the drawer, he demolished it in a matter of seconds.

'Is it okay if Ellie comes round?' he asked, tossing the empty pot in the bin. 'We've a project on climate change. Thought we could work on it together.'

'Of course.'

Lifting the lid of the empty bread bin, he pulled a tragic face. 'Weren't you going to do a shop?'

'Didn't have time. I'll do it tomorrow.'

'I sort of promised Ellie she could eat with us,' he said, hopefully.

Maggie's spirits sank. She'd been counting on a free evening to get on top of her paperwork. Still, Colin's girlfriend was a good influence. George Laird had left the force under a cloud and their son's schoolwork had suffered. She was thankful to see him back on track.

Wearily, she scraped back her chair. 'That's fine,' she said, rising. 'There's probably something in the freezer.'

'We could send out for pizzas.'

'Not this week,' Maggie said firmly. Since taking on George's fledgling detective agency she'd struggled to stay afloat, many a sleepless night spent agonising over how to pay the bills.

She dropped to a crouch and started pulling out freezer drawers, peering at fogged labels in an attempt to establish the contents. 'Here,' she said, thrusting one out. 'Tell me what it says.'

'Butternut Squash Casserole. Eugh!' Colin wrinkled his nose. 'We had that on Tuesday. Gross.'

'Well,' Maggie said. 'It's either that or...' Rubbing ice crystals off the lid with one finger. 'Macaroni Cheese.'

'Why do we have to eat Gran's stuff all the time?'

'Because, if your gran helps with the housekeeping, it frees me up to earn money. If I don't earn, I can't pay the mortgage, or...'

'Go on, say it: my school fees. Isn't that the root of the problem, that we're always short of money? If I wasn't at Gordons...'

'And if you'd applied yourself,' Maggie retorted. 'I wouldn't have to pay a tutor.'

Colin sneered, 'Now we're getting to it.'

'If you'd kept your head down like your sister.' The words were out before Maggie could stop herself.

'Don't throw Kirsty at me.'

'I'm sorry.' She reached out, contrite.

Colin batted her hand away.

Trying to keep her voice even, 'Your school fees are only one of the many outgoings I have to meet. Your sister's uni accommodation doesn't come cheap. Then there's...'

'Can't you at least get Gran to cook healthier stuff?' he interrupted. 'Like pizza?'

With a resigned shrug, Colin passed the foil container back.

'If you tell me what Ellie likes to eat,' Maggie compensated, 'I'll be better organised next time.'

Scratching his forehead, 'Salad? Avocadoes? I dunno. Oh, and you won't like this,' he said, not meeting her gaze. 'I ripped my rugby shirt at practice. You couldn't sew it up, could you?'

'I don't believe this.' Maggie threw her hands up in despair. 'That shirt is only weeks old. Have you any idea how much it cost?'

'Sorry,' he mumbled. Turning, 'Can I go and get changed now? Only, Ellie...'

'Whatever,' Maggie cried. Seething with frustration, she thrust the container back into the freezer and slammed the door.

Ian

'Total madhouse up there,' Wilma said. 'Ambulances nose to tail, folk parked on trolleys.'

'Don't know why you stick it,' Ian grumbled. He'd picked Wilma up after her shift as a healthcare assistant, and they were in the Aldi supermarket at Cornhill. 'When we got together first I could see the point. But now we're well set up, there's no need.'

'It's early days. There's things I want to do, places I want to go.'

'Still...'

'Pay's not great, right enough. But I've built up benefits: super-annuation and that. Plus, the gossip's good,' she added, dropping a pack of beef mince into their trolley.

'That's more than you get from her next door.'

'Don't be so sarky.' A garlic and herb chicken joined it with a thwack.

Ian said, 'Speaking of gossip, have you heard anything on that suicide?'

'Nah.' She reached for a black pudding. 'Too busy.'

'The guys were talking about it at the garage. Turns out Dodd Benzie services the wife's car.'

'How come?'

'His mum's a neighbour. Asked a favour.'

Wilma eyed a tray of sticky toffee pudding. Salivating, she turned her back. 'That right?'

'Me, I wouldn't be seen dead in a pair of knickers.'

'Aye.' She quirked a sculpted eyebrow. 'Weel.'

Cupping a hand to his lips, Ian mouthed, 'Pervert.'

'Don't rush to judge,' Wilma said, cognisant of Maggie's stric-tures. 'There's folk that feel trapped in the wrong body.'

'Try telling that to your lot. Isn't a poofter who'd last a minute in your street.'

'Times have changed.'

'And not for the better.'

'Torry has changed: all those young Polish families that have settled there.'

Jutting his chin, Ian said, 'My point exactly. Poles canna be doing wi shirt-lifters.'

'That's a bit strong.'

'God's honest truth. In their country they have no-go areas to keep the LGBT lot out.'

'Do you mind?' objected a woman standing nearby, a couple of school-age kids in tow.

'Sorry.' Red-faced, he propelled the trolley forward at speed.

Reaching the comparative safety of the next aisle, Wilma said, 'In any case, you're confusing gender with sex. They're two separate things.' She grabbed a pack of Tunnocks Caramel Wafers and dropped them into the trolley. 'Gender identity is about who you are, sexual orientation is about who you fancy.'

Ian's jaw dropped. 'Where did you get that from?'

'Maggie says…'

'Own brand are cheaper.' Fishing the biscuits out, he put them back on the shelf.

'Aye, but the chocolate's not half as good. Flakes off. I'm sick to death picking it off the settee.' She replaced the biscuits and added another two packets for spite.

'You've changed your tune. When we first got together, you used to agree with me on every last thing.'

Wilma lofted a giant bottle of Diet Coke, swiftly followed by a two-litre bottle of Irn Bru. 'I've learned a thing or two since.'

'Aye. Load of perversions.'

'That's not what you're saying when you're glued to the telly, watching Eddie Izzard.'

'What's he got to do with it? '

'Identifies as gender-fluid.'

'"Gender-fluid",' Ian mimicked. 'Where did you get that one? No, don't tell me: Maggie Laird.'

'Jumbo haddock or battered cod?' Wilma demanded, hand hovering over an open chest freezer.

'Excuse me.' A burly man in a hi-vis vest shouldered her out of the way.

Her head swivelled. Ian was bent over a wire bin full of hand tools.

'Make your mind up,' she urged. 'This is freezing my tits.'

His head came up. 'Haddock.'

'See,' she said, 'That wasn't so hard.' She tossed a giant bag of oven chips into the trolley and slammed the freezer lid shut.

'It's not enough you've started to dress like her,' Ian persisted.

'I do not.'

'Talk like her.'

'Bollocks.' Eyeing the Caviar Face Cream, Wilma debated whether it would cure her crows' feet.

'You never used to use fancy words.'

Decided it would take more than £6.99 to do the job.

'You're beginning to sing from the same hymn sheet.'

Sighing, Wilma said, 'Can we talk about something else?'

Stony-faced, 'What's for dinner?'

Jerking a thumb at the trolley's contents, she replied, 'Take your pick. And before you say another word, all that's on my mind is a strong drink and a lie down, so you'll be making it yourself.

II

Seaton School

Maggie stood in the middle of the playground. In her second job as a part-time Pupil Support Assistant, supervising outdoor activities was just one of the duties she performed in a role that involved getting the classroom ready for lessons, helping teachers plan learning activities, complete records, manage challenging behaviour, and working one-to-one with pupils needing extra help.

On days like today, when the sky loured grey as an army blanket and an icy wind whipped sideways off the North Sea, she could have seen the job far enough. But the few hours she put in at Seaton were critical to supplementing her income from the struggling business set up by her late husband. If she lost that comfort margin, who knows how she'd end up.

All around, children tumbled, divided down the middle - as if by an invisible wall - into girls and boys. The boys awkward, all knees and elbows. The girls more collected, determinedly pursuing games or gathered, heads bent, in conspiratorial huddles.

And then one. Maggie had seen it so often, some poor child made an outcast by dint of being different. Kids were quick to sniff out weakness. Single-minded in exploitation.

Swiftly crossing the asphalt, she called, 'You okay?'

The girl continued to worry a loose stone chip with the toe of her trainer. She didn't look up.

'You must be Frances,' Maggie guessed. Her timetable hadn't yet taken her into Primary 6, but she'd been alerted by head teacher, Anne Shirreffs, to a late entrant.

The girl nodded gravely. She was tall for her age. Fine-boned. Dark hair in spikes around an elfin face. Lifting her chin, she regarded Maggie with defiant eyes. 'I'm fine.'

Maggie smiled. 'Glad to hear it. A new school can be pretty scary.

To start with, anyhow. Takes a wee while to make new friends.'

'I can look after myself.' Frances Bain said. 'And the name's
Frankie.'

Some Men

'It's what they do. Men. Some men,' Jean Sellars qualified with a furtive sideways glance. 'Handcuffs and that. Canna mind the word.'

'Fetish?' Susan queried, not daring to look at Douglas. From her experience in the job, handcuffs weren't the half of it.

'That's the one. Didn't bother me, not to begin with. You know what it's like when you're married first.' She looked to Susan for confirmation. Found none. 'You'd do anything to please your man. Well...' Biting her lower lip, '...I'd draw the line at some things.'

Jotting a note in her pocketbook, Susan continued, 'The cross-dressing, did it start straightaway?'

Jean's eyes clouded. 'Canna mind.' She'd been in her housecoat when they arrived, drowsy from the sedative her GP had prescribed.

'Was it an ongoing feature of your marriage?'

'Until the kids came along. When I fell pregnant with the first I wasn't in the mood to play games in the bedroom, and by the time we had two, well...' She drew a work-reddened hand across her forehead. '...to be honest, I'd lost interest in sex altogether.'

'How about Vinnie,' Douglas came in. 'Had he lost interest, too?'

'In the dressing up? Must have. Never happened again. As for intercourse, once a week, like most folk, I suppose. And before you ask if he got it elsewhere, the answer's no.'

'Any other sexual proclivities you can think of?'

Jean's head jerked up. 'Don't know what you mean?'

'During sex,' Douglas said, leaning in. 'Did your husband ever attempt to strangle you?'

A bitter smile curved her lips. 'Wouldn't dare try. Vinnie was a good husband. Let me have free rein in the house. Never grudged the kids a treat. Me neither. Nor raised a hand to any of us. So I don't understand why...' She broke off, shoulders heaving.

'Drink some of this,' said Susan. She'd brewed a mug of hot, sweet tea in the hope of clearing Jean Sellars' head.

Jean accepted the offering and took an obedient sip. Then, cradling the mug in both hands, she repeated, 'I don't understand. Not any of it.' She set the mug down.

'There weren't any warning signals. Anything at all that seemed a bit off?'

'Nothing. Not unless...' Picking nervously at a cuticle, she added, '...this past while, I've noticed things going missing.'

Douglas pounced. 'What things?'

'Make-up. Underwear. Nothing of any consequence. I put the blame on Lauren. Years she's been helping herself to my stuff.' She shook her head in disapproval. 'Never stopped. But she's not around that much. Even so, I asked her straight out.'

'What did she say?'

'Denied it. Said she wouldn't give my stuff house room and was I going through the change.'

Susan's eyes flashed alarm signals at Douglas. If he put both feet in it she'd kill him. 'Is Lauren staying with you?'

'Aye, but she's out at the shops.'

'How about your son?'

'He works away from home. I've tried phoning him, but he's not picking up.'

'If that's all.' Douglas pocketed his notebook and made to rise.

'And another thing,' Jean Sellars added.

He sat down again.

'Vinnie got into TV. Never showed any interest before. Not that he got the chance, not till our two left home. Up to then, bairns would be sat in front of the set day and night. Well...' Chewing off a piece of dead skin, she stuck a finger in her mouth and sucked. '...till after teatime anyroads. Then, I'd get a sit down to watch my programmes: Corrie, Eastenders. Only time I got a minute's peace.'

'You said your husband got into TV,' Douglas said, suddenly animated. 'Are we talking mainstream channels, or—?'

Susan threw him a warning look. She knew what he was after. Doubted Vinnie Sellars would have watched porn in his living room when he could do it in total privacy online.

'That's just it,' Jean Sellars said. 'The only telly I've ever known Vinnie watch is football, and that's usually on BBC1. We spoke about getting Sky. Decided it wasn't worth the money.'

'What, specifically, did your husband watch?' Douglas pressed, patently running out of patience.

'Art.'

'Art?' he queried, eyes out on stalks.

Susan felt a giggle bubble up inside. Clamped a hand to her mouth.

'One specific art programme, or a variety?'

'Same one, far as I can remember. Vinnie was mad on it. Never missed an episode.'

'Can you remember what it was called?'

Jean Sellars shook her head. 'Didn't pay a great deal of heed.'

'Okay,' Douglas acknowledged. He looked enquiringly to Susan.

'Anything stick in your mind?' she asked gently. 'Anything at all?'

'Never sat down long enough to catch the gist of it.'

'So there's nothing—'

'Only thing struck me was the artist. Funny-looking. Funny-comical,' she qualified. 'Not funny – you know – weird.'

'Can you give us a name?' Susan fished.

Jean shook her head. 'Sorry.'

'Take a moment or two.'

'Not a name I'm familiar with,' said Jean. 'Perry, maybe. I mind thinking "Babycham", but that's daft, isn't it?'

'Perry?' Susan repeated, racking her brains. She vaguely remembered reading something in the Sunday papers. But what?

For a few moments, she sat, deep in thought. Then, 'Grayson Perry?' she said, as much to herself as the others.

Vigorously, Jean Sellars nodded. 'That's the one.'

Frankie

They're talking about me. That tall girl – the one in the North Face jacket – just pointed. Then she said something, and they all looked in my direction and laughed.

I'd go over. But the way they're standing, all bunched up together, don't think I'd be welcome. Doesn't help I don't know all their names yet. The wee blonde one with the ponytail is called Chloe, and the fat girl is Emma. The others I forget.

Seaton's rubbish. Our new house isn't nearly as nice as the old one in Tullos. Neither is Seaton School. And if that lot over there are anything to go by, my classmates are no different from the last. That first day, when Mrs Shirreffs showed me into P6 and they were all staring and whispering behind their hands, I was so embarrassed I wanted to wee.

I told Mum there was no point us moving, it wouldn't change anything. But she wouldn't listen. I'd have tried to talk to Dad, but he's never here. It was bad enough before. Now he's living in town, I only see him on Saturdays, and then only when he's onshore. When he does come to ours – and that's hardly ever – it always ends up in a fight.

That wee gang of girls has moved away, now. The rest are with their pals, playing games or just hanging out. No one's asked me to join in. Who'd want to be bestie with a weirdo like me? And if Mum gets a job, like she's talking about, I'll have to go to Breakfast Club, another thing they'll hold against me.

I'd try and talk to some of the boys, but I'd be wasting my time. They wouldn't want their mates to catch them talking to a girl – not one like me at any rate – and anyhow they're on the other side of the playground, kicking a Coke can about.

The PSA's on playground duty today.

She's watching me right now.

I duck my head.

She already asked me how I was getting on.

What a joke.

Said it would take time to get to know people.

I said I was fine. Anything to be shot of her.

I could have told her: it's not them that's the problem, it's me.

Dad's Wee Hobby

'How long have you known?' Susan asked gently.

'Must have been eleven, twelve maybe,' answered Harvey Sellars. 'It was a Sunday, I remember, clear as day. He was working in the garage: joinery, supposedly. "Dad's wee hobby", Mum called it. We – my sister Lauren and me – weren't supposed to disturb him. But that Sunday Lauren was at a friend's, and Dad had promised me we'd go to the football, just the two of us. I was that excited.' He looked to Susan for understanding. 'My dad worked all hours, so we didn't see a lot of him.'

'What happened?'

'He didn't hear me at first. He was bent over, his back to the door. He must have been pulling on stockings, I twigged, much later. Anyhow, all he had on was a padded bra and a pair of lace knickers.'

'What did you do?'

'Just stood there, rooted to the spot. I must have made a noise, because he turned and saw me. The look on his face!'

Douglas asked, 'Were there other incidents?'

'Not as such. All through my teens we pretty much avoided one another, but I knew Dad was still at it. Sometimes I'd sneak into the garage when nobody else was at home. Suss where he hid his stuff. I even…' He admitted, shame-faced. '…sniffed the knickers once or twice to check if he'd been jacking off. And before you ask, it's a no.'

'You didn't happen on anything else?'

'Like what?'

'Porn? Sex toys?'

Susan gave him a surreptitious nudge. Douglas could be antsy at the best of times, but this was pushing it.

'No.' Harvey eyed Douglas with hostility. 'What are you getting at?'

Consulting his notebook, 'You were in Dumfries on business when your father's body was discovered?'

'You know bloody well where I was,' Harvey said. 'I've already told the uniformed coppers.'

'How long were you in Dumfries?'

'Overnight.'

'Can anyone vouch for you?'

'The bed and breakfast I stayed in. The companies I had meetings with.'

'When did you leave?'

'Dunno. After lunch.'

'You didn't think to check your phone?'

'It was in my inside pocket. On silent.'

'What time did you get back?'

Harvey looked pointedly at Douglas. 'Two hundred miles, give or take. Work it out.' Stabbing a finger, 'I don't like your attitude. Are you accusing me of something?'

'I'm not accusing you of anything,' answered Douglas, squaring up. 'I asked you to account for your whereabouts on the day of your father's death, that's all.'

'Well, I've done that. And I was no sooner through the door than the cops came knocking, gave me the news. Then I went straight to Mum's. That satisfy you?'

'I'm sorry for your loss,' Susan offered before her partner could aggravate the situation further.

'Right,' Douglas said, pocketing his notebook.

Susan looked daggers. Not for the first time, she speculated how she could offload him onto some other unsuspecting DC.

Turning to Harvey, she said, 'Thank you for answering our questions at this difficult time. It's much appreciated.'

*

'Just because you went to uni,' Susan seethed, when they got back to the car. 'There's no reason to behave like an arse.'

'What are you on about?'

'Harvey Sellars. Guy has just lost his father and you go in there with both feet.'

'Nothing of the sort. All I did was put questions pertinent to the investigation.'

'You really are a pompous load of shite.'

'Just because you have an inferiority complex.'

Susan flinched as the barb struck home. She held her ground. 'You don't seriously think Harvey Sellars was complicit in his father's death?'

'I'm saying Vinnie could have had help.'

'Who from? The wife? The daughter? The bleeding neighbours?'

'Whoever has most to gain,' Douglas said stubbornly. 'My money's on the wife. Jean Sellars must have known about the cross-dressing. Do you really swallow that in all those years she never once went in that garage? Not to check up on him? Offer him a cup of tea?'

'Maybe she was scared,' Susan argued. 'She didn't come across as the assertive type.'

'She could have seen her husband's behaviour was escalating. Worried he would lose his job, and with it his pension. As for the son, Harvey Sellars couldn't look his father in the eye. He said as much. And you saw how stroppy he was.'

'How do you get on with your dad?' Susan asked disingenuously.

'What's that got to do with it?'

'Bet he thinks – like I do – you have an inflated opinion of yourself.'

Straightening in his seat, Douglas said, 'I hold an honours degree in—'

'Yeah, yeah. You've rammed that down our throats since the day you joined the team.'

'Haha. Coming back to Jean Sellars, we should have checked if he had life insurance.'

'Luckily,' said Susan, 'I had the presence of mind.'

'When was that?'

'She came through to the kitchen when I was making the tea. I may not have an honours degree, but I've more life experience, that's for sure. Real life,' she added with a satisfied smirk.

31

Small but Growing

The office had that airless feel peculiar to legal firms.

Like your Granny's front room, Maggie thought, as she waited for him to speak. She'd rushed straight from her stint at Seaton School and was apprehensive, not just about the outcome of the interview, but whether she looked a mess.

Jowly, in a funereal three-piece suit, 'We've had a long association with Ace Solutions,' the solicitor said, from the far side of a desk drowning in ribbon-tied folders.

True. She'd done her research.

'They've executed good work for us.'

Liar. The one nugget of gossip she'd managed to glean: the investigations agency in question had made a major cock-up, so spectacular there were rumours of impending litigation. Maggie had got on the phone tout suite and blagged an appointment.

'What makes you think Harcus and Laird can do better?'

Nervously clearing her throat, she replied, 'We have a proven track record in solicitor support. Can cover all your requirements: tracing beneficiaries, probate enquiries, locating business assets, evidence gathering, matrimonial surveillance, process serving...' Breathless, she broke off. 'I myself have a legal background, unlike...'

'I wasn't aware of that,' he interrupted, visibly perking up. 'Are you an Aberdeen graduate?'

'N-no,' Maggie stuttered. 'I was a legal secretary. A PA,' she added hopefully.

'I see.' Mouth turned down, he sat back in his seat.

Maggie drew a calming breath. If she could land the contract, it would take the pressure off, short-term. 'As I was saying, unlike many of our competitors, who rely on call-centre operators, we can offer a service tailored to your needs.'

'Mmm.' He didn't look convinced.

'Our company may be small, but...'

'So small,' he broke in. 'You're virtually a one-man-band.'

Leaning across the desk, 'You still with me?'

'Of course,' said Maggie, starting like a frightened rabbit.

He cast a glance into the corner of the room, 'You seem somewhat distracted.'

Oh to hell! Maggie cursed that wandering left eye. Not so much a squint as a lazy slither to one side, it became exaggerated when she was stressed.

'We're small, I grant you. Small but growing,' she emphasised. 'We're actively recruiting,' she added, marvelling at how easily a lie tripped off the tongue when it was uttered with confidence. Something else she'd learned from Wilma. 'That notwithstanding, my partner and I are determined to maintain the high level of service upon which we've built our reputation.'

Between the thumb and fingers of his right hand, the solicitor rolled a fat fountain pen. The nib was gold. Maggie wondered how much it had cost.

'You could have a word with someone at Innes Crombie,' she offered in desperation. 'I'm sure they'd be happy to vouch for the quality of our work.'

'I've already done that.'

'Oh.' The wind evaporated from Maggie's sails.

Setting the pen down, he rose from his seat.

'Leave it with me,' he said, showing her the door.

Famous Last Words

The company occupied a squat red-brick building on an industrial estate at Bridge of Don. Douglas slid the Vauxhall Astra into a visitor's space. 'Jeez,' he said, greedily clocking the customised Audi TT that sat alongside highly polished BMW and Mercedes saloons. 'Get a load of that!'

'Don't hang about,' said Susan. 'We've a ton of actions to get through and we're already in the boss's bad books.'

'We've only to get a bit of background. We'll be in and out.'

Famous last words, Susan thought as, finally, they were shown through to Human Resources. They'd been corralled in Reception for almost half an hour – no offer of refreshments – and the dog-eared copies of Building magazine and Construction News hadn't held much appeal.

'Sorry to keep you.' From behind a desk overflowing with paperwork, the HR Manager – a Rosa Klebb lookalike in a mannish grey suit – explained, 'We've a rush job on.'

'Won't take up much of your time,' Douglas assured her. 'We just need to ask a few questions about one of your site managers, Vincent Sellars.'

The woman, who had been introduced as Isa Pirie, glanced around the open-plan office, a flicker of apprehension on her face. She looked back at Douglas. 'Can't help you. Data protection.'

'I'm sure you're aware, the legislation doesn't prevent an employer providing information requested by the police.'

'Have you got a disclosure request form?'

His eyes darted sideways and back again. 'No.'

Ms Pirie made to rise. 'There's your answer.'

'But, surely,' Douglas wheedled, 'In the circumstances...'

Susan cut in. 'Can I take it you're aware of Mr Sellars' death?'

Isa Pirie nodded. 'Heard it on the local news.'

'Must have been a shock. He's been with the company a long time, I understand.'

'Was,' Ms Pirie emphasised.

Her eyes scanned the office.

Leaning forward, she said in a low voice, 'We had to let him go.'

*

In Asda's Middleton car park, Susan sat in the passenger seat. Staring ahead in cold fury, 'You said you would do it.'

Chewing his way through a Chicken Triple sandwich, Douglas shrugged. 'Ran out of time.'

She turned. 'How long does it take to get a bloody form signed?'

'I did try. DCI was on a conference call, then… to be honest, I didn't think there would be a problem.'

'You reckoned you'd be able to charm the pants off whoever had the misfortune to be on the other side of the desk, is that it? Well, you met your match there.'

'Wouldn't like to end up in the ring with that one.' Wide-jawed, Douglas took another giant bite. 'What do you reckon to that last remark?'

'Hard to tell. Company looks to be doing well. If it was a question of redundancy, they'd likely have been upfront about it.'

'Or Mrs Sellars would have said.'

'And why would you make a long-serving manager redundant ahead of someone just through the door? Especially someone valued, by all accounts. Doesn't make sense.'

Douglas said, 'I reckon Ms Pirie was cagey for a reason: misconduct, maybe, or…'

'One thing I do know,' Susan interrupted. 'You better not carry on chancing your arm or you'll land us in trouble, you and me both.'

'I suppose you never cut corners.'

'Is that what you call hacking into a suspect's computer?'

'That was yonks ago,' he replied, through bulging cheeks.

'And nearly writing off a pool car. Not to mention—' She broke off as Douglas started to choke. Shoving him roughly forward onto the steering wheel, she thumped him between the shoulder blades.

'Stop that!' he mouthed, spitting gobbets of mulched chicken onto the dashboard.

'Only trying to help.' Susan said, backing off. 'Here.' She passed him a clean tissue.

Douglas wiped his mouth and dabbed ineffectually at the dash, then stuffed the last of his sandwich back into its wrapping and stowed it under his seat. Jerking a thumb at the untouched pot of fruit salad in Susan's lap, 'You going to eat that?'

'Nope. You've put me right off.' Wedging it in the door-well, she turned. 'Seriously, Douglas, if you want to avoid a disciplinary...'

Her words were drowned as, switching on the ignition, he revved the engine and roared out of the car park with a squeal of tyres.

Easy-Peasy

Gripping the gun in clammy fingers, Wilma took a quick shufti over her shoulder. Not a soul on the street. She scanned the parked cars for occupants. Found none. The windows of the neighbouring houses were blank-faced. No twitching net curtains here.

Holding the gun close to her chest, she inserted the needle into the lock. Originally designed for law enforcement and the emergency services, the pick gun was – so the advertising blurb promised – now used by professional services that require fast, convenient entry as a complement to manual lock picking.

Professional services. Wilma's bosom swelled. She'd been stuck in the house for days and was pissed off with Maggie's hectoring. Had taken on this wee freelance job in the hope of evening the score.

In and out, the client had said.

Couple of happy snaps.

Easy-peasy.

Wilma pulled the trigger, felt the needle flick at the pins.

Bugger! The job was taking longer than she'd expected.

When she'd checked out pick guns online, Wilma had been tempted by the electric version, which claimed to flick hundreds of times with one pull of the trigger. Complete with picking chuck and a selection of needles, the model she favoured came in a nifty, zipped case. But it was twice the price of its manual equivalent. And would need charging, besides. It would be just her luck if she were to roll up to a situation, only to find the thing out of juice. If that happened, she could hardly rap on a neighbour's door and ask them to re-charge it.

She took another shufti behind her, heart skipping a beat as a black and white cat slid from beneath a VW and shot across the pavement. Wilma was in two minds whether to cut and run. Maybe she should have asked more questions before rushing in headlong: like if it was that easy, why didn't the client do the job himself? Then again, the guy had a record as long as your arm. Probably couldn't chance getting banged up.

With shaky hands, she inserted the tension tool that would ensure when the pins were flicked above the shear-line they would stay there.

Bingo!

Removing the gun, she pushed the door open and crept inside. Standing stock still, she weighed her options as to which of the closed doors to try first. The flats had a pretty standard layout: public rooms at the front, bedrooms at the back.

Entering what she reckoned to be a spare bedroom, she hit lucky. Still in their outers, the stolen goods were piled to the ceiling.

Reaching for her digital camera, Wilma rattled off a series of shots, then quietly closed the door behind her.

She was standing in the hallway, deliberating which room to scope next, when a naked figure emerged from what looked to be a bathroom.

'Christ,' he yelled, hands dropping to cup his privates. 'What the hell are you doing here?'

Wilma was wondering the exact same thing as she turned on her heel and fled.

Graffiti

'Would it surprise you to learn your husband had parted company with his employer?' Susan enquired.

'"Parted company"?' Jean Sellars echoed. 'Given in his notice, you mean?'

'It's not entirely clear,' Susan hedged, with a sideways glance at Douglas. 'What we do know is his employment terminated some weeks before his death.'

'But he went out every morning same as usual,' Jean said plaintively. 'Came back at his regular time. Even took his dinner piece.'

Susan and Douglas exchanged knowing looks. The number of times they'd encountered a situation where someone had been made redundant, but couldn't bring themselves to tell their partner.

'You must have got it wrong,' Mrs Sellars insisted. 'Me and Vinnie, we've been together since school. He'd have told me. Even he hadn't...' Her chin wobbled. 'I'd have known.'

'I'm sorry,' Susan said. 'We've spoken to his employer. There's no mistake.'

Face stripped of colour, Jean Sellars closed her eyes. 'Where did he go all day? What did he do?' Her eyes snapped open. 'He should have told me,' she said angrily. 'I could have helped.'

'Sometimes, people feel they're beyond help,' said Susan, feeling inadequate.

'Anyone for a cuppa?' ventured Lauren Sellars, sticking her head round the door.

Her mother ignored her. 'When will I get him back?'

'Hard to say.' Susan had explained that a post-mortem would have to be carried out. 'But, believe me...' She offered a sympathetic smile. '...we'll do everything in our power to return your husband to you as quickly as we can.'

'In the meantime,' Douglas added, 'Is there anything more you can think of that might explain his actions?'

Jean's lip curled. 'More than losing a job he'd held down all his working life?'

Ducking his chin, 'There is that.'

'Ever since our two moved out, Vinnie hasn't known what to do with himself, is all I can say. Working to tight deadlines, he's never been able to keep up a hobby. There's the football, and wee bits of joinery, but other than that… This past couple of years we haven't seen much of our kids.' Jean Sellars gave a hopeless shrug. 'When it gets to the weekend, you can't blame them if they'd rather see their pals. They've their own lives to lead.'

'Absolutely,' Susan concurred. 'That aside, did they get on well with their dad?'

'Lauren's a right daddy's girl, always has been. As for Vinnie, he doted on her from the day she was born.'

'How about her brother?' Douglas insinuated. 'Did he dote on him too?'

Jean gave a bitter laugh. 'Went at it hammer and tongs, the pair of them.'

'Did they ever come to blows?'

'No. Not since Harvey was in his teens, at any rate. They both have a short fuse. Blew up once in a while.'

'Would Harvey have had any reason to wish his father harm?'

'Far from it. Vinnie set him up in a nice wee house when he got hitched. Marriage didn't last, more's the pity. Did the same for Lauren a couple of years back.'

'Is there anyone else,' Douglas pressed, 'who might have wished your husband ill? Has there been a dispute with a neighbour, perhaps? An incident at work? Think carefully. Take your time.'

For long moments Jean sat, brow knitted, teeth gnawing on her lower lip. Then, 'No. Vinnie could be a bit short when he was tired, but he was a softie.' Looking at the detectives' sceptical faces, she added, 'Ask anyone.'

'So there's nothing,' said Susan, 'that would explain why Vinnie should want to take his own life?'

'Only thing comes to mind, few weeks back someone wrote graffiti on the side of his van.' With a shrug, '"Thing was asking for it", Vinnie said at the time, it was that clarted.'

'Can you remember what?'

'Aye. It's not something you'd forget in a hurry.'

Proffering her notebook and pen, Susan asked, 'Will you write it down for me?'

Frowning in concentration, Jean balanced the notebook on her knee.

The detectives strained forward.

Followed with their eyes as she wrote in laborious capital letters, UR DEAD.

A Dog's Life

'Cheers!' Wilma said, taking a greedy slurp from her glass.

Maggie mirrored the gesture. The two were sitting in Wilma's conservatory, an open bottle of red wine on the glass table between them.

Noisily smacking her lips, 'Did I need that,' Wilma went on. 'The day I've had, you wouldn't believe.'

'Mine wasn't much better. And the phone's been ringing off the hook since I got in: mostly time-wasters. Either they were in need of a lawyer, a marriage guidance counsellor or psychiatrist, or they balked at the hourly rate.' Taking a judicious sip, 'I'll have to work this evening to get the Harlaw Insurance report finished.'

'Harlaw again?' If you ask me, you put in more time on them than the contract's worth.'

'I wouldn't do it if it wasn't necessary,' Maggie said, tight-lipped. 'And may I remind you, our corporate clients may not be the most lucrative, but they provide a steady income stream.'

'Spare me the sermon.'

'Well, if that's your attitude...'

'Here,' Wilma thrust a giant bag of Cheesy Wotsits under Maggie's nose. 'Bet you haven't eaten all day.'

'I had a good breakfast.'

'That's no use. There's little enough of you as it is.'

'I'll grab something later. Colin has rugby practice. He's going to a friend's for tea.'

Scooping a handful of Wotsits, Wilma crammed them into her mouth. 'This detective business,' she mumbled through crackling noises. 'It's a dog's life.'

'Speaking of which, one of the calls I took was from a Mr Buchan wanting us to investigate a stolen pet.'

Wilma banged a fist down on the table. 'No more cats.'

'It's not a cat. It's a dog.'

'I don't care if it's a bloody unicorn. After the dance that ugly Malthus led us.' Rolling up her sleeve, Wilma said, 'I've still got the scars.'

'We got a result,' Maggie argued. 'Client got her cat back. Plus, the job paid well. Kept us afloat.'

'You didn't take the case on?'

'Said I'd get back to him. Listen, we can't afford to be picky. Fraud's still huge. And on the increase: it accounted for nearly 40% of reported crime in 2020–2021, according to Police Scotland. But our corporate insurance fraud cases are drying up, more companies taking the work in-house. That's a worry. They've been a steady earner. Pet theft, on the other hand, is on the rise.'

Wilma took another slurp of wine. 'So?'

'If you've been reading the papers, you'll know demand for puppies skyrocketed during lockdown. The price for the most sought-after breeds almost doubled.'

'You don't say.'

'Imports from Romania increased by 70%,' Maggie persisted, 'a significant proportion of that attributable to exploitation by criminal gangs.'

Yawning widely, Wilma asked, 'What's your point?'

'As travel corridors were shut down, bringing dogs into the country became riskier and more expensive, so it's hardly surprising thieves are targeting family pets. For them it's easy money: the animals can be sold on to another owner or for breeding to a puppy farm. They fetch high prices. And the risks are negligible.'

'Forget it.'

'You're the one wanting outside work. And the job would be a piece of cake: scout around the neighbourhood, post an appeal on social media, put a call in to the DogLost dog-napping charity helpline.'

'That's what you said last time,' Wilma huffed. 'We're supposed to be professional private investigators, not a feckin animal sanctuary.'

'It could be lucrative. The Buchan family is devastated. They're prepared to pay a substantial reward.'

'What about the police? Are they not in play?'

'They're overstretched as it is. Only about 20% of stolen dogs are returned to their owners. Think of the potential.'

'Think of the danger,' said Wilma, fingering the weals on her arm.

'Have you got a better idea?' Maggie demanded. 'We can't go on, losing clients at this rate. We'll be out of business in a matter of months, if not weeks.'

'Don't be so negative.'

'I'm being realistic. Times are tough. Our current client list barely covers our outgoings. I've kids to support. I can't go on living from hand to mouth.'

'Ach,' said Wilma. 'Dinna fret. Things will pick up.'

'That's you all over,' Maggie retorted. 'Winging it. What's the story on new business?'

'Same old.' No way was Wilma going to share the details of her latest exploit. 'Background checks for employment, housing, pre-nup, security clearance. Debtor traces. Nothing exciting, that's for sure.' Reaching for the wine bottle, 'Top you up?'

'No, thanks.' Maggie moved quickly to cover her glass with her hand. 'I've already drunk more than I should. To make my day complete, Colin has torn his new rugby shirt. Once I've finished my paperwork, I've that to mend.'

'Just as well my loons are grown,' Wilma said, taking another consolatory swallow. 'Wayne and Kevin have gone quiet this past while.' Crossing her fingers, 'Hope they stay that way. Now, I've only Ian to think of.'

Her husband appeared in the kitchen doorway.

'Talk of the devil!'

Eyeing Maggie, 'Can't keep away from here,' he remarked.

'We're just finishing up,' she said hurriedly.

'Keep your hair on,' Wilma chided. 'Dinner's in the oven. Away and have your shower.'

'Pet theft,' Maggie repeated, gathering her things. 'If we're going to rule that out, we'll have to come up with some other way to boost our income.'

Upending the bottle into her glass. 'I'll think on it,' Wilma said

III

A Midlife Crisis

'Sellars case,' Chisolm said, kicking off the morning team talk. 'What have you got?'

Susan was in like a shot before Douglas had a chance to respond. 'We've taken statements from the son and daughter. Lauren Sellars was in the dark where the cross-dressing is concerned. Not so her brother. There was animosity between him and his dad on account of it.'

'Enough for him to top him?' asked Duffy.

'Doubt it. Plus, he was in Dumfries at the time of the suicide. He was able to rule out any sexual element, however. We've also paid a return visit to Vinnie Sellars' employer.'

Jumping in, Douglas volunteered, 'After some persuasion, they finally conceded Vincent Sellars was dismissed due to...' Consulting his pocketbook, he pronounced, '"...behavioural issues".'

'Meaning what, exactly?'

'Seems he started wearing makeup: tinted moisturiser...'

'Same as you?' Susan supplied, face the picture of innocence. 'Clinique, didn't you say?'

Douglas gave her the full evils. 'As I was saying, moisturiser at first, then mascara. After that, he turned up on-site from time to time dressed "inappropriately" for the job, for which...' Rolling his eyes. '...I take it they mean wearing items of women's clothing.'

'Can you imagine?' Bob Duffy muttered out the corner of his mouth. 'Dame Edna Everage in builders' boots.'

Chisolm threw him a black look. 'Go on.'

'To the extent the navvies were taking the piss,' Douglas continued, obviously riled. 'Got to the stage Sellars couldn't keep order. Business began to suffer, and...'

'Came as news to his wife,' Susan interjected. 'Poor woman had no idea her husband had lost his job. The other thing that came out: someone had written a threat on his works van.'

'Where was the vehicle at the time?'

'In the driveway. Could be a total red herring. For one thing, it happened weeks before the suicide. Plus, the van was due its weekly wash, so the graffiti may have been there for some time. Any one of his workmates could have done it as a prank. Sellars put it down to local kids.'

'Still,' said Chisolm, 'Get back to the employer. Ask them to draw up a list of his workmates, then set up interviews, see if you can find anyone with a grudge.'

'Will do.'

'Anything from the neighbours?'

'Negative,' answered Douglas, rushing back in. 'Other than the statement from the guy who found the body. There's a Mrs Benzie, pal of Jean Sellars, but she was out when we called. Another old dear, lives across the road, said she saw a man coming out of the Sellars' garage, but she couldn't give a description. Wasn't even sure which day.'

Chisolm said, 'Follow those up. And get back in touch with the building company. Establish if there's been animosity.' Shuffling his papers, 'Moving on...'

His words were interrupted by a uniformed officer entering the room. Addressing the inspector, 'Interim post-mortem report for you, sir.'

'Thanks,' Chisolm acknowledged. 'Timely,' he remarked, when the officer had departed. Skim-reading the contents, 'Diagonal marks on the neck. Tongue forced out of the mouth and almost severed by the force of the jaw clenching. Hands bunched into fists in the process known as posturing.' Looking up, he added, 'All indicative of suspension hanging.'

'Sounds to me like the guy was having a midlife crisis,' Brian said, with some feeling. Divorced from cheating wife, Bev, his move from the Urquhart Road bed-sit to the flat in Spring Garden had upped his comfort level. It had done zilch for his love life, which had languished since his doomed pursuit of Maggie Laird.

Duffy said, 'I'm with you. Kids have flown the nest. He's left sitting in an empty house. Is it any wonder he feels redundant?'

'That's all very well,' argued Douglas 'But it doesn't strike me as sufficient motive to kill yourself.'

Brian came back. 'Losing a job that was his whole life, that's a pretty major…'

He was interrupted by Chisolm. 'According to this report, there were claw marks on Vincent Sellars' neck.'

'Gut reaction,' Duffy growled, 'when the rope started to burn.'

'Either that,' said Chisolm, features twisted in a wry grimace. 'Or he didn't intend to go through with it.'

Kirsty

'There's a girl in Kirsty's bed,' Colin panted, his bulk filling the doorway.

Maggie jolted awake. She'd sat up until well after midnight anxiously issuing invoices, then painstakingly mending the rugby shirt. "Go big or go home" was Wilma's mantra when it came to money matters. Maggie was less bullish, not wanting to lay on billing hours or expenses to the extent they lost even more clients.

'What girl?' she enquired, knuckles rubbing sleep from her eyes.

He shrugged.

Maggie shot from under the duvet.

Shouldered past him.

Charged up the stairs.

On the landing she checked herself, questions scrambling in her head. What was Kirsty doing there? She was supposed to be in Dundee. And sleeping with a girl? There hadn't been a boyfriend on the scene for ages, but this was something else.

Taking a deep breath, she grasped the door handle.

Thought better of it.

Stealthily, she retraced her steps, wincing as a stair tread creaked, crossing the hall in two long strides until she reached the comparative safety of her bedroom.

Maggie tore off her fleecy pyjamas and scrambled into yesterday's clothes. As she hurried though to the kitchen, Colin was nowhere to be seen. For which – unusually – she was grateful. Filling the kettle, she pulled a half-loaf from the breadbin and stuck a couple of slices in the toaster, then set about laying breakfast on a wooden tray, a relic of the old Methlick farmhouse. She had a cloth somewhere. Maggie's blood pressure ratcheted up as she rummaged in the Ercol sideboard, so dated it was back in fashion. Extracting a rust-spattered linen tray-cloth embroidered with pastel daisies, tutting, she stuffed it back in the drawer. High time she had a clear-out.

Ten minutes later she climbed the stairs again, tray tightly gripped in both hands. It was set with a paper napkin, laid diagonally, on which sat a fat china teapot, a small cut-glass milk and sugar, two mugs and teaspoons and a plate of toast cut into neat triangles. Wedging the tray against the door jamb, she gave a tentative knock.

No answer.

She knocked again, louder this time.

'What?' came Kirsty's angry voice.

Plastering a bright smile on her face, Maggie opened the door. 'Breakfast,' she announced, her voice filled with false cheer.

'Don't want any,' Kirsty grumbled, raising a tousled dark mop.

'But your friend,' Maggie protested, eyes riveted on the neon green head lying, face down, next to her daughter.

Kirsty scowled. 'Cat doesn't eat breakfast.' Tugging the duvet up to her chin, she added, 'And get out of my room.'

*

'You're early on the go,' Wilma said, when Maggie came rushing in. 'Something up?'

'No,' Maggie replied, plucking privet leaves out of her hair. She'd dumped the breakfast tray by the sink and taken a nose-dive through the hole in the dividing hedge. 'I just needed to remind you about tomorrow's presentation,' she ad-libbed, realising – too late – taking Wilma into her confidence was a bad idea.

'You already did.' Hitching the straps of a satin camisole that exposed a chasm of cleavage, she gave Maggie a sly nudge. 'Loon got a bidey-in?'

'No.'

'Who's the quine?'

'Friend of Kirsty's,' Maggie replied, with as much nonchalance as she could muster. 'How do you know we've a visitor?'

'Happens I was at the window.'

'As if!' Maggie exploded. 'They must have rolled up in the middle of the night.'

Holding up her hands, 'Okay,' Wilma owned. 'I couldn't sleep. When I heard the door, l had to have a nosey. Just in case it was your polis pal.'

'Who, Brian?'

'Dinna be daft. Thon inspector.'

'But,' Maggie puzzled. 'Why would Allan Chisolm be at my door in the wee small hours?'

Innocent-faced, Wilma said, 'You tell me.'

*

'You should have let me know,' Maggie said when, eventually, Kirsty surfaced.

'It was late. Didn't want to wake you.'

'All the same, I'd have made up a bed.'

'Wasn't any need.'

'I'll be the judge of that.' Reproachfully, Maggie added, 'What that girl must be thinking. This house is chaotic at the best of times.'

'Whose fault is that?'

Bristling, Maggie said, 'Don't go blaming it on the business. That brother if yours is the untidiest—'

'Cat wouldn't care. She only came along for the ride.'

'And you let her sleep in a bed that hasn't been changed since I don't know when?'

'She wouldn't have noticed. Sleeps like a baby.'

'Where is she now?'

'In the bathroom. Won't be long. One of her more endearing traits.' Kirsty's normally combative expression softened. 'Totally without vanity.'

She's in love.

'Sorry to land on you like this,' Cat said, coming through the kitchen door. 'Hope we didn't give you a fright.'

'No,' Maggie lied. 'Kirsty's never predictable. Likes to keep me guessing. '

This was met with a scathing look.

'Social visit?' she fished.

'Hardly,' Kirsty scoffed. 'The last Megabus from Dundee's not my idea of a picnic. I needed a reference book for an essay. It's due in on Monday. This seemed the quickest way.'

'Couldn't you have borrowed it from the library?'

'Obviously not.' Said with studied sarcasm.

'Oh, well.' Maggie fought to keep her voice light, though she would have liked to strangle Kirsty. 'It's always good to see you, even it is only a flying visit.' Heart thudding, 'It is a flying visit?' she enquired. This day – of all days – following her morning's work at Seaton she had a pressing lunch appointment.

'Totally. We have to be back by two.'

Maggie's heartbeat slowed. Turning to Cat, she asked, 'Are you doing the same course?'

'Her?' Kirsty said, pointing. 'Doing law?'

'I'm an art student.'

'So,' Mind racing, Maggie said, 'How did you two meet?'

'In a club.'

So they are an item.

'Oh,' was all she could muster.

54

A Bit of Alright

Allan Chisolm walked into the CID Suite, a young woman in his wake. Picking up a stray ruler from the nearest desk, he rapped it briskly. 'Your attention, folks.'

Conversation stopped dead, all eyes fixed on the newcomer. She looked to be in her late twenties. Tall: five-six at Brian's guess. Blonde hair cut in a shoulder-length bob. Pristine white shirt under a well-fitting charcoal trouser suit.

'Let me introduce our new team member, DC Elizabeth Haldane.'

From the back of the room came the beginnings of a low wolf-whistle, hastily suppressed.

Frowning, Chisolm craned his neck. Decided to let it go. He'd been blind-sided when his DCI had summoned him. Taken further aback to find installed in Edward Scrimgeour's office a young woman, looking very much at ease.

'Elizabeth has joined us from Tayside Division,' Chisolm said, now. 'I'm sure you'll join me in making her welcome.'

From workstations came murmurs of assent, which the new constable acknowledged with a confident smile.

'Brian, I want you to partner Elizabeth. Show her the ropes. But for now, we have formalities to complete.' Followed by the newcomer, he turned on his heel and strode from the room.

*

'What d'you reckon, Sarge?' Susan asked, the minute the door closed behind them.

Brian grinned. 'Big improvement on Dave Wood.' Secretly, he was torn between disappointment they hadn't been sent another sergeant and relief there would be less competition in his struggle for promotion.

'Bit of alright, I'll say,' Douglas added.

'You would,' said Susan. 'One-track mind, the pair of you.'

'Don't lump me in with him,' Brian protested.

'Just joking.' She cocked her head. 'We all know you're the perfect gentleman.'

Pulling a rueful face, 'Not that it's done me any good.' If he'd had more bottle, Brian might have stood a better chance with Maggie Laird, or with the occasional ill-fated dalliance he'd embarked upon since.

'Maybe you'll get lucky,' Susan said, with a pretend nudge.

Douglas sniffed. 'Speaking personally, I wouldn't touch anything that came out of Tayside.'

'Dream on. Dame like her wouldn't look twice at a wuss like you.'

Squaring up, 'Who are you calling a wuss?'

Ever the peacemaker, Brian intervened. 'Pack it in. As the DI said, we'll have plenty time to get to know the woman. Let's wait and see.'

A Yellow Bag

I knew I'd wet myself, but I thought if I kept quiet the dark bit would dry by lunchtime. I could have died when Miss Archibald asked Mrs Laird to take me out of class.

She's outside the door of the girls' toilets right now, waiting for me to get changed. Then she'll put my trackie bottoms in one of those yellow bags, I suppose, like they did at Tullos. And my knickers. I've tucked them inside the joggers so she doesn't see.

I thought it would be easy, nicking my skin with a razor blade, but it was hard. And that one wee cut bled more than I thought it would. Stung as well. I would have asked Mum for a plaster, but she'd want to know how it happened, up there on the inside of my leg.

When I saw the blood on my pants today I thought my periods had started. Yuk! Bad enough getting boobs on your front without bleeding between your legs. Grosses me out.

There's a knock on the door.

I draw up my knees.

Hold my breath.

A voice says, 'Frankie. I know you're in there.'

That will be Mrs Laird.

'Frankie,' the voice says, 'Are you okay?'

Too right. I could sit here all day, reading the names scratched on the walls. And I'm not one bit hungry. But I know they'll come looking for me: Mrs Laird and Miss Archibald and maybe even Mrs Shirreffs.

'I need you to come out now.'

I look down at the floor. The things they've given me to put on are minging. If those P6 kids aren't killing themselves already, they will be when I go back into class.

I stand up.

Tug on the pants and joggers.

Unsnib the door.

Mrs Laird nods at my wet things.

I pick them up.

She holds out the yellow bag.

*

'Might just be down to too many fizzy drinks,' Lynsey Archibald posited, with a look that said it all: many of the school's low-income families seemed to subsist on a diet of junk food.

'Don't think so,' said Maggie, stowing art materials in a cupboard. 'I haven't ever seen her drink rubbish. Haven't seen her with a drink at all, come to that.'

'She must have the constitution of a camel.'

'Plus,' Maggie continued, 'I've seen Frankie's mum at the school gate. Looks a decent soul. Even so...' She'd learned how deceptive appearances can be. '...there's something going on.'

'She's probably started her periods. And we both know what does to our hormones.'

'Frankie's how old?'

'Nine. Bit early, but not that unusual, not these days.'

'I suppose.'

'Did you put the question?'

'Sorry. Didn't think. We'd been out of class so long by that time, my mind was on getting back.'

'I still think it's a one-off,' Lynsey insisted.

'Wish I shared your confidence.'

'Well, don't take it home with you.'

'Hard, when children are so deprived they start school at a disadvantage in terms of reading and maths. When a third of them qualify for free school meals. When almost half of P1 are already suffering dental decay.'

'Agreed. And we can make a difference, but we can't save them all. That includes Frankie Bain. You wouldn't want to get too close to things. Not after...' Catching Maggie's wounded expression, Lynsey added, 'Sorry. I didn't mean to rake over old coals.'

'Doesn't matter,' Maggie said lightly. Her first big case as a private detective – when a gang of Seaton schoolkids had become embroiled with a drug runner – still gave her nightmares. And had long-term consequences for the boys. One in particular. She'd often wondered what had become of Kieran Chalmers. Another nine-year-old. A clever, sensitive boy. She'd learned a hard lesson there. Fervently, Maggie hoped he was thriving at his new school.

Worry's My Middle Name

Allan Chisolm rose from his seat when Maggie approached. Started forward. Clasping both her hands in his, he asked, 'How have you been?'

Suffused with happiness, she smiled up at him. 'Doing away.'

They hadn't met in the flesh since the resolution of the agency's last major case – a sociopath targeting vulnerable women – and a series of missed calls had made her realise how much she missed him. When he'd rung to propose lunch, she'd suggested Banchory Lodge, an easy half-hour drive from the city centre. She hadn't visited the hotel in years, not since before her husband's sudden demise. A Grade II–listed Georgian building set in twelve acres on the banks of the River Dee, it had undergone an extensive refurbishment. Maggie had read about it in the newspapers, but hadn't been prepared for such an adventurous take on country chic.

'What do you reckon?' Chisolm enquired, once she'd settled into one of the lounge bar's upholstered tub chairs.

Maggie took in the wall-mounted row of reproduction stags' heads, the funky black and white wallpaper, the retro carpet. 'Not sure.' Gesturing to the room's focal point, a heavily carved Gothic oak bar, she joked, 'That's more my style. But, then, as my kids keep telling me, I'm old-fashioned.'

'You've good taste. The barman tells me it originates from Culloden House. But I digress. How are your kids?'

'Good. Kirsty's in her Honours year, so she's been keeping a low profile. Colin, well, we'll have to wait and see.'

He laid a consoling hand on her arm. 'Don't worry. He'll come right.'

'Worry's my middle name,' Maggie said lightly, though her heart was hammering, the memory of their passionate kiss still vivid in her mind. 'So my granny used to say.'

Withdrawing his hand, 'You've had your troubles, for sure. But hopefully all that bad business is behind you.'

'I hope so, too,' she said fervently. She'd wasted time and effort in fruitless attempts to clear George's name of the stigma associated with the collapse of a drugs trial. 'It's my firm intention to move forward.'

'Does that include me?' he teased.

Maggie felt her colour rise. Ducking into her handbag, she pulled out a tissue and made a show of blowing her nose.

'I'm sorry,' he said quickly. 'Didn't mean to put you on the spot. It's just, we haven't had a chance to talk, not properly, since...' His voice trailed off.

'Zoom doesn't quite cut it,' Maggie mumbled, not meeting his eyes

Leaning in close, he said, 'We've been dancing around one another for quite long enough. Do you think we can make a go of this?'

Hesitantly, she answered, 'Maybe.'

His face creased into a smile. 'I was hoping you'd say that. I know it's early days. But if we take things slowly. If we're honest with each other – and that has to include our respective work situations.'

Maggie dropped her gaze. In her dealings as a private investigator, she'd compromised a police investigation on more than one occasion and still smarted from the memory of the inspector's wrath.

'Mrs Laird?' A voice spoke at her back.

Heart sinking, she whirled.

Thrusting out a hand, the young man flashed a toothpaste smile. 'Gary Moir. I came out to value—'

'I remember,' Maggie said, colour flooding her face. To make ends meet, she'd begun the process of putting her house on the market with disastrous consequences when, through her own lack of judgement, she had put her life in danger.

'Did you achieve a sale?' Gary was asking, now.

Covertly, she looked over his shoulder. On a banquette against the far wall, a perma-tanned teenage blonde was listlessly toying with her hair extensions. 'No,' she replied. 'Changed my mind.'

Gary slid a hand into his breast pocket. Proffering a business card, 'I've set up on my own. Keenest commission rates in town. Give me a call.'

'Thanks,' Maggie said weakly.

Yanking his head towards the blonde. 'Got to run. Business calls.'

'That's Aberdeen for you,' Allan Chisolm quipped, as Gary beat a retreat. 'Can't go anywhere incognito.'

Maggie sighed. 'If I'm not playing invisible on behalf of the agency, I'm dodging folk.' Like Wilma, a small voice cried inside her head. These past few months it seemed her partner was not only watching Maggie's back, as she'd done in a succession of dangerous situations, she was trying to take over her entire life.

'As I was saying,' Allan Chisolm picked up. 'For our relationship to work, it's critical we compartmentalise our private and working lives. No more meddling with police inquiries, Maggie. No tapping my officers for information. Do you agree?'

Chastened, she found herself nodding, then pulled herself up. 'It's unfortunate police resources are so stretched people turn to agencies like mine, but it's a fact of life. My primary duty is to my clients.'

Chisolm threw her a quizzical look. Then, voice softening, he said, 'We plough the same furrow, you and I, in taking on other people's burdens. Where we differ is I have a support network, whereas you – you're a plucky woman, Maggie Laird, but you can't take on the world single-handed.'

'I'm not,' she protested. 'There's Wilma.'

'Ah, yes,' he said, the corners of his mouth twitching. 'Big Wilma.'

Maggie was on the point of leaping to her friend's defence, when, 'Enough of the soul-searching,' Chisolm said. 'Shame it's not warm enough to sit on the terrace, but this isn't too shabby.' Signalling to the barman, 'Why don't we enjoy our lunch and take it from there?'

A Pair of Boxers

Ian squinted at his plate. 'What's this?'

'Lamb casserole,' said Wilma. 'Looks right tasty.'

His head jerked up. 'Where's it from?'

'Tesco.'

Gingerly, he prodded the contents of the foil tray: a sea of gelatinous brown sauce punctuated by hillocks of what might be meat and vegetables. 'I wasn't born yesterday.'

Wilma shrugged. 'King Street mini-mart. I was pushed for time.'

'I thought we agreed no more ready meals.'

'Aye, but you have to make allowances. Our case was held up. Been hanging around court like a pair of curtains.'

'Your choice.'

Her temper flared. 'Don't start.' Then, sidling closer, she fondled the nape of his neck. 'I'm sorry. A man needs a square meal when he comes in from his work, but there's nothing else. Give it a go.'

Ian speared a forkful and chewed laboriously.

'Okay?'

He swallowed painfully. 'Lamb's pushing it. More like auld mutton.'

Sighing, Wilma said, 'I could fry you an egg. And there's chips in the freezer. Take a wee while, mind.'

'Forget it.' he fished out what looked like a lump of turnip. Or it could have been carrot, maybe even potato. Put it in his mouth.

Scrabbling to redeem the situation, Wilma lowered herself onto the seat opposite. Leaning across the table, she fluttered false eyelashes, 'How was your day?'

Ian raised his head. 'Same old.'

'Dodd have any more to say about thon suicide?'

Grumpily, 'Do you think we sit around talking all day?'

Wilma threw him a wink. 'Not about the news, mebbe.'

'If it's skirt you're thinking, think again. We're that snowed you wouldn't believe.' Carefully separating another piece of vegetable, he chewed and swallowed. 'Garage is bursting at the seams. We've cars parked on the forecourt and right down the street.'

'You'll be in line for a bonus, then,' she said with satisfaction, a new kitchen never far from her mind.

'Now you mention it,' Ian mused, 'there was a picture of that fella in the P&J.'

'What fella?'

'Him committed suicide. Dodd was reading it during his break.'

Wilma's antennae twitched. 'That right?'

'Weird thing is...'

She strained forward, giving him the full benefit of her embonpoint.

'...According to Dodd, last time he picked up the wife's car, the bloke answered the door didn't look anything like the one in the newspaper.'

Wilma sat back with a thud. 'Call that news? Could have been anybody: neighbour, relative, even the feckin plumber.'

'Except,' said Ian, shoving the ready meal aside. 'Bloke was wearing nothing but a pair of boxers.'

'Bloody hell!' exclaimed Wilma, china-blue eyes popping.

Her brain went into overdrive.

Slipping a hand inside her bra, she jiggled one breast, then the other.

Running a moist, pink tongue around parted lips, she leaned in close.

'You must be knackered,' she said. 'What d'you say we have an early night?'

Old Blackfriars

'Elizabeth,' Chisolm began. 'Bit of a mouthful, if you don't mind my saying.' He'd returned to the station and the team had decamped to the Old Blackfriars in Castle Street for a welcome drink. 'Is it okay if we call you Liz?'

'I'd rather you didn't,' she responded lightly. Smiling up into his face, 'My friends call me Lisa. I'll settle for that.'

'Lisa it is, then.' Raising his pint glass, 'Let's drink to that.'

The two clinked glasses. The rest of the team followed suit, Brian and Bob standing either side of the newcomer, Douglas and Susan behind and slightly to the side, propping up the bar.

'What prompted the move north?' Chisolm asked. 'Can't be the weather,' he cracked a feeble joke. It had been teeming rain all day.

Lisa's pupils flared. For a split second she hesitated. Then, 'New horizons. Bit like yourself, if my information is correct.'

'Spot on,' said Chisolm, his face a mask. Last he heard, his estranged wife, Clare, had found herself a new man. There was nothing to take him back to Glasgow, that's for sure.

Laying a hand on his arm, Lisa said, 'I was rather hoping you'd help me get to know the city.'

Chisolm threw her a piercing glance.

'If your partner doesn't object,' she added with a disarming smile.

Cupping a hand over her mouth, Susan whispered to Douglas, 'Bet those are false.'

His eyes widened. 'Tits?'

'No, dummy, eyelashes. And clock how she's cosying up to the boss.'

Turning his back on the group, 'Wouldn't you,' said Douglas, 'if you'd just started a new job?'

Susan wrinkled her nose. 'You're only sticking up for her because you want into her knickers.'

'I do not.'

'Just as well. You'd never know who'd been there.' With a yank of the head, she added, 'And get a load of Brian.'

Turning back, Douglas zeroed in on his sergeant, whose mouth hung open as he listened to whatever Lisa Haldane was saying. Her voice was too low for Douglas to catch, but she must have told a joke, because all three men erupted, suddenly, into hearty laughter.

'Never mind Brian,' Susan added darkly. 'They're all over her, the three of them.'

'I do believe you're jealous.'

'Of Brian? Don't be ridiculous. If anything, he thinks I'm trying to mother him.'

'Of Lisa.'

Susan squared up. 'Her neither. But I'll tell you one thing, sunshine. Bang goes our chances of being put forward for sergeant.'

All Good

'Val,' Maggie exclaimed when her friend's face appeared on the screen 'What a surprise.'

'Sorry I haven't been in touch,' said Val. 'My other half had leave he needed to use up.'

Maggie's spirits soared. 'You're back home?'

'Didn't run to that, sadly. Just enough for a quick holiday.'

'Oh,' Maggie said, deflated. She hadn't seen her old school chum for more than a handful of fleeting exchanges since she moved overseas. A good old heart-to-heart would have been just the tonic she needed. 'Somewhere nice, I hope,' she added lamely.

'The Seychelles. Nothing there but sea and sand.' Val pulled a sad face. 'As if I don't get enough of that already. Still, they're only a short flight from Dubai.'

'Sounds idyllic,' said Maggie. In truth, she was green with envy. It had been years since she'd enjoyed the luxury of even a weekend break.

'How are things?'

'Doing away.'

'Kids fine?'

She tapped closed fingers to her skull. 'Touch wood.'

'Business booming?'

'You wouldn't believe.' Maggie wasn't going to admit how close she sailed to the wind when her old school friend was living the good life with a houseful of servants.

'How's that business partner of yours?' Val enquired, with a mischievous twinkle. 'Still running rings round you?'

'I'd be the first to admit we've had our ups and downs. But now the agency is bedded in, we're getting along famously.'

Crossing the fingers of both hands out of Val's line of vision,

Maggie said a quiet prayer she wasn't tempting fate.

'By the sound of it, she sails close to the wind. You want to be careful. One of these days she might land you in jail.'

'Wilma has a good heart. She just gets a bit carried away.'

'You need to think about number one,' said Val. Getting no response, 'Seriously, I worry about you.'

So much so you can't pick up the phone?

From what Val had told Maggie of life in Dubai, she had nothing to do and all day to do it in.

'You've gone quiet on me.'

'Sorry,' Maggie said, mind jumping back to the present.

'You're not getting any younger. Your kids will have flown the nest in no time at all. And then what?'

'Haven't thought about it.'

'Well, I'm asking you now: what is it you want out of life?'

'To clear George's name. And before you say another word, I accept that's not going to happen, not after all this time.'

'What else?'

Maggie deliberated for a few moments, then, 'Two things: financial security, so I can get my kids through their education without lying awake half the night.'

'That's a no-brainer. Remember what I said last time we spoke.'

'And that was?' Maggie asked, feigning ignorance.

'Offload Wilma. Get yourself an intern: some bright young thing would work for free.'

'I did look into it,' Maggie lied. 'Decided it wasn't worth the hassle.'

'Two things, you said.'

'A man.' Seeing Val's concerned face, 'Not so much a love interest as—' In the dark, lonely nights since she'd been left a widow, Maggie had prayed, not just for financial succour, but that – someday, somehow – she'd find loving companionship once more. 'You've no idea how hard it is raising teenagers on your own.'

'What about George's buddy?'

'Brian? Not my type.'

'You need to join a club, get out and meet new people.'

'Haven't the time.'

'Have you considered a dating site?'

'Wouldn't have the nerve. The things you read—'

'How about your folks? Are they being supportive?'

'To a point. But they're getting on.'

'I guess.'

'There's Wilma of course. She's been a rock.'

'When she's not grandstanding.'

Maggie said, 'Forget it. There's no need to worry. We're all good.'

With Bells On

IV

With Bells On

'Where have you been?' Wilma asked tetchily. 'I've been calling since yesterday. Phone went straight to voicemail.'

'I've been up to my eyes,' Maggie replied. They were sitting in Wilma's car, having rendezvoused on the Esplanade, mid-way between Seaton School and the city centre, where Wilma had been acting as a professional witness. 'If it was that urgent, you could have popped in.'

'I would. Except…' Despite pleasuring Ian in imaginative ways, Wilma has failed to elicit more information. Only when he was lying, spent, had she extracted a promise: he'd press Dodd to ask his mum if she could put a name to Jean Sellars' man friend.

'Well, now I'm here?'

Trying to sound casual, Wilma said, 'Picked up some intel on that suicide.'

'From ARI?'

'Nope.'

'Where, then?'

'I have my sources.'

Maggie burst out laughing.

'You're not the only one with connections.'

'At least mine aren't shady.'

'Well, if you really don't want to know…'

'Go on, then.'

Coyly, Wilma spoke from under her lashes, 'Vinnie Sellars' wife has a fancy man.'

'What has that got to do with anything?'

Wired with excitement, Wilma breathed, 'The two of them could have bumped the husband off.'

Maggie said, 'You're not seriously suggesting that poor woman colluded with a lover in staging a fake suicide.'

'Stranger things have happened. We both know from experience...'

'...not to indulge in flights of fancy. That's always been your problem: you never know where to draw the line.'

'Not true.'

'How about the cannabis farm? And the chop shop? Illegal use of a GPS tracker? Breaking and entering? I could go on.'

'That was yonks ago.'

'Nonetheless, you could have got us both locked up.'

Jabbing a finger, Wilma said, 'You're not so squeaky clean yourself. It was you got us mixed up in the drugs trade. There could be folk out there now, trying to track us down.'

'I'll say, again, we need to put all that nonsense behind us. Concentrate on serious investigation.'

'Conspiracy to murder,' Wilma persisted. 'You can't get more serious than that.'

Eyes fixed on the horizon, where an oil barge sat, seemingly immobile, Maggie said, 'We are not going down that road, and that's all there is to it.'

Wilma sulked for a bit. Then, you got anything to eat?' She rummaged in the depths of a vast black patent handbag. 'I'm starved.'

'Sorry, no.'

'Bingo!' Straightening, she brandished a half-eaten Bounty Bar. 'Bang goes the diet.' She bit a ragged chunk off the end.

'If it's action you're looking for, you'll have to come up with something else.'

Chewing vigorously, Wilma mouthed, 'Romance fraud. It's on the up.'

'Not in Aberdeen. Folk are far too canny.'

'You're wrong. There was a case not long since: Kemnay man met a Russian woman on the Plenty of Fish website. During an online "courtship", the woman repeatedly asked for small amounts of money. He was on the way to Aberdeen Airport, convinced he was going to meet her, when he heard his "girlfriend" had been arrested in London and needed him to pay a £4,000 fine in order to free her.'

'Then what?'

'Daft bugger paid up. Turned out she didn't exist.'

'Okay. But that's an isolated incident.'

'Not so. An Inverness woman was conned out of thousands of pounds through a friend request from a man on Facebook. The previous year, a West Lothian conman was jailed for tricking an Aberdeen woman he met online out of £60,000 over a period of four years.'

'You're well-informed.'

Wilma demolished the last of the Bounty Bar. 'I've been reading up.' She scrunched up the wrapper and tossed it into the foot-well. 'There have been twenty-three incidents in the region in the last twelve months, fraudsters fleecing their victims out of a total of almost two million.'

'Point taken,' Maggie said dubiously, watching wind-whipped waves crashing onto the beach below. 'But I don't think it's something we'd want to get involved in.'

'Why not?'

'Much romance fraud, especially so-called catfishing – where someone sets up a fake online profile to trick people who are looking for love – is perpetrated on the internet. Wouldn't it follow most of our investigation would be online?'

'Only after we'd done the legwork. Think on it, we could be out there interacting with all sorts of folk. Single folk and all. You might even find yourself a man.'

Maggie ignored this. She hadn't breathed a word of her lunch date with Allan Chisolm.

'Think on it,' Wilma continued, unabashed. 'We'd be like agony aunts.' Eyes alight, she spread her hands. 'With bells on.' Picking a piece of coconut from between her front teeth, 'How hard can it be?'

'Look, Wilma, granted you know your way around a computer. You've taught me a lot. But we're neither of us hotshots.'

'You don't have to be a geek.'

'You have to know your limitations. We don't have the technical know-how. Police Scotland has Cybercrime Investigations and Digital Forensics departments that provide specialist support to local policing.'

'So? PIs can work in ways the police can't.'

'Give me one example.'

'Oh,' said Wilma airily, running a mental inventory of her dodgy detection gadgets. 'This and that.'

'Don't even go there. You can forget your so-called 'investigation tools' once and for all. As I was saying, we don't have the resources. The police can draw on office backup, forensics, IT systems, tech support. Then there's our competition to consider. The larger investigation firms have both the manpower and technical resources to leave us standing.'

'Don't give me that,' Wilma huffed. 'Aren't you the one who argues women make better investigators: female intuition and that.' Tapping the side of her nose, she added, 'Between the two of us, we'd be able to sniff out a honey-trap nae bother.'

Maggie said, 'Good try. But many of these fraudsters have multiple profiles. Use burner phones. Operate from foreign internet accounts. Accept it, where romance fraud is concerned, we're on a hiding to nothing.'

'A global market. Think of the potential.'

'Plus, how would we go about getting victims' money back? These scams typically involve three unrelated people, so they can be almost impossible to trace. And the code some of the banks are signed up to is voluntary. Newspapers are full of stories: people who've lost their life savings.'

Wilma jutted a petted lip.

'We're not even talking banks here. I read about some poor woman chatted on WhatsApp to a man she met on Facebook Dating. He said he would help her make a lot of money investing in bitcoin. Closer to home, Police Scotland reported an email sextortion scam, where fraudsters threaten to publish online footage of victims watching pornography unless payment is made in bitcoin. Cryptocurrency is held in a digital account called a wallet,' she explained. 'It contains a security key that corresponds to the wallet's address. But...'

'I know. You don't have to spell it out.'

'Maybe I do,' Maggie said forcefully.

Scowling, Wilma said, 'Aren't you the one always banging on about fraud?'

'Yes, but we have to be realistic. Stick to the sort of cases that are within our capabilities. Admit it, romance fraud isn't a goer.'

'It's a bloody sight more of a goer than chasing someone's feckin pet dog.'

Maggie gripped the edge of her seat as the Fiesta was buffeted by a squall. 'Not. Going. To. Happen.'

'Well, you might be happy sitting in front of a computer for the rest of your natural.' Angling the rear-view mirror, Wilma wiped a smear of chocolate from her upper lip. 'But it sure as hell isn't how I see my future.'

No More Notes

'Frankie Bain,' the PE teacher calls. 'Get a move on. You can't sit on that bench all day.'

I bend down, make a show of unlacing my trainers.

Most of the other kids have stripped off their uniforms, and some of them are already down to their underwear. Next to me, Chloe is unbuttoning her school shirt. She's wearing a pink bra, one of those angel jobs I wouldn't be seen dead in.

I've a loose T-shirt on, but they still show. Maybe I could get Mum to buy me a crop top. Anything to hide the swellings on my chest. Mum says they're not proper breasts and she'll get me bra when I develop. Develop what? Great big droopy tits like my Auntie Vera? I'd kill myself first.

Last time we did PE, two of the boys nudged one another when I took my top off and one of them whispered something, then they fell about laughing. The girls in my class aren't much better. They're forever taking selfies and slagging each other off. I asked Mum to write me a note: say I've been feeling dizzy or something. But she said I've run out of excuses. No more notes.

They've all got changed, now, everyone but me.

They're standing in line, whispering and scuffing their feet.

The PE teacher looks across.

'Frankie,' she calls, 'I'm not going to tell you again.'

The Torry Battery

In the car park of the Torry Battery, Souter sucked brown sauce off a sodden chip. Located on the road that loops around Girdle Ness, the Battery's cannons and coastal defences have protected Aberdeen harbour since the late 1400s, but it was in 1840 that today's battery was built.

In the passenger seat of the patrol car, Miller wolfed down a fish supper. 'Any developments on that suicide?' he mumbled through a mouthful of haddock.

'Haven't heard.' Glugging from a bottle of orange Fanta, Souter added, 'Not since the interim PM.'

'When's the final report due?'

'Way things are, wouldn't hold my breath.'

'You have to ask,' said Miller, sooking on a vinegar-soaked chip. 'What makes somebody do a thing like that?'

'Sex.'

'Tell me about it,' Souter sighed. 'I'm up to here with the job. Same goes for Shirley. Says if we never see one another what's the point?'

'You reckon Sellars wasn't getting his?'

'Who knows?'

'Might have got his rocks off dressing up.'

'Could have wanted a sex change. Just never got the length.'

Miller popped the ring on a can of Irn Bru. 'Transvestite, transgender, it's all a mystery to me.' Taking a thirsty swallow, he said, 'Imagine getting your old man chopped off?'

'Eugh!' Souter spluttered, choking on his battered sausage. Face screwed up in distaste, he dropped it into a polystyrene box and closed the lid. Swiftly changing the subject, 'Ferry's on the way out.'

'Aye.' The car park offered a commanding view over Aberdeen harbour. First established in 1136, over the centuries it had been the subject of pirate raids, even withstood being bombed by the Luftwaffe. More recently, a new chapter in its history began when work started on the £350 million Aberdeen South Harbour expansion project. 'What do you reckon to my chances of making CID?'

Souter turned. 'Seriously?'

'Straight up. I don't want to be toting a utility belt for the rest of my working life.'

Suddenly transfixed by the Girdle Ness Lighthouse which dominated the peninsula, Souter asked, 'Did you know that's the only lighthouse in Scotland to have twin fixed lights?'

'Nope. '

'They're still operational, controlled automatically from Edinburgh.'

Miller yawned. Checking his watch, 'Couple of hours to go.'

'Much as that?'

"Fraid so. And you haven't answered my question.'

Feigning forgetfulness, 'Which was?'

'What you reckon to my chances?'

Souter rolled his eyes. 'And pigs might fly.'

Ten Minutes

Lauren Sellars whirled at Wilma's tap on the shoulder. 'What?' Feet planted, she took up a defensive stance.

'Whoops,' said Wilma. 'Didn't mean to give you a fright.'

Curiosity piqued by Ian's revelation, she'd resolved to do a bit of digging. She'd been disappointed by the results: no debt or misdemeanours sullied the outwardly unremarkable life of Vincent Sellars. Nor was anything recorded against his wife. The son had married. No children. With the daughter, she'd landed lucky: Lauren Sellars worked at the hospital, albeit in Ophthalmology, a department Wilma had no reason to frequent.

She'd shadowed Lauren for as long as she could get away with. Tried to establish a pattern of movement. But either the young woman was paired with a colleague or it was too risky to make an approach.

Now, Lauren looked her up and down. 'Do I know you?'

'We sat next to one another on a training course.'

'Did we?'

'While ago.'

'Don't remember.'

'Why would you?'

Eyeing Wilma's light blue tunic, Lauren asked, 'Where do you work?'

'Fourth Floor.' Keep it vague. 'I heard about your dad.'

Her mouth twisted. 'You and the rest.'

'I'm sorry for your loss.'

'Thanks. I don't mean to be rude, but these past few days have been a total nightmare. If it's not the police, it's reporters. And if it's not them, it's someone pushing me to get counselling. I can't even nip down for a drink of juice without someone at my back.'

'I know the feeling,' said Wilma. She'd loitered so often in WH Smith – flicking through whatever magazines weren't shrouded in plastic and scrutinising the paperback bestsellers – she'd been challenged on suspicion of shoplifting. It was only by serendipity, when she'd followed a sudden craving for Maltesers, she'd spied Lauren at the soft drinks. 'I had a sudden bereavement myself not long since,' she fibbed. 'I'm surprised you're here at all.'

'I was offered compassionate leave, but what use is that?'

'I suppose.' Indicating the nearby cafe, 'Tea and sympathy's the best I can do.'

Checking her watch, Lauren said, 'Thanks, but I've got to get back. My colleague will be going off shift soon. I'll need to cover the desk.'

'Ten minutes,' Wilma pressed. 'They'll never even notice you're gone.'

'Well…'

'Even they did, they'd think you were in the toilet.'

Lauren scanned Wilma's top for ID. 'What did you say your name was?'

With a deprecating grin, 'They call me Cupcake on the ward. Can't imagine why.' When she'd spotted her prey, Wilma had whipped off her lanyard and slipped it into her pocket.

That brought a smile to Lauren's lips. Reaching for a bottle of Orangina, she turned towards the checkouts.

Wilma laid a staying on her arm. 'Don't go. It might not seem like it right now, but it would help to talk to someone who's been through….'

Lauren put the juice bottle back on the shelf.

'Ten minutes,' she said.

A Dish of Fish

'Thanks,' Maggie said from the passenger seat of the Mercedes. 'I enjoyed that.'

Smiling, Allan Chisolm responded, 'Me too.'

They'd enjoyed an early evening drink at Maryculter House, a historic hotel founded in the 13th century by the Knights Templar. Picturesquely situated the banks of the Dee and just fifteen minutes from Aberdeen, its Poachers Brasserie offered casual dining in atmospheric surroundings. More important, the venue was discreet.

Stooping to retrieve her bag from the foot-well, she added, 'Back to the grindstone.'

He stole a glance at the time display. 'Can't you give yourself the night off?'

'No way!' Guiltily, Maggie wondered what Wilma was up to – her red Fiesta was missing from the drive – then remembered it was one of her shifts at the hospital.

'Well,' she began, fiddling nervously with the clasp of her handbag.

An awkward silence ensued.

Maggie's mind raced. Does he expect me to invite him in?

The last time Allan Chisolm had been in her house was when they'd had a showdown over the murdered socialite, Annabel Imray. She'd called him "officious" and "humourless", she remembered. He'd retaliated with "cussed" and "infuriating". But that was before he'd taken her in his arms. Her heart lurched. She could summon, still, the sensation of his lips on hers.

Maggie did a quick mental calculation. Colin had rugby practice. He wouldn't be home for at least a couple of hours. Same went for Wilma. Ian invariably worked into the evening. Just as well. He'd be bound to notice a strange car.

What if Chisolm makes a pass?

She made a virtual tour of the house.

Did I hoover the front room?

Has Colin left dishes in the sink?

How did I leave the bedroom? She'd be mortified if it was a tip.

Looking up, she caught a twitch at the corners of his mouth.

What the hell!

'You're right,' she said. 'I'm due a break. Can I offer you a cup of coffee?' Opening the car door, she motioned for him to follow.

Pulse racing, Maggie strode up the drive and turned her key in the front door. 'Grab a seat.' She indicated the sitting room. 'I'll put the kettle on.'

She had just turned on the tap when she heard a shrill cry, closely followed by a thud. Still in her coat, she ran back through the hallway, to find her mother lying on the sitting-room floor, Allan Chisolm stooped over her.

'What's going on?'

Netta McBain pointed an accusing finger. 'I was having a wee nap when this fella…' she eyed Chisolm with distaste, 'appeared. Gave me such a fright I fell off the settee.'

'I do apologise,' Chisolm said. 'I didn't mean to…'

Maggie cut him off. 'Where's Dad?'

'Sent him to Sainsbury's at Bridge of Dee,' her mum replied. 'I'm needing tinned tomatoes.' It was Maggie's turn to get the gimlet eye. 'You're right out.'

'Sorry,' she said lamely. She'd clean forgotten it was the day her folks drove into town from Oldmeldrum to help with the house. 'Let's get you up.'

Taking an arm each, she and Chisolm hauled Netta onto her feet.

'Can we take a rain-check on that coffee?' he whispered, backing out the door.

*

'What were you thinking,' her mum demanded when Chisolm had gone. 'Bringing a strange man into your house in the middle of the day?'

Maggie thought better of pointing out the time. Instead, 'If I'd seen the car…' She'd parked her own Astra a couple of streets away.

'Don't go blaming it on your dad. It's not his fault you keep such a poor home.'

Maggie wasn't going to go there. 'And he's not a strange man. You've met him before.'

'Don't think so.'

'Police inspector.'

'Could be the chief constable,' Netta said, in a voice would have stripped paint. 'Couldn't tell him from Adam.' Perched stiffly on the edge of the sofa, she added, 'What will the neighbours think?'

'Bugger the neighbours,' Maggie exploded.

'Dolled up like a dish of fish,' her mother ploughed on. 'Face clarted with…' She broke off. 'Have you been drinking?'

'What if I have? I'm a grown woman. I can do what I like. When I like. Dressed how I like.'

Eyes fixed on the big chair in the window, Netta said, 'If George was alive—'

'Don't bring him into it.'

'Did you never stop to think of your children?'

'Them neither,' Maggie snapped. 'I've had a bellyful of thinking about other people.'

'Well,' her mother began. 'If that's your attitude…'

Maggie didn't wait to hear the rest of the sentence. Slamming the front door behind her, she shot out of the house.

A United Front

Douglas sat awkwardly in a low Parker Knoll chair, a Denby coffee mug clasped in both hands. 'Lived here long?' He cast a sharp eye over Susan's mid-century Schreiber sideboard.

Following his gaze, she found it wanting. She'd thought the piece cutting-edge when she'd spotted it in Milne's North Silver Street auction rooms. Now, it looked tired. A weight settled in her stomach. She'd probably paid too much. Collecting her thoughts, 'Couple of years.'

'Place working out?'

'I wouldn't go as far as that.' Located on the North Deeside Road past the affluent western suburbs of Cults and Milltimber, the village of Peterculter offered little in the way of amenities: a couple of supermarkets, a hairdresser, a chippie and an ice cream parlour, improbably named Fits the Scoop. 'It's on the quiet side. But it suits me,' she added quickly, unwilling to admit it was all she could afford. 'How about you?'

'Love my pad,' he crowed. 'The Boulevard's so central. And the views are amazing.'

Susan couldn't resist. 'Isn't there a cladding problem with that development?'

'There is,' he responded airily. 'But it's on the other side, so no worries.'

Jammy bastard.

'Right,' she said. These past few months, she'd been sorely tempted to move back into town. The flat, on the top floor of a rundown semi-detached villa, had seemed quirky on first viewing. Now, Susan found the dormer-windowed living room dark, the kitchen cramped, the bathroom dated. The only bedroom was spacious enough, but stifling in summer, Baltic in winter. The commute could be a real pain, not to mention the cost of petrol. Aberdeen house prices had taken a nosedive. Landlords were selling up. City centre flats going for a song. Problem was, she never seemed to get the space. If she wasn't actually on duty, she was thinking about it. As a consequence, her social life had suffered. She was too tired to go out on the razzle. Had lost touch with friends. Unlike Douglas, who seemed to combine the job with a succession of girlfriends.

Leaning forward, he said, 'I thought it was time we got together.'

Susan held her breath. Her car had gone into the garage that morning for its MOT, and needed a part. When Douglas had offered to run her home, she'd reluctantly accepted. When he'd invited himself in, she'd thought for one fleeting moment he was planning to make a move on her. Dismissed the thought. True, he had an inflated sense of his own importance, but they'd worked together long enough. Surely, he'd know better.

'Things being as they are...'

What things? Her mind scrambled. The job? The economy?

Douglas balanced his mug on the chair's wooden arm, where it teetered precariously for a moment or two before he had second thoughts. Set it down on the carpet instead.

'...We need to present a united front.'

Giddy with relief, Susan stifled an urge to giggle.

'I don't see what's so funny,' he complained, colour flooding his face.

'It's just...' Susan could contain herself no longer. She erupted into uncontrolled mirth.

'Well, if you're going to be like that,' said Douglas, jumping to his feet.

The half-drunk mug of coffee tipped over.

They both watched as a dark stain crept over the carpet.

'Shit!' he exclaimed.

Susan said. 'Doesn't matter.' She sprinted into the kitchen and returned with a cloth.

Douglas was on his knees, desperately mopping the carpet with a fistful of sodden tissues.

'Here.' She dropped to a crouch, 'Let me.'

Raising his head, their eyes met, faces barely six inches apart.

Susan spread the cloth, patting it down to absorb most of the liquid. 'You were saying?'

Douglas sat back on his heels. 'Haldane. I know we've had our differences. But you're right, that dame's a piece of work. She could seriously damage our chances. What I'm saying is…' He looked down at his feet, the pair of pointed tan Oxfords incongruous against the retro floral carpet. '…Why don't we stick together? Let bygones be bygones? Way I see it, that can only benefit us both.'

Less Talk, More Action

In her conservatory, Wilma relaxed into the plump cushions of a capacious cane chair, a booklet in one hand. After the day she'd had, she'd been buoyed to find the prospectus on the mat.

'What have you got there?' asked Ian, peering over her shoulder.

'Nothing,' said Wilma, swiftly moving to cover the booklet with a brown envelope.

His hand shot out.

Holding it at arm's length, he read, 'Diploma of Higher Education in Criminology and Sociology.'

Wilma snatched it back.

Clutching it to her breast, 'It's mine.'

'What's it in aid of?'

Defiantly, 'You can read, can't you?'

His brow furrowed. 'Yes, but…'

'The Open University, if you must know.'

Ian's eyes stood out on stalks. 'University? You?'

Squaring up, Wilma retorted, 'Why not me?'

'Wondered how you'd find the time,' he back-tracked, 'you keeping up two jobs and all. Plus, don't you need Highers and stuff?'

Wilma fixed him with a challenging look. 'The short answer is no.'

'Then there's the question of…'

'It's the money,' she interrupted. 'That's what's bothering you, isn't it?'

'That's not what I said.'

'It's what you bloody meant. How am I supposed to better myself, tell me that, if I don't have an education?'

'You have,' Ian insisted. 'Same as me.'

'Call that an education: leaving school on the Friday and gutting fish on the Monday?'

'Well...'

'I've left Torry behind, along with that thieving bastard Darren.'

'Leave your ex out of it. All I'm trying to say is, we're fine as we are, without you...'

'I knew it,' said Wilma, whacking the prospectus back onto the table. 'You're that far up yourself – you and the rest of them miserable sods around here – you're feart to broaden your horizons.' Lip curled, she added, 'Talk about the living dead.'

'That's not what I was thinking at all,' Ian protested. 'And if you're set on further education, why not study English? You'd get more use out of thon dictionary your head's aye stuck in.'

'Because,' said Wilma, jabbing the prospectus, 'I need to up my skillset. This will benefit the business and me, both.'

'What about that new kitchen you've been on about? There's no way we could run to...'

His words were drowned by the sound of a slamming door.

*

'Yasss,' Ian breathed, as Wilma bent over him, fingers creeping up his inner thigh. 'Don't stop!' he moaned, as they moved to his groin. 'You big darlin',' he sighed, as they found their target. After their earlier disagreement, he'd plied her with beer and sat – unprotesting – through several episodes of CSI.

'Big?' she shrieked, fingers frozen mid-move. 'I've lost two feckin stone since we tied the knot.'

'Take your word for it,' he murmured, burying his nose in her cleavage.

She sat up ramrod straight. 'Gone down two dress sizes. You mean you haven't noticed?'

Backing off, Ian eyed her generous breasts. 'Mebbe in other places. But these...' Jiggling them in both palms, he licked his lips. '...Look just the same to me.'

'Get off,' Wilma hissed, shunting over to her side of the bed. 'All that effort, and I might as well not have bothered.'

'Nobody asked you to lose weight,' he remonstrated. 'I liked you fine the way you were.'

'That's as may be. But if I'm going to better myself—'

'I knew it. That Open University nonsense, it's down to her.' Voice rising, Ian pointed an accusing finger at the party wall. 'Next door.'

'Phooey,' said Wilma. 'It was flagged up at the end of some TV programme. Thought it wouldn't hurt to have a look.'

'As if.'

Wilma sat up. 'Don't you "as if" me. Every last thing goes wrong in this house you blame on Maggie Laird.'

'With good reason. Ever since you pair got in cahoots, there's been nothing but trouble: you stay out till all hours, fraternise with criminals, bring police to our door.'

'Goes with the territory.'

'And gey shady territory is, too. We were perfectly happy before she came waltzing in, begging favours.'

'Favours?' Wilma shrilled. 'Maggie Laird has changed my life.'

'And not for the better.'

'If it wasn't for her I'd still be…'

'…Content,' said Ian, finishing the sentence. 'You look different, I'll grant you. Talk different. Next thing I know you'll be looking for a different fella.'

'Dinna talk shite.'

'If she's not got a man,' he persisted. 'Don't take it out on me.'

'If Maggie Laird doesn't have a partner,' Wilma said in a pretend-posh voice, 'it's because she's…'

'…Miss Picky. Isn't that what you were calling her not long since?'

'Well,' Wilma conceded. 'I might have.'

'It's make your mind up time. Her or me.'

'Och,' she said, cosying up. 'Don't be like that.' She'd got a major fright, when a previous bust-up had resulted in a short-lived separation. Wasn't looking for a repeat. 'I was just saying…'

'Less talk, more action,' Ian said, hands roving her body.

'Ooh,' Wilma squealed. 'That's nice.'

Justice for George

V

Justice for George

Brian threw a nervous glance over his shoulder. 'I shouldn't be doing this.'

'Why the sudden change of heart?' Maggie said accusingly. They'd fallen out over her repeated attempts to extract police information. That, and Brian's clumsy advances.

'Our friend Brannigan has surfaced. Thought you'd want to know.'

They were in a quiet corner of The Wild Boar in Belmont Street. His idea. The scene of past assignations, it was handy for the station, quiet at this time of the day.

Now, 'Where?' Maggie asked. 'When?'

'Liverpool. Bobby Brannigan was remanded to Walton Prison three months ago.'

'How did he end up in Walton?'

'Drugs offences. No surprises there.'

'What's he saying?'

'Not a lot. He's dead.'

Maggie started in shock.

'Life he led,' Brian said, laying a hand on her arm. 'It was always on the cards.'

She shook him off. 'Are you sure you've got the right information? Brannigan can't be that old.'

'Quite sure. Pneumonia, it says on the death certificate, though I gather from my source he died of complications from an injury: stabbed with a shiv when he was inside.'

Clasping a palm to her forehead, Maggie slumped back on her seat. 'All that heartache for nothing.'

'Not entirely. Before he was taken to hospital, Brannigan confided in his cellmate: goes by the name of Pat Toomey. Put his hands up to a fair few things. Upshot is, Bobby Brannigan gave a sworn statement exonerating George from all culpability.'

'I don't believe it.'

'It's true. Merseyside have committed to send a copy through to our Executive as soon as it has been properly authenticated.'

Maggie said, 'To think I've spent all this time chasing justice for George.' She turned an angry face. 'The risks I've taken. The things I've gone without.' With a shake of the head, 'I'd never have dreamed of taking on a half-baked detective agency for a start. Never have got involved with…'

Wilma Harcus? Brian threw her a quizzical look. He'd speculated how long it would take for the unlikely partnership to implode.

'…A criminal kingpin like James Gilruth.' Her brow furrowed. 'Any news on that front?'

'Haven't heard a word.' Ineffectually, Brian patted her arm. 'Don't beat yourself up.'

'I ran at it like a mad thing,' Maggie wailed, pulling away. 'Thinking I'd clear the family name. When that didn't happen, I told myself I'd have to be patient, that it would come right in the end. But now…' Her eyes brimmed with tears. '…I feel robbed. Like I've been bereaved all over again.'

A server materialised at Brian's elbow. 'Can I get you something?'

He turned. 'Maggie?'

'Not for me.'

'You sure? A stiff drink might do you good.'

'Quite sure. I've Seaton to think about. Coffee would be good.'

'Cappuccino and a flat white, thanks.'

'What if I hadn't managed to make something of the business?' Maggie went on. 'We could have lost the roof over our heads. My children's education would have suffered. They could have been taken into care.'

'Didn't happen,' Brian argued, once their drinks had been set in front of them. 'What you need to do now is move on.'

Maggie flinched from his searching gaze.

What was Brian trying to say? Move on from agonising over

George, or was there more to it? Queen Street was a hotbed of gossip. She wondered how much of her burgeoning relationship with Allan Chisolm was common knowledge.

Taking a sip, she responded, 'Easier said than done. It has been such a struggle. If I hadn't had Wilma...' Seeing Brian's mouth twitch, 'What?' she demanded.

'She still as big?'

'That's fat-shaming,' Maggie snapped.

He grinned. 'Just joking.'

Changing the subject, 'What will I tell the kids?'

'What you've always told them: their dad was a good copper and straight as a die.'

*

Wilma's face loomed out of Maggie's phone. 'That it?' she queried, when Maggie broke the news about Brannigan.

'What did you expect? Fireworks?'

'More than a damp squib, that's for bloody sure. When you said Brian had been in touch, I thought mebbe you'd manage to winkle some intel out of him on thon suicide.'

'In your dreams. I've learned my lesson there. But getting back to the matter in hand, you'd have had Bobby Brannigan die bound to a chair, I suppose. Being tortured by a power drill, like you and your boys tried before.'

'It was a steam iron,' Wilma protested. 'And we never laid a finger on him.' Smirking, 'But you're right, I'd see the bastard in hell.'

'Hell's too good for him,' said Maggie.

'Never thought it would end up like this. Or take as long. There's no justice in this world.'

'If you'd been married to a cop for as long as I was, you'd know these things don't always wrap up tidily.'

'And if you'd come from where I did, you'd have...'

'I know. Summoned a hit squad and gone looking, armed with baseball bats and God knows what.'

94

Wilma said, 'There's no call to take the piss.'

'I'm sorry. But you do have a tendency to...' she chose her words with care, '...find the most direct route to problem-solving.'

'Can I take that as a compliment?'

'Take it whatever way you like. 'To tell the truth, I'm sick and tired of the whole sorry business. If it hadn't been for that, we'd never have become private investigators and landed up like this.'

'You saying we should pack it in?'

'That's exactly what I'm saying. The whole point of us carrying on George's agency was to use it as a springboard to clear his name.'

'But...'

'We've knocked our pans out. And for what: a prison confession that might not be worth a row of beans?'

'Think what we'd have missed,' Wilma teased. Then, seeing Maggie's sour expression, 'We've nobody to account to but ourselves. Isn't that worth having?'

'We've no steady income,' Maggie exploded. 'No job security. No...'

'...Baggage,' Wilma offered with a cheeky grin.

'You're forgetting about my kids.'

'Kirsty's independent of you already. Colin won't be far behind.'

'Okay. But what about you? There's Ian to think of.'

'Forget about him.'

'That's all very well,' said Maggie.

Her head spun.

If things were to develop with Allan Chisolm—

'With luck, Merseyside will come up with the goods. George will be cleared. And...'

'Even if that happens, where do we go from here?'

'Crack on,' Wilma insisted, mouth set in a determined line.

A Secret

'I'm not going to tell you again,' Maggie warned, assuming her sternest expression.

Head lowered, the small boy scuttled back to his classmates, who stood slack-jawed on the far side of the playground.

She felt a tug at her elbow. 'Miss?'

Maggie whirled to find Frankie Bain standing at her back.

'Can I speak to you?'

'Of course.' She'd been relieved to see the girl starting to join in group activities. Concluded her own anxieties ill-founded.

Shifting from foot to foot, Frankie began, 'The other day...'

'Don't worry about it,' Maggie said. 'Accidents happen to everyone.' It was on the tip of her tongue to ask if Frankie had started her periods. Decided it was neither the time nor place.

Speaking from beneath lowered lids, Frankie went on, 'Still, I didn't say thanks.'

'Forget it, ' Maggie said dismissively.

'Can I ask you a question?'

'Go ahead.'

'Why is your eye funny?'

Sighing, Maggie said, 'It just goes its own way some of the time.'

'Does it hurt?'

'No. But I'll let you into a secret.' She bent to whisper in Frankie's ear. 'Sometimes it makes me feel really embarrassed.'

Nodding, Frankie asked, 'Do you have kids?'

'Two: a girl and a boy.'

'Do they have a dad?"

'No,' Maggie said with a renewed stab of loss. 'He died.'

'Huh.' Frankie deliberated for a few moments, then, 'Do you miss him?'

'Sometimes.' With a jolt, Maggie realised how true this was. Now she thought about it, the times she missed George the most was when she needed support with their kids.

Checking there was no-one within earshot, Frankie dropped her voice. 'If I told you something, would you keep it a secret?'

'I would if you asked me to.'

Head bent, Frankie scuffed the grass with the toe of her shoe.

Maggie scanned the playground. Two knots of boys were scrapping over a trophy, three others in a tight huddle, heads bent over something. Her antennae twitched. Looked like they were in possession something they shouldn't be. Nearby, a group of girls giggled conspiratorially and flicked their hair.

Stooping, 'Wouldn't say a word,' she whispered. 'Not to a living soul.'

The bell clanged.

Frankie's head shot up, a look of panic on her face.

All around them, excited children were making last-minute exchanges as they filtered into line.

'You can talk to me anytime,' Maggie said. Seeing the doubt in Frankie's eyes, she added, 'In confidence. That's what I'm here for.'

Sunset Court

'Finished?' Wilma asked, eyeing the untouched bowl of soup.

This was met with a vacant stare.

Scooping a spoonful, she held it out.

Lightning-quick, the old woman knocked the spoon out of her hand.

Fuck!

Wilma's snatched conversation with Lauren Sellars had yielded scant intel: she was in a long-standing relationship. Her mother worked at a Northfield care home. Didn't talk much about her workmates, had more to say about the residents, living or dead. The brother was an agricultural equipment sales rep. Divorced.

She was cock-a-hoop when Ian broke the news: Dodd Benzie's mum had delivered the goods. Or almost. Couldn't put a name to him, but she'd divulged Jean Sellars' lover was a work colleague.

Wilma proceeded to make overtures – both by telephone and in person – to Jean's workplace. Got knocked back each time. Mrs Sellars, she ascertained, had been signed off sick. But as for gaining entry, the security at Sunset Court would have put Alcatraz in the shade.

She debated rocking up to Jean's house, under the guise of a work colleague, with a bunch of supermarket flowers. Decided that was a step too far. Since the day the news broke, there had been very little in the papers, but for all she knew there could still be reporters hanging around. In desperation, Wilma rang the local recruitment agencies until she landed a temp job at Sunset Court.

Now, snatching a paper napkin, she began to mop up the mess.

'Don't waste your time,' instructed a fellow care assistant, identified from her name badge as Aggie. 'Starter, main, pudding...

Most of them canna tell the difference. Dish it up. Whack it away. Faster you go, quicker you'll get your break.'

'Thanks,' said Wilma, sussing an opportunity. She'd made an abortive start, time wasted pumping mostly East European employees for information they clearly didn't possess. This one looked more promising. Slapping an ingratiating smile on her face, 'I owe you one,' she said.

*

Lunch over, the residents were nodding off in the conservatory and Wilma had bolted down a plate of shepherd's pie, followed by a dollop of rhubarb crumble and custard – one of the few perks of the job – when Aggie beckoned.

Wilma followed her down a corridor and through a set of fire doors.

Ducking around the corner of the building, 'Ciggie?' She drew a pack of JPS from her trouser pocket.

Wilma shook her head. 'Jacked them in.'

'Too bad,' said Aggie, lighting up.

'How long have you worked here?'

'Coming on six months.'

'You'll know Jean Sellars, then.'

'Aye.'

'Terrible, losing her husband like that.'

Aggie took a long drag. 'You could say.' Blowing smoke rings, 'On the other hand…'

Wilma quirked an eyebrow. Sniffing blood, 'Don't keep me in suspense.'

Aggie shook her head.

'Pal of yours?'

'No way. Old timers like her, run the place like they own it. Leave the shite jobs to the likes of us.' Holding her ciggie at arm's length, she dropped to a crouch, rummaged under a hydrangea bush, and fished out a half-empty water bottle. Brandishing it aloft, 'Drink?'

'Had a cuppa not long since.'

Aggie grinned. 'Never say no to a wee vodka.'

Unscrewing the top, she took a thirsty swig.

'Now you're talking,' said Wilma, reaching out.

*

Wilma leaned back against the office door, heart hammering fit to bust. Once they'd emptied the vodka bottle, it had taken no time to ferret out of Aggie that Jean Sellars was in a relationship with the care home's cook. And time was of the essence. Unless Wilma came up with the intel fast, Maggie would come asking questions. And once Maggie started asking questions…

There was just one problem: it was the cook's day off.

Wilma weighed her options.

Decided there was only one thing for it.

Behind the desk, a grey filing cabinet stood in one corner. Crossing the room, Wilma tugged open the top drawer.

Unlocked. Her pulse rate slowed, just a tad.

She scanned the tabs: Accounts, Dental/Medical, Finance, Insurance… Slid the drawer shut.

The second drawer was more promising. Stooping, she read, Property Maintenance, Receipts… Then, Staff.

Wilma's pulse quickened.

She was about to dive in when she heard the murmur of conversation in the corridor outside.

Lightning-quick, she shut the drawer and leapt into the chair that sat in front of the desk.

There was a tap on the door.

A head appeared.

'Boss not here?' A carer whose name she couldn't remember, even she could pronounce.

'Just nipped out.' Wilma said a silent prayer. She'd been introduced to Cathy Adamson, the care home manager, when she reported for duty. Knew she'd met her match.

'Tell her we're low on incontinence pads.'

'Okay.'

The door had no sooner closed than Wilma was back at the filing cabinet. Her fingers flew: Anderson, Buchan, Chalmers, Dunbar...

Wilma faltered when she reached the letter 'S'. Weighed for an instant whether Jean Sellars' file would yield useful intel. Decided against.

Then there it was: Keith Williams.

Wilma lifted out the file and laid it on the desk.

Fishing her phone from a trouser pocket, she selected the photo icon and pressed the button.

A Dummy Run

'You must think me an old fool,' Bill MacSorley mumbled, head in hands.

'Not at all,' said Maggie, from her hard chair at the kitchen table. When she'd finished at Seaton School, she'd driven out to Inverurie, sixteen miles north of the city. A market town, home to the biggest livestock market in Scotland, it has grown in recent years to become a commuter satellite of Aberdeen.

'Dummy run,' Wilma pronounced, when MacSorley made his initial contact. 'If it doesn't work out, we can try something else.' Then, having quashed Maggie's objections, 'You go. You're the one was brought up on a farm.'

Slowly, he raised his head. 'In my defence, ever since I lost my wife...' His voice wavered. 'Beginning of last year. Lung cancer.'

That explained a lot. The house had a sour smell, not wholly attributable to the muck-clarted wellington boots at the back door.

'I'm sorry,' Maggie responded. 'But you mustn't blame yourself. So-called romance fraud is commonplace these days.'

'Not in Inverurie.'

'There have been a number of cases in the north-east,' she assured him. 'And they say statistics don't accurately represent the true scale of the problem. Many victims are too embarrassed to report their experiences.'

'I suppose that should make me feel better,' he said. 'My friend – Yelena is her name – was so convincing I let my guard down. Not like a farmer, eh?'

Maggie nodded her understanding. The MacSorley farm in Chapel of Garioch wasn't far from where her folks had farmed all their lives. She wondered how she would feel if it were her own father who had been so cruelly deceived. 'You mentioned, when you called, you met the woman online.'

'That's right. I checked the reviews of quite a number of dating sites over a period of months.' He offered a rueful smile. 'I'm not a complete novice. Plus, I wasn't at all sure I was ready to commit. But living out here on my own – life's hard at the best of times.'

'You don't need to tell me.'

'Online dating websites and apps are one of the most popular ways to meet a new partner,' she said. 'Users are at an all-time high. But, sadly, so is the number of people becoming victims of online dating scams.'

'If it feels too good to be true then it probably is,' Bill MacSorley bemoaned. 'If only I'd trusted my gut.'

Opening her notebook, Maggie asked, 'Can you give me details of the fraud?'

'It was small amounts of money to start with: a new pair of shoes, an unexpected utility bill. And Yelena seemed embarrassed to ask. Promised to pay me back when she sorted out her finances.'

'When discussions quickly turn to money, that's a real giveaway.'

Grim-faced, MacSorley continued, 'As the weeks went by, her demands increased: she'd lost her mobile, couldn't afford the plane fare to visit her sick mother. Sounds ludicrous when you say it out loud, but at the time—' Shrugging, 'She's a good-looking girl. I'd defy any man to keep his head, far less someone like me: a fifty-something, balding, overweight widower.'

'These requests for cash, they didn't raise your suspicions?'

'Not at first. You have to understand the relationship developed very fast: we were chatting several times a day, half the night sometimes. I was too caught up to question her motives, though with hindsight I realise this was all about building trust.'

'And after that?'

'Yelena suggested we move our interaction away from the website to a more private channel: phone, email, instant messaging.'

'Another giveaway.'

'Oh, there was a niggle in my mind, now and then: some detail in her online profile not consistent with what she told me, excuses as to why she couldn't talk on the phone, camera not working when I wanted to Skype.'

'The money,' Maggie pressed. 'How was it transferred?

'Via Western Union.'

'Mmm.' It was, she'd learned from a previous case, one of the fastest ways to send criminal cash, transactions irreversible.

'Thankfully, I managed to cotton on before I lost the shirt off my back. It's not even the money,' MacSorley said. 'Though in my business we know the value of a shilling. To be honest with you, Mrs Laird, it's my pride at stake. If the family – not to mention the farming community – get a whiff of this, I'll be a laughing stock. That's why, when police enquiries hit a brick wall, I turned to you.'

'They didn't manage to make contact with Yelena?'

'They said because I had shared personal information, including my phone number, it made their job more difficult. Can't say I blame them. From what I've read since, these scams have become so sophisticated, Russian fraudsters even use lists of ready-made excuses to cover all eventualities.'

'I see,' Maggie said, though she hadn't the foggiest. 'Given what you've told me...' she extemporised, a prelude to turning him down.

'I'm under no illusions,' he said earnestly. 'I may be throwing good money after bad, but I don't like being taken for a mug. And if anyone can get me satisfaction it's another woman, hence the reason we're sitting here today.'

Poor man.

Maggie's heartstrings tugged. Bill MacSorley looked so vulnerable, sitting in his cheerless kitchen: no one to brew him a cup of tea of a morning, bid him goodnight at the end of a long day. She could identify with that.

'You will help me, won't you?'

Use your head. Turn him down.

'Please?'

Her resolve wavered. 'I can't make any promises,' she said cautiously.

'Thank you.' He leaned forward. 'That means a lot.'

'We'll do our utmost to achieve a resolution.'

Closing her notebook, Maggie couldn't help but think, 'Who's the dummy, now?'

Watch Your Back

The logo – four orange squares on a bright blue background – was instantly recognisable. Sandwiched between Poundland and Paddypower, Greggs the bakers occupies a double-fronted retail unit on Aberdeen's main thoroughfare, Union Street.

'Better watch your back,' Bob Duffy warned, as they waited to be served.

Brian looked over his shoulder. The lunchtime queue snaked out the door and down the street. 'Don't get you.'

Cupping a hand over his mouth, Duffy leaned in close. 'Haldane,' he said in a low voice. 'That story about requesting a transfer, it's total bollocks.'

Frowning, Brian queried, 'She didn't ask to come out of Bell Street?'

'Let's put it this way: she jumped before she was pushed.'

'Where did you get that from?'

Tapping a finger to his nose, Duffy said, 'Pal of mine. Story goes, Haldane shagged her way up the chain of command.'

'She can fairly turn on the charm,' Brian allowed. 'Working with her this past while, I've seen her in action.'

'Bit of a ball-breaker, by all accounts. Dumped the poor buggers without a backward glance.'

*

Takeaway in hand, the two crossed the street and cut through McCombie's Court. The narrow pend led from the former Esslemont & Macintosh department store building to the Marischal Square development, where they could take the air on the roof terrace of the St Nicholas Centre.

Once parked on a bench, Brian asked, 'Why are you only telling me this now?'

'My pal's been on sick leave. Stress,' Duffy confided.

Chewing on a vegan sausage roll, he nodded in sympathy. Police Scotland statistics showed days off due to "psychological disorders" had rocketed over the past three years, averaging nearly four days annually for each of the 17,000 plus workforce.

'Only came back on duty this morning,' Duffy continued, biting into his steak bake. 'Got on the blower straightaway.'

'All the same, I wouldn't lend too much credence to hearsay. A looker like Haldane, folk are bound to be jealous.'

'Fair dos.' Brushing flakes of puff pastry off his chin with the back of his hand, Duffy took a mouthful of milky tea. 'But seems she deliberately targeted guys who could advance her career, with no regard to the comeback.'

Brian's stomach lurched. It had been on the tip of his tongue to suggest Lisa join him for a quick drink, maybe a bar supper. She was new to the city, after all.

Now, 'Didn't get her far. She's still a DC.'

'That's where you're wrong,' said Duffy. 'She got promotion to sergeant in double-quick time.' Taking another swallow of tea, he added, 'Would have made inspector by now, I shouldn't wonder, if she hadn't picked on the wrong guy.'

'"Wrong guy"?' Brian echoed, taking another bite. Suddenly, the sausage roll didn't taste so great.

Duffy nodded. 'Fell head over heels.'

Sipping his coffee, 'How did it end up?'

'Broke up the poor bastard's marriage. And that was for starters. When the affair got out, Haldane landed him right in it.' Glancing behind, Duffy's voice sank to a whisper. 'He'd told her things she had no right to know.'

'What was the upshot?'

'Disciplinary leading to demotion. And him with a disabled kid and all.'

'How about her?'

'Back where she started.'

Duffy scrunched his paper bag into a ball.

Aimed it at a nearby litter bin.

'I'm telling you, mate…' He laid a cautionary hand on Brian's arm. 'Better watch out.'

A Test of Initiative

'Russian? That's a stroke of luck.'

'I'm glad somebody thinks so,' Maggie said dourly, leaning back against the kitchen worktop. She'd barely been through the door before Wilma came knocking, and was desperate for a lie down and a cup of tea. 'I spent hours holding that poor man's hand.'

'Good-looking, was he?'

Maggie frowned. 'I didn't mean that literally. And if the police cybercrime people can't help him, we haven't a hope in hell.'

'We may not have their resources, but we've more life experience between the two of us than some young nerd sitting in a back office. Look at it as a test of initiative. Isn't that why we became PIs?'

'As I recall, we took on the agency because we were skint. That, and ill-qualified for anything else. Admit it, this is a complete non-starter.'

Chin jutted, Wilma said, 'Client's prepared to pay.'

'That's not the point.'

'It's what you said when we took on that feckin cat.'

'That was different. Bill MacSorley has been defrauded once. I don't want to be the one to add to his pain.' Sneaking a peek at her watch, 'Look, can we talk about this another time?'

'You needing to make Colin his tea?'

'No, he's out tonight. It's just…'

'How's about we crack open a bottle? Ian's working overtime. After the news you've had about Brannigan, you should switch off for a bit.'

'Sorry, I've work to do.'

'What work?'

Maggie's mind raced. The last thing she'd do was share her plans for the evening. 'Admin,' she said.

'Bugger the admin.' Wilma patted her hand. 'You look tired. Take the night off. Do you good.'

'No can do.'

'Then take the weight off your feet.' She steered Maggie though to the dining room. 'I'll make you a cup of tea.'

'I'm fine,' Maggie protested, sitting down.

'Okay,' said Wilma, plonking herself down opposite. 'But as I was saying…'

'If you're so sure of yourself,' Maggie interrupted. 'Then how are we going to go about this investigation, tell me that?'

'Do a trace on Yelena.'

'Oh, yeah? Like she's sitting up in Northfield? The woman's not even in the UK. And a country the size of Russia—'

'We'll start with Skype handles,' Wilma said matter-of-factly. 'Establish if the name she's using is genuine, though it's unlikely. Then we can upload her photo onto search engines, do a reverse image lookup, see if anything matches.'

'How come you know all that?'

'Don't ask. If that doesn't do it, we'll have to get more creative.'

'You mean dodgy. Since the day we set up in business, Wilma Harcus, you've used tactics that are questionable to say the least. I turned a blind eye because I was desperate. But the dark web, that's a step too far.'

'The dark web would be a good place to get stuff like this, I grant you. But it's not limited to there. A huge black market exists for information, and Russia is quite heavily involved. There are hundreds of leaked databases folk can access if they know where to look.'

'Leaked?' Maggie shrieked. 'You mean stolen. There's no way I'm going to break the law. We could lose our licence. Even go to jail.'

'We wouldn't be breaking the law,' Wilma said. 'Internet forums would probably throw up a seller.'

'You're proposing we pay some low-life for information?'

'Not our fault. It's all down to corruption. We're not even talking big bucks. And we'd be doing good: saving poor lonely souls like Bill

MacSorley money and heartache.'

'Don't come the bleeding heart with me. I know you too well.'

Wilma had the grace to look abashed. Recovering swiftly, 'If we make a go of it, think of the potential. We could be up there with the big boys.'

'You're getting ahead of yourself.'

'Better that than feart.'

Maggie said, 'I'll be the first to admit I tend to err on the side of caution. But right now...' Struggling to her feet, '...I really need to...'

'Hang on. How did you leave it with MacSorley?'

'Said we'd do our best,' Maggie muttered through clenched teeth.

'Good on you,' said Wilma. 'We're going to hit the jackpot with this one. I've a feeling in my bones.'

Between the Sheets

Maggie bent forward to check the level on the cafetiere. Turning, 'More coffee?'

'Not for me,' Chisolm replied with a slow smile.

They were sitting side by side in Maggie's front room, having not long returned from a leisurely supper at Borsalino, a small Italian restaurant in the outskirts of Peterculter.

'How's your mum?' he teased, a wicked glint in his grey eyes. 'Has she recovered?'

Maggie's face burned. 'Don't know. We haven't spoken since.'

'Oops,' said Chisolm. 'Hope I haven't upset the apple cart.'

'Not a bit,' Maggie lied. 'My folks are set in their ways, that's all.'

He chuckled. 'That's a relief. I was half expecting them to parachute in at any moment.'

'No chance of that. They're in bed by nine o'clock.'

Not only them.

Colin had a sleepover at a friend's, the reason she'd felt confident enough to agree to a dinner date. Maggie would have the house to herself.

Her and Chisolm.

Her insides clenched uncomfortably.

'Then, relax.' Laying a hand on one shoulder, he drew her back.

Settling into the soft upholstery, Maggie let her eyelids droop, felt the stiffness start to ebb from her limbs.

'Better?'

'Mmm.'

'You need to ease up.'

Her eyes shot open. 'You can talk.'

'Wasn't meant as a criticism.'

'I know.' With a small shake of the head, 'I'm sorry. Didn't mean

112

to bite your head off. 'It's just…' Her eyes swept the familiar room, George's big chair in the bay window.

'You're apprehensive.'

She nodded.

'Me, too. Never thought I'd be in this situation.' With a rueful grin, 'Not at this age, anyhow.'

This last brought a smile to Maggie's lips. 'What are we like?'

'Couple of teenagers,' Chisolm said, moving his arm to encircle her shoulders.

✳

'You don't need to do this,' said Chisolm, as they stood, fully dressed, in her bedroom.

'No.' Maggie's voice sounded unconvincing, even to herself.

That morning, before driving across the city to her job at Seaton, she'd hoovered and dusted. Changed the bed. Sprayed her bedroom with expensive room spray – Floris, a past birthday gift from Val – all the while telling herself she had no intention of ending up in bed with Allan Chisolm.

None.

At.

All.

Now, she stood trembling with fear and exhilaration: nerves taut, stomach in knots, adrenaline coursing through her veins.

Slowly, Allan drew her into his arms.

Gently, he dropped a kiss on the crown of her head.

Still, Maggie trembled.

Then, 'Sod it!' She broke free.

Feverishly, she stripped off her clothes: shoes, socks, jeans, top.

She unhooked her bra.

Peeled off her knickers.

Leaving them where they lay, she drew back the covers and got into bed, pulling the duvet up under her chin.

For a few moments Maggie lay motionless, appalled and heartened in equal parts by what she'd just done.

Lifting her head from the pillow, she said, 'Well?'

Chisolm shook his head. 'I don't believe you just did that.'

With studied calm, he undressed and slid into bed beside her.

Maggie's lips turned up at the corners. 'I surprised myself.'

An alert pinged on her phone.

Chisolm's voice in her ear, 'Ignore it.'

It pinged again.

Distracted, Maggie turned onto her side.

She groped in the bag she'd left by the bedside cabinet.

Checked the display.

Turning back, 'Colin.'

'Didn't you say he was…'

'…Away overnight.' Maggie's heart raced. What if Colin had a change of plan? He might be on his way home that very minute. 'I'd better take it.'

When the call connected, 'You're at Torquil's, right?' she asked, heart in mouth.

'Right.'

'Then, why are you calling?' she managed to squeeze out, though her throat was bone dry.

'Forgot we're going out for a pizza. Can you put some cash in my account?'

'That it?'

'Pretty much.'

'Okay. I'm tied up right now. I'll do it later.'

'Thanks, Mum. Bye.'

Maggie put her phone on silent and stowed it away.

Turning to face Allan Chisolm, she said, 'Where were we?'

'Back where we started.'

He drew her close. 'But there's no hurry.'

With exquisite slowness, he stroked her bare skin. 'We have all the time in the world.'

VI

Missing

Maggie burst into the head teacher's office. 'Frankie Bain,' she mouthed, between laboured breaths. 'She's gone missing.'

Anne Shirreffs' head jerked up from the paper she'd been studying. 'Where from?'

'She isn't in class this morning,' Maggie panted.

'Calm down,' Mrs Shirreffs said. 'There's probably a straightforward explanation: they may have overslept, forgotten to tell us about a dental appointment, something like that.'

'That's just it,' said Maggie, eyes wide in alarm. 'Lynsey gave it an hour, just in case. Then she thought better safe than sorry. Called Mrs Bain.'

'What did Frankie's mum have to say?'

'That she'd put her daughter out at the usual time, and she'd trotted off quite the thing.'

'That puts a different complexion on the matter.' Clicking the button on her pen, Anne Shirreffs asked, 'Doesn't mum usually take her to the school gate?'

'For the first week she did, yes. After that, Frankie said she'd rather go on her own.'

'Where do they live?'

'Seaton Walk.'

'Not far, then. Still...'

'There aren't any major roads to cross,' Maggie fretted. 'So it's unlikely she'll have met with an accident.' Scrunched fingers worrying at her mouth, 'She could have made a detour. King Street shops are a magnet if kids have money burning a hole in their pockets.'

'Let's hope that's the case. I'll give the police a ring, all the same. It's not as if they have far to come.' Together with Starfish developmental nursery, catering for three to five year olds with additional support needs, Seaton School has the benefit of a police station in the adjacent Community Wing.

'Thanks,' said Maggie. 'Lynsey's quite upset. It would help ease our minds.'

Brow furrowed, 'Have either of you noticed anything to suggest Frankie would go off like this?'

'Not really. She's been on the quiet side in class, but that's not unusual in a late entrant. The only thing springs to mind: Frankie approached me in the playground the other day. Said she wanted to tell me something.'

'What was it?'

'No idea.' said Maggie. 'Bell went before she could say. But it has been bugging me. You never know what's going on in their wee heads.'

With a sigh, 'You're right there. The stuff that happens on the internet. Doesn't bear thinking about.'

'The world we're in,' Maggie said ruefully, 'they don't stay innocent for long, that's for sure.'

'Get back to P6,' the head instructed. 'Keep them occupied. Send Lynsey along here. I'll see what she has to say.'

'Will do.'

'I'll get onto the police.' Reaching for her phone, Anne Shirreffs said, 'This might be a storm in a teacup, but a situation like this, better safe than sorry. Anything could have happened to that child.'

Cover the Bases

From the doorway of the first-floor CID Suite – The Big Room, as it is known – Allan Chisolm surveyed a sea of computer consoles. Open-plan, the detectives' desks divided by partitions, it appeared to him a microcosm of modern policing.

Chisolm felt a sudden twinge of nostalgia: a hollow longing for the days when detectives got results by dint of solid legwork. Over the two decades since he'd hit the Glasgow streets as a rookie cop, policing had changed beyond all recognition, an explosion in online crime demanding a correspondingly technical response.

Clapping his hands, he called, 'Your attention, folks. We have a report from Seaton Police Office of a child missing from home: Frances Bain, aged 9, known as Frankie.'

'Missing?' queried Bob Duffy. 'Or abducted?' Bob had a reputation for never looking on the bright side, not even on a July day in Majorca.

'Let's not jump the gun. The Community Policing Team have searched the immediate area. There have been no sightings yet. You all know the protocol. Brian, notify the usual organisations. Get hold of a photograph. Ask the press office to circulate it to newspapers and post an appeal for information on social media.'

'Boss.'

Chisolm perched on the corner of a desk. 'See what we've got in the way of manpower. On the subject of which, where are the uniforms? Souter and Miller keep popping up like a pair of bad pennies.'

'Elrick's off sick,' Brian replied. 'Far as I know, Esson's on a training course at Tulliallan.'

'What about Anderson and Patel? Are they on duty?'

'I'll check that out.'

'Douglas and Susan, pay a visit to the home address. Establish the last point of contact: when and where Frankie was last seen and by whom. Fill out the family background. Talk to the neighbours. And have a good look around the house.' Bristling, 'Are you hearing me, Douglas?'

He snapped to attention. 'Boss.'

'Pay particular attention to Frankie's bedroom, if she has one. Find out her interests. Look for anything she might have taken with her that would give us a lead as to where she's gone. Got it?'

'Sir,' Douglas and Susan said, as one.

'Bear in mind, all of you, that roughly half of children who go missing are found at their home address, the next quarter at friends, about 20% walking in a public place. And don't forget, sometimes children hide. Or are hidden. Remember Shannon Matthews?'

Lisa asked, 'Wasn't she found drugged in the base of a divan bed?'

'That's right. Like Frankie Bain, Shannon was nine years old and last seen on her way to school. In 2008, she was the victim of a fake kidnap in Dewsbury, West Yorkshire, resulting in a major missing person investigation.'

'In a house belonging to the uncle of her mother's boyfriend,' Susan supplied.

Douglas was quick to throw in his tuppence-worth. 'Closer to home, volunteer charity worker, Laura Milne, was brutally attacked in a Union Street flat by Stuart Jack and two accomplices.' Eye-balling Lisa, he added, 'You probably aren't familiar with the case. Laura's partially dismembered body was found in a kitchen cupboard.'

'There was a similar incident in Perth last year,' Lisa justified. 'Thirty-five-year-old Martin Reeves hid a missing fifteen-year-old girl under his bed after twice having sex with her.'

Chisolm looked from one to the other, a perplexed frown on his face. The running rivalry between Douglas and Susan was an ongoing source of irritation. He hoped Lisa Haldane wasn't going to aggravate the situation. 'Sort out a Family Liaison Officer,' he instructed. 'And alert the Dog Unit, just in case.'

'Yes, boss.' Lisa flashed a smile of even, perfectly whitened teeth.

Susan looked daggers.

'Bob, check on CCTV opportunities: shops, petrol stations, buses, what have you. We could be looking at a possible crime in action.'

'Will do.'

'And establish the whereabouts of registered sex offenders. At this time here's no indication foul play is involved, but best cover the bases.'

Chisolm rose. 'That's it for now. Thanks, everybody. Go to it. And get me a result.'

Seaton Walk

The three-storey block of flats mirrored a more substantial pre-war council block across the street. Its grey render was stained, the pend which gave access to the security entry little short of a wind tunnel.

In the living room of the ground-floor flat, 'Take a deep breath,' Susan urged.

From her perch on the edge of a tired faux-leather settee, Isla Bain regarded her, wild-eyed.

'I need to ask you some questions to help us find your daughter.'

'I've already talked to the Community Police Officer,' said Isla. 'Shouldn't you be out looking?'

'I understand your concern. But there's no immediate cause for alarm. We had a similar incident at Hazlehead Primary: pupil reported missing around 10 a.m. after failing to report for lessons. The child was found safe and well an hour or so later.'

'But...' Checking the display on the phone by her side, Isla Bain protested, 'It's gone eleven o'clock.'

'I know.' The first hours were critical, Susan was only too aware. 'But let me assure you, where a vulnerable child is concerned, we act without delay. Uniformed officers are already on the case. So...' She leaned forward in anticipation. '...if you could start by giving me a full description of Frankie.'

'She's slim,' Isla said woodenly. 'Short, dark hair. Blue eyes.'

Douglas and Susan exchanged glances. Covered half the kids in Aberdeen.

'Does she have any distinguishing features: birthmarks, scars?'
'No.'

What was Frankie wearing when she left the house?'
'School uniform.'
'Specifically?'

'White blouse, navy blue sweatshirt and jogging bottoms, black shoes.'

'Did she have a coat?' Susan prompted.

'Black padded jacket.'

'Any logos?' Douglas asked, jumping in.

'Folk like us can't afford designer stuff,' Isla responded, face the picture of contempt.

'How about a phone?'

'That neither. Kept losing them, either that or they were taken off her or she cracked the screen. I told her if she broke another one, that was it.'

'Would she have any cash on her?' Douglas persisted.

'Doubt it.'

'Do you have a recent photograph?' Susan moved to change the subject. With high unemployment and those in work having a prevalence of unskilled or low-skilled jobs, Seaton residents were reported to have the lowest median income in their locality.

'Somewhere.' Hauling herself off the sofa, Isla crossed to a wall unit. 'Since the move, I can't lay my hands on a thing.' Unearthing a cardboard box, she rummaged for a few moments, then, 'This do?' She held out a school photo in a dark brown mount. 'It was taken last year. Her hair was longer, but—' Her eyes welled up.

'Thanks,' Susan said. 'Can we borrow this? We'll return it,' she added with a reassuring smile.

'I suppose.'

'Frankie's dad...'

'We're separated.'

'On amicable terms?'

Isla's face darkened. 'What do you think?'

How did you come by that bruise on your cheekbone? was the question Susan was itching to ask. She decided to save it for later. 'Do you have any other children?'

'No.'

'Is her dad still in touch?'

'When he's able. Stuart works offshore. The way things are, job's not always out of Aberdeen.'

Susan nodded. Twelve thousand jobs had been lost in the oil industry over the past year as a result of plummeting oil prices, eighteen thousand losses forecast for the year ahead. 'Has he maintained a good relationship with Frankie?'

'He tries. But it's not easy. Stuart finds it difficult to stick to access arrangements. He can be away for weeks on end. Even when he is onshore, it's hard to keep a kid entertained for long.'

Douglas cut in. 'Do you have a boyfriend?'

With a resigned shrug, Isla Bain mumbled, 'Off and on.'

'When was the last time you saw him?'

'Saturday night.'

'Did he stay over?'

For a split second she hesitated. Then, 'No.'

'He the one who whacked you on the face?'

Susan looked daggers. Insensitive bastard!

Isla's hand moved protectively to her cheekbone. 'I caught it on the cupboard door.'

Douglas sneered, 'That right?' Then, getting no response, 'We'll need contact details for them both.'

Susan was ready to land one on him. Instead, 'How about grandparents? Do they live locally?'

Isla shook her head.

'You mentioned a move, when was that?'

'A few weeks ago.'

'Where did you live before?'

'Tullos.'

'Was there a particular reason for the move?'

'Bit of bother at school.'

'What sort of bother, may I ask?'

'There was a bunch of girls picking on Frankie. They wouldn't let up, not even after the parents had been called in. Upshot was, I thought moving schools was the only way.'

'Why Seaton?'

Contemptuously, 'Have you looked at the City Council house exchange website lately? Seaton's the only place I could get a swap.'

'Are there any friends from your last address Frankie might have been trying to get in touch with?'

'None that spring to mind.'

'Would she go off with a stranger?'

Her eyes widened in alarm. 'You don't think—'

'We have to keep an open mind. You've been very helpful,' Susan added with a reassuring smile. 'We'll get a Family Liaison Officer to keep you company while investigations are ongoing. Meantime, if there's anything else you can think of, anything at all...' Pulling a card from her pocket, she held it out. '...don't hesitate to give me a call.'

Isla laid the card down without looking at it.

'One more thing. Does Frankie have her own bedroom?'

'Yes.'

'We'll want to have a look around.'

'Why? The size of this flat, it's obvious she's not here.'

'Standard procedure,' Susan replied. 'We have to search the last place the person was seen.'

Wearily, Isla said, 'On you go.'

Spot On

'I was spot on!' exclaimed Wilma, pride oozing out of every pore.

Maggie said, 'What about?'

'Thon suicide.'

They were driving along Cromwell Road, heading for Westhill to give a presentation.

'You're not still harping on about that,' protested Maggie. 'I thought we'd put it to bed.'

'Ran some background checks, all the same. Just to satisfy myself.'

'Thought we'd better things to do.'

'Like signing up a bunch of farty old solicitors?'

'Like romance fraud which, may I remind you, was your idea.'

Wilma ignored this. 'Don't you want to know?'

'Not, really.'

She bit her lip. Then, unable to keep it in any longer, 'The wife was having it off, right enough. Fella from her work.'

'Big deal,' Maggie said dismissively. Then, suspicious, 'Where did you get that from?'

'Someone at Ian's garage.'

'There's Aberdeen for you.'

'So,' Wilma said, 'the two of them had a motive.'

'Wife could have filed for divorce. Plus, where's the opportunity? The paper said the body was found in the afternoon. They'd have been at work.'

'Right enough. Except…' Eyes bright, she turned to Maggie. '…I've a witness saw them heading off in her car after lunchtime.'

'What witness?'

Wilma wouldn't meet her eyes.

'I wondered where you'd disappeared to. Have you been up to your old tricks again?'

Negotiating a roundabout, she took the third exit onto Anderson Drive. 'Might have spoken to one or two folk.'

'What folk?'

'Staff at the care home.'

'How did you gain access? No, don't tell me. I'm better off not knowing.'

'It was you that said female intuition was our USP. I was only going where my PI instincts took me.'

Maggie scoffed, 'Your nose, more like. I can't believe, after the conversations we've had, you would brazenly invade people's privacy, and at a time when they're at their most vulnerable.'

'And I can't credit you're happy sitting on your arse, pushing paper, when you could be out there—'

Maggie braced herself with a hand on the dash as Wilma zipped through another roundabout onto Queen's Road. 'Doing what?' she shrilled. 'Chasing my tail?'

'Solving a murder.'

Sitting back, 'Even if I was to buy into this theory – that Jean Sellars and her lover nipped home from work in the middle of the afternoon and bumped the husband off – how did he happen to be there?'

'Wife could have called him home, said she'd been taken ill.'

'How did they get him into the garage?'

'Drugged him first.'

'Post-mortem would have thrown that up.'

'Not necessarily. Something like GHB has a short half-life.'

'What about the women's clothes?'

'Her and Keith could have nipped back for a quickie. Found him, dolled up. Then—' Flooring the accelerator, Wilma shot past a Stagecoach bus.

'How did they hoist a grown man onto a stepladder, tell me that? This Keith Williams, he a big chap?'

'Middling.' Wilma was going by Dodd's description. She'd only seen an ID mugshot.

'Well-built?'

'Typical chef: overweight, bit flabby. I get where you're coming from but, by all accounts, Sellars wasn't huge either.'

'No,' said Maggie. 'But doing the job he did I bet he was all muscle. And the lovers, how long did you say the affair had been going on?

'Years.'

'So it wasn't exactly white-hot?'

Hazlehead Park flashed by. They were on Skene Road, now, passing the crematorium entrance.

'There's something fishy about thon suicide,' Wilma insisted. 'I feel it in my bones.'

'One question: did any of these "folk" retain our services?'

'No, but…'

'Then it's none of our business. Let the police get on and deal with it. Speaking of which, one of my P6 students has gone AWOL.'

'Par for the course,' said Wilma. 'By that age, I was hardly at school. Does the kid have a mum and dad?'

'Yes, but they're living apart.'

'There's your answer. If she's not with one, she'll be with the other.'

'I hope so.'

The road had merged onto the A944. Wilma changed down, took another roundabout at speed and accelerated away, saying, 'Cheer up. It hasn't happened.'

Changing tack, Maggie said, 'MacSorley case. Any progress?'

'I was at it till three this morning,' Wilma groaned. 'Every time I got a lead, something else cropped up. It's like peeling an onion, or one of them dolls fits one inside the other.'

'Matryoschka?'

'Take your word for it. Russian, anyhow. And before you say "I told you so"—'

'I'll re-state what I've said already: we don't have the resources to investigate this sort of thing. Plus, it's too labour-intensive for what we'll earn from it. You've just admitted as much.'

With a sly nudge, Wilma said, 'I got an address.'

'How?'

Flicking the Vs at a white van driver, 'Never mind.'

Maggie threw her a searching look.

'It was nothing illegal,' she protested.

'You didn't pay for it?'

'Not a lot: hundred dollars.'

'Wilma,' Maggie shrilled. 'We can't afford—'

'Cheap at the price,' Wilma countered. 'We can bill the client.'

'This address,' Maggie asked suspiciously. 'Where is it?'

'Woking.'

'Woking in Surrey?'

Wilma grinned. 'You know another one?'

'That's not funny,' said Maggie. Knitting her brows, 'Can't be right? If the client has been emailing this Yelena back and forth, surely she'll have a Russian .ru email address?'

'She's just as likely to be using Gmail or Outlook.'

'Okay. So what do we do now?'

'Check out the Woking address.'

'How?'

'Same way we find absconding debtors: Google Maps.'

'Then what?'

'I dunno.'

'That's you all over,' Maggie complained. 'Charging into something without an exit strategy. So much for hitting the jackpot.'

'I suppose you'd have done better?'

'Woking,' Maggie scoffed.

Lip curled, Wilma sneered, 'One thing you have to admit, it's a bloody lot closer than Vladivostok.'

There's a Thing

'We'll start with the missing from home,' Chisolm said, when his team had gathered for an update. Flipping open a file. 'Brian?'

'Nothing yet from the search co-ordinator, but Frankie Bain's photograph has gone out to press and TV. I'm hopeful we'll see calls coming in very soon.'

'Bob, what's the story on CCTV?'

'Good news is we've harvested footage from a number of locations. The bad news: techies will take hours sifting through it.'

'Lisa?'

With a flash of Colgate-white teeth, she said, 'Confirm Dog Unit on standby and FLO in place.'

'Douglas and Susan?' Chisolm looked from one to the other. 'What did you get from the parents?'

Douglas rushed to answer. 'Took a statement from Mrs Bain. We haven't managed to raise the husband yet. They're separated.'

'We didn't get much out of her,' Susan volunteered, 'other than Frankie was bullied at her last school. Neighbours didn't give us useful intel either. Frankie and her mum haven't lived in Seaton long enough to make connections.'

'However,' Douglas said portentously, 'a search of Frankie's bedroom turned this up.' He dangled a plastic evidence container in front of his face. 'Razor blade. Found under the bed.'

'Looks like it belongs to a Stanley knife,' Duffy observed.

'Figures,' Susan said. 'What struck me about Frankie's bedroom was how sterile it was. Walls were bare of the usual pre-teen pop posters, and I picked up a lingering smell of paint. Turns out, there had been a decorator in. Just to do that one room. Money's tight, from what I can gather.'

'You're suggesting the painter might have dropped the blade?'

'It's a possibility.'

'What did Frankie's mum have to say about it?'

'Denied all knowledge.'

Brian joked, 'Doesn't say much for the housekeeping.'

'Didn't get there by accident,' Douglas pontificated, a self-satisfied look on his face. 'Bed has a slatted base. Blade was stuck to the underside with a piece of Blu Tack.'

Susan's eyes narrowed. When they'd checked out the Bain house, Douglas had made a beeline for Frankie's bedroom, leaving her to do the rest. Discovering the blade, he'd bagged and tagged it in double-quick time. He hadn't mentioned anything about Blu-tack.

Chisolm asked, 'You're suggesting self-harm?'

'Possibly.'

'Consider this hypothesis,' said Susan. 'Painter leaves the blade lying around. Frankie picks it up and decides to hide it. That's the sort of thing kids will do.'

Holding up a second evidence bag, Douglas argued, 'It doesn't explain the underpants we later found under the mattress.'

Brian said, 'Let me ask you this: when you were a kid, did you never soil yourself and hide the evidence?'

'We get the picture,' Chisolm said sharply. 'Let's move on.'

Smug-faced, Douglas continued, 'If you look closely, you'll see what appear to be bloodstains.' He sat back in his seat and folded his arms.

'Blood-stained knickers and a razor blade,' Bob Duffy marvelled. 'Now there's a thing.'

'Indeed,' Chisolm remarked. 'There might be a perfectly innocent explanation. Frankie Bain may have started menstruating and been too embarrassed to say. But, taken with the fact that room had been recently re-painted, let's get both items analysed. See if they're forensically fruitful. Meantime, persons of interest: any thoughts?'

'Mum has a boyfriend,' Susan offered. 'Hasn't been around lately.'

Douglas sneered. 'So she says.'

Susan ignored this. 'I've PNC'd the husband. Nothing there.'

'How about the boyfriend?'

'Couple of pre cons: affray, breach of the peace.'

'Brian, I need full background checks and both interviewed.'

'Boss.'

He looked around. 'Anyone else?'

Duffy spoke. 'The Offender Management Unit have identified five registered sex offenders in the vicinity.'

'Make sure every last one of them is pulled in for interview.'

He riffled through a bundle of case files. 'Before we move on, what do you have for me on the Sellars suicide?'

'Zero on the graffiti, boss,' said Susan. 'It's a transient labour market. We weren't able to locate everyone on the list of Sellars' workmates. Those we did speak to reckoned it was par for the course to write insults on dirty vans.'

'What about the neighbours?'

'Said it was a quiet round there. Didn't have too many problems with vandalism.'

'How about the son and daughter?'

Douglas answered. 'Lauren Sellars was visibly distressed, but in the dark where the cross-dressing was concerned. The son was another story. If Harvey Sellars is to be believed, his dad was in the habit of dressing up on a regular basis. They'd fallen out over it.'

'Where was he at the time of the decease?'

'Dumfries.'

'His story checks out,' Susan chipped in, with a smirk at Douglas. So much for his theory that someone could have given Vinnie a helping hand.

Lisa asked, 'Does anyone stand to benefit from Vinnie's death?

'Not that I can establish.'

'No insurance policies taken out recently?'

'Nothing.'

'Had he made a will?'

'Years back. Left everything to Jean. She should be comfortable. The house is hers. They had savings. I checked back with Vinnie's employers. They confirmed he 'retired' with full pensions benefits.'

'What I don't get,' said Duffy, 'is why didn't the bloke just come out?'

Ticking off the fingers of one hand, Chisolm replied, 'But come out as what? One: cross-dressers self-identify as different from both gay men and trans people. Two: it may be Vinnie Sellars knew he was different, but didn't know quite how. Three: attitudes were very different thirty years ago when he'd have been in his teens.'

With a conspiratorial look to her boss, Lisa added, 'Either way, he wouldn't have had any legal protection. The Gender Recognition Act didn't come into force until 2004. Same sex marriages weren't legal until 2014. And even now, whatever his identity and legal status, he still lost his job.'

'In my opinion,' said Duffy, 'you're blowing this whole thing up. I don't think there was any more to it than a guy wanting to escape a dull marriage.'

'Talking from experience?' Brian joshed.

Duffy ignored him. 'If Vinnie Sellars was that way inclined, do you think he'd have chosen to marry and have kids?'

'As the boss said, we don't know what 'way inclined' he was, and anyway, times were different, then. You did what was expected.'

Platitudes

'Can you speak?' Maggie asked when Kirsty accepted her FaceTime call.

'Obviously. What's up?'

Maggie's nerves jangled. Not a good start. 'Just wanted...' She began cautiously. '...to say hello.'

'Hello.'

'How have you been?'

'Okay.'

'Just "okay"?' Maggie said anxiously. 'You're not sickening for something?'

'What is this? I've only just been home.'

'I know,' Maggie soothed. 'I was glad to see you. Cat, too,' she added hastily. 'But you'd no sooner arrived than you were away again.'

'I've seminars to attend. Essays to write. I'm not going to get a good degree sitting on my arse.'

Maggie balked at her daughter's use of language. Hoped it didn't show in her face. 'I'm well aware of that,' she said stiffly. Then, lightening her tone. 'Studies going well?'

Kirsty shrugged. 'I'll find out at exam time.'

'You've done well so far. Hard work really does pay off.' Platitudes, Maggie thought. She'd worked day and night to make the agency a success without much in the way of reward.

She could hear voices in the background.

Distracted, Kirsty said, 'If that's all you're phoning about—'

'How is Cat?' Maggie blurted.

'Fine.'

'Seen much of her?'

'Too much. She's been crashing at our place since the beginning of the semester.'

They're living together?

A small 'Oh!' escaped Maggie's mouth. Much as she tried to be open-minded, life as a single mother had rendered her more fearful than ever for her children's futures.

'She's driving Sarah mad,' Kirsty went on. 'You know how OCD she is. Cat leaves her stuff lying all over the place. Doesn't clean the shower. Leaves the milk out the fridge. I could go on all day, but...' She gave a theatrical sigh. '...I wouldn't want to bore you.'

'I can imagine,' Maggie said weakly. 'How come she's sharing with you?'

'Had digs up Blackness Road, but they didn't work out.'

Where does she sleep?

It was on the trip of Maggie's tongue to put the question. Then, *None of your business.* Kirsty had been fortunate to hang onto the same flat – and flatmate – since the start of her course. If the landlord was okay with an extra occupant, who was she to interfere.

'Mmm,' was all she said.

Stuart

'When did you last see your daughter?' Brian asked.

They'd roused Stuart Bain from sleep at the second attempt. Sitting on the edge of an unmade sofa-bed, he said, 'Three weeks, I suppose, give or take. Been offshore.'

'When did you get back?'

With a sideways glance at Brian, 'Flew in this morning.'

'So between the hours of 8 a.m. and 12 noon you'd have been where?'

'On the rig, either that or somewhere over the North Sea.'

'Can anyone vouch for you?'

'Loads of people: my supervisor on the rig. The guys I was with on the helicopter.'

'How often do you see Frankie?'

'Not as often as I should. It was hard enough before…' He broke off, running his fingers through unkempt hair. 'There used to be plenty work in the energy supply sector, either the North Sea or Norway. But now, things being what they are, you can be in Doha, Qatar. Jobs are hard to come by. And if I'm not in work I can't contribute towards Frankie's upkeep. Everybody suffers. Vicious circle, eh?'

'You've split from her mum?'

Stuart's mouth twisted into a sour smile. 'On me. One drunken night. Shagged some quine I didn't know from Adam. Isla threw me out.'

'How are relations between you, now?'

'One night,' he repeated, stroking a jaw dark with stubble. 'And she calls it quits. How do you think?'

'Can you shed any light on the bruise she recently sustained to her face?'

'Obviously not. I've been offshore.'

Brian said, 'When you do see Frankie, what's the arrangement?'

'I pick her up from Seaton every other weekend.'

'She couldn't take the bus?'

'No way. She's only a kid. I wouldn't let her get a bus on her own.'

'Does she stay over?" Lisa asked.

'Sometimes.'

'That must be fun,' she remarked, giving Brian a loaded look.

'In this place?' Stuart waved a hand at the cramped bedsit. 'You've got to be kidding. And before you ask, we don't share the bed.' Tugging the crumpled duvet straight, he added, 'If you can call it that. There's a sleeping bag in the cupboard.'

'Can't be easy to keep a kid entertained,' Brian observed, rejoining the conversation.

'Easy enough if you let them sit glued to a tablet or the TV. Me, I think kids should get out in the fresh air. We go to Duthie Park a lot. Frankie's too old, now, for the junior playpark. Self-conscious. Not like when she was wee. Wooden Adventure Playground's more her thing.'

'Right,' said Brian. Not having kids, he was none the wiser.

'And the Winter Gardens,' Stuart ran on. 'The Tropical House especially. She's forever on about the Amazon rainforest. My wee eco-warrior, I call her.' His voice broke with emotion. 'Sorry.' He scrunched balled fists into his eyes.

'Take your time,' Lisa said.

'Then there's McPuddock, the mechanical frog in the Fern House,' he expanded. 'That always raises a smile. When the weather's bad – which is most days – it's a Godsend. The cafe too, though it shuts at four.'

'Anywhere else?'

Shifting position, Stuart replied, 'Sometimes we go to the cinema in Union Square. Or have a wander uptown. I'm not keen on shopping myself. Thought Frankie would be into fashion by now, but she's not bothered.' He shrugged. 'Maybe later on.'

'Is there anyone she might have paid a visit: a friend or relative?

Anywhere else she might have gone? Where she lived before, perhaps?'

'I doubt it. From what she's said she hasn't been happy at school, lately, and Isla doesn't have many friends: keeps herself to herself.'

Lisa said, 'Am I right in thinking your wife has a boyfriend?'

'Is that what she's calling him?'

'What would you call him?'

'Total wanker.'

'I gather you don't approve?'

'Who Isla shacks up with is her business. When it comes to Frances. Frankie,' he corrected. 'Can't get used to calling her that. It's a recent thing.' With a shrug, he added, 'All part of growing up, I suppose. But I don't want some bampot sharing a roof with my daughter. The things you read nowadays—'

'Indeed.'

'You don't think…?' he began.

Brian cut him short. 'We're following a number of lines of enquiry.'

Squaring up, Stuart said, 'Then shouldn't you be out there, instead of…'

Lisa extended a staying hand. 'Returning to your wife's boyfriend, Jason Eadie. You referred to him as a "bampot". Is there anything you want to tell us could substantiate that?'

'Aside from the obvious: that he's fucking my wife?'

She darted a glance at Brian.

Has Haldane heard something? He averted his eyes. Time hadn't lessened the ignominy he felt at a colleague's dalliance with ex-wife Bev.

Stuart shook his head. 'Nothing I can put my finger on. I've only met the guy a couple of times. Didn't have a lot to say, but I got the feeling there was stuff he was keeping from her: Isla, I mean.'

'What sort of stuff?'

'I dunno.' He looked from one detective to the other. 'Why don't you ask him?'

VII

The Bide a Wee

'Here's tae us,' Wilma said, raising her glass.

Over their pints of heavy, Wayne and Kevin eyed her uncertainly. They'd been summoned at short notice. Not that her call took them away from anything of importance: Wilma's two sons had joined the ranks of the Torry long-term unemployed not long after leaving school.

'Not behind the bar?' Kevin remarked.

'No.' Wilma had given up her evening job when the detective agency began to gather momentum, but still did the odd shift when they were stuck. Now, she didn't waste time. 'Fancy a wee holiday?'

With a disbelieving expression, he asked, 'Whereabouts?'

'Benidorm would be good.' Hands making bull-horns on his head, Wayne offered a lusty rendition of Viva Espana.

'Nice one!' exclaimed Kevin approvingly.

'Nae chance,' Wilma said.

'Blackpool?'

'That neither.'

'Did you have somewhere in mind?'

'Aye,' Wilma replied. Taking a long draught of her lager, 'Woking.'

Kevin's jaw dropped. '"Woking"?' he repeated.

'Where's that?' Wayne piped up.

Scratching his balls, 'Wales,' Kevin answered. Then, catching Wilma's withering expression, 'Down south, anyhow.'

'Aww,' Wayne said. 'Disna count.'

'Count or no,' Wilma threatened. 'I've a job I'm needing done. And you're just the ones to do it.'

'No way,' Kevin spluttered, choking on his beer. 'Last job we did near got us killed.'

Wilma pooh-poohed. 'Wee message to my boxing gym?' In

desperation, she'd borrowed from Joe Grogan to bail Maggie out of a corner and been threatened with violence when she couldn't repay. 'All you had to do was play postie.'

'Aye. An' near get ma heid stoved in.'

Eyeing his undercut, she observed, 'Looks okay to me. Bit soft, mebbe.'

'Seriously,' said Kevin. 'What's in Woking to interest you?'

'None of your business. I need the job done ASAP. Can you go today?'

The penny dropped. 'It's one of your detective jobs.' Leaning in close, 'How much is it worth?'

'I'll pay your petrol,' Wilma said, all business. 'Plus subsistence.'

'Fit's that?' Wayne queried.

'Meals. A night's B&B if it comes to that.'

'Ma,' Kevin protested. 'That's not what I'd call a holiday.'

'Dinna you worry.' Jerking her head at Wayne, Wilma added, 'You'll have money enough for a stick of rock and a straw hat.'

Jason

'Jason Eadie?'

'Who's asking?'

Showing their warrant cards, 'DS Burnett and DC Haldane.'

Brian led. 'We'd like to ask you a few questions regarding a missing child, Frances Bain.'

Stiffening, he responded. 'Nothing to do with me.'

'Is it alright if we come in?' Brian asked, taking a small step forward.

Jason stood his ground. 'It's not a good time. '

'Suit yourself,' Lisa said with a disarming smile. 'Now or later, makes no difference.'

'Well, I suppose,' Jason grudged. Taking a step backwards into the hall, he held open the door.

The detectives followed him down a short corridor into a kitchen-diner: worktop littered, rubbish overflowing from a flip-top bin.

With studied casualness, Jason leaned back against the room divider, feet apart, elbows splayed on the worktop. 'Fire ahead.' He didn't ask them to sit down.

Brian spoke. 'Where were you this morning between the hours of 8 a.m. and 12 noon?'

'In the sack.'

'Can anyone corroborate that?'

Jerking upright, Jason said, 'Why would they? Kid goes walkabout. Fuck all to do with me.'

Brian looked to Lisa, who responded with a raised eyebrow.

'I'm on my own,' said Jason, recovering his bravado. 'What do you think?'

'We understand you're in a relationship with the missing child's mother, Isla Bain.'

'Who told you that?'

'It's irrelevant,' said Brian. 'Can you confirm that you're in such a relationship?'

He shrugged. 'Been with her once or twice.'

Brian caught Lisa's eye. Why would Jason Eadie want to play down the relationship? '"Been with her",' he repeated. 'As in?'

'Shagged her.'

'At her home in Seaton Walk?'

With a dismissive sneer, Jason replied, 'Anywhere that was handy at the time. I'm not fussy.'

Lisa asked, 'When you were at Isla Bain's house, was her daughter at home?'

'Sometimes.'

'How did you get on with her?'

'How do you think?'

'You didn't find her a nuisance?'

His lip curled. 'She's a kid. They're all a bloody nuisance.' His eyes darted right and left. 'Look, what is this? "A few questions", you said. Am I suspected of something?'

'We're only trying to fill in the background,' Brian explained. 'When did you last see Isla Bain?'

'Don't remember.'

'Take your time.'

Jason's eyes narrowed to slits. 'What has Isla told you?'

'I'd rather hear it from you.'

'Saturday night, if you must know.'

'In Seaton Walk?'

'Yup.'

'Was Frankie there at the time?'

'She was in her bedroom, far as I know.'

Lisa again, 'Did you stay the night?'

'I would have, but the bitch threw me out.'

'Did you and Isla part on good terms?'

'What has that got to do with anything?'

'When we spoke to her, she was sporting a rather large bruise on her face. So I'll ask you again, did you part on good terms?'

'Not exactly.'

'Why was that?'

Thrusting out his chest, 'We had a row,' Jason replied, 'You happy, now?'

Kincorth

The Council-built block of flats was like many the length and breadth of Scotland: three storeys, grey-harled, two scrubby patches of grass bordering a concrete-flagged path.

The door gave at a push. So much for security entry. Behind it, amidst crumpled cans and empty crisp packets, lay a small Everest of junk mail.

Anderson kicked the debris aside. There was a strong smell: cheap cleaning fluid and piss. He inspected the soles of his boots in turn for dog shite. Or worse.

Patel preceded him up the stairs, Anderson's breath laboured as they reached the top floor. Lee Marshall's front door was like every other on the stair: regulation wood with an obscure glazed panel. No fancy UPVC upgrades here.

Anderson's knock reverberated around the stairwell.

Patel recoiled. They hadn't had time to take a lunch break, and his head was splitting.

Getting no answer, Anderson poked open the flap of the letter-box. Stooping, he put one eye to the aperture.

'Any joy?'

'Can't see a bloody thing.' Straightening, 'There's something stuck to the inside. Looks like a black bin bag.'

'Figures.'

Anderson acknowledged this with a nod. The internet was increasingly being used to identify Registered Sex Offenders within communities – commonly referred to as 'Outing' – and organise public protests at their home addresses. Whilst most protests were peaceful, there had been instances where property was damaged and individuals assaulted or threatened with physical violence.

Patel turned to his partner. 'What do you want to do?'

'Give it a minute or two. Marshall might be asleep.'

'If I'd just come out of prison,' Patel joked, 'I'd sleep for a week.'

'Too right.' Prisons were noisy places.

'He a user? Might have OD'd. He could be lying inside.'

'Recreational, far as I know.' Anderson put an ear to the keyhole. Shook his head.

'You thinking what I'm thinking?' Patel asked.

'Something could have happened to him. Might even be a copycat of thon Walker case.'

'Fella that was turned in by vigilantes?'

'Aye.' Anderson gave the door another hammering. 'Wanker contacted two fake dating website profiles set up by different paedophile-hunter groups pretending to be underage girls.'

The door opposite flew open.

'Fuck's sake!' A figure stood, dressed only in vest and Y-fronts. 'Can a man no get a night's sleep.'

Pointedly, Anderson looked at his watch.

'I work nights,' the neighbour complained. 'If you're needing in, I've a spare key.'

Hidden Lives

'Got ten minutes?' Chisolm asked, passing his sergeant on the stairs.

'No problem,' Brian answered eagerly. His request to be put forward for inspector had yet to be answered. Perhaps this was his moment: the day his bid for promotion would finally bear fruit.

Once they were seated in his office, Chisolm said, 'Sellars case. Final post-mortem report has come through. Nothing untoward there. Just wanted to bounce a couple of things off you before I put it to bed.'

Brian's heart flatlined.

'I did think – momentarily – the son might have been implicated. They had a tense relationship by the sound of it. Fathers and sons,' Chisolm remarked. 'Never did see eye-to-eye with my own dad.'

It was on the tip of Brian's tongue to draw him out. For all the time Allan Chisolm had been DI, he'd not spoken about his private life. 'Never ceases to amaze me,' he confided, 'how anyone can live that long under a veil of secrecy. And I'm not just talking sexuality. When you think of the fraudsters, the bigamists, the murderers. Makes me want to punch the air every time some bastard gets nailed by his DNA decades down the line.'

'You and me both. Forty years it took to get Angus Sinclair convicted of The World's End murders, thirty-five the McLaughlin case in Glasgow. But that doesn't help us here. I'd have been more comfortable putting the case forward to the PF,' Chisolm qualified. 'Had it not been for the graffiti.'

Brian asked, 'You think there was something behind it?'

Steepling his fingers, Chisolm replied, 'Sellars must have been mentally fragile to take his own life. He was conflicted, at the very least, borne out by the history of cross-dressing. The loss of his job must have come as a hammer-blow. Seeing that on his van might

147

just have been enough to push him over the edge.'

'What I don't understand is why didn't he just open up?'

'By the time people reach middle age, they are often in a long-term heterosexual relationship or life path, with no room to deviate. They've passed an age where they feel comfortable going to gay clubs, have fallen into straight circles, or convinced their families and themselves that there isn't a problem. They feel caught between two worlds: they don't fit into the straight world anymore but they don't fit into the gay world, either.'

'That might have been true once,' Brian argued. 'You said yourself attitudes have changed.'

'Nonetheless, most people fear disrupting the lives of those closest to them. They risk losing their marriage, their kids, their standing in society. Sometimes – as happened with Vinnie Sellars – their job. These people lead hidden lives, one secret away from losing everything they love. That's a very lonely place to be.'

Meeting Chisolm's unflinching gaze, Brian couldn't help but reflect on his own failed marriage. He wondered how much his boss actually knew about his wooing of Maggie Laird, and how Chisolm's own suit was faring? 'And I thought I had problems,' he joked, in an attempt at lightening the mood.

'The more I've thought about it,' Chisolm continued. 'The less likely I've concluded Vinnie Sellars was a closet gay. Working in the building trade, don't you think if he had certain proclivities he'd have been outed in a flash?'

'Fair point. But why commit suicide?'

'That, Brian, is what has been exercising my mind these past few days: what was it that tipped him over the edge? Vinnie had been pushing the boundaries at work. One day he wore a bit of make-up, another an item of women's clothing. He wanted to present as female. The way I see it, he was – in his own terms – coming out.'

'As what?'

'Doesn't really matter.'

Brian snorted. 'Mattered to him.'

'Maybe he hadn't thought it through. Panicked when he was confronted. Didn't know where to turn when he lost his job. Whatever, looks like we'll have to put it down as an unexplained...'

There was a sharp rap on the door.

'Enter,' Chisolm instructed.

'Sir,' a civilian officer stuck her head into the room. 'The Misper. DCI Coutts wants you both in the incident room ASAP.'

The Chanonry

Souter stood in the doorway of the double garage. 'Can you tell me what's missing?'

'Other than my joint stool…' Celia Pendreich's fingers fluttered in front of her mouth. '…It's hard to say.'

Souter followed her gaze. Beyond the elderly Mercedes estate and more recent Fiat Punto which sat side by side, the rear of the space was piled high: brown furniture, old kitchen units, defunct Hoovers, tired Christmas decorations, black bags bulging with who knows what.

'There was a tent, I think. Green. Rolled up in a sort of duffel bag. Hopeless thing. We only used it once.' Craning her neck, she added. 'And an old sleeping bag. Blue. But it was so mouldy we may have thrown it out.'

He looked in frustration to his colleague. Folk like her had so much stuff, small wonder they couldn't keep track.

Miller responded with a hopeless shrug.

Souter's eyes travelled upwards. Several pairs of ancient skis bridged the crossbeams, alongside a bundle of long-handled garden tools. He couldn't help but think of the last garage he'd stood in: the lifeless corpse of Vinnie Sellars, eyes bulging carp-like, tongue obscenely engorged.

'What I can tell you,' Mrs Pendreich continued. 'Is that stool has most definitely gone.'

'You couldn't have…?' Miller began.

'I saw it with my own eyes only the other day.'

'You sure?'

'Quite sure. In fact, I made a mental note to bring it back into the house. Stools are quite the thing these days.'

'That right?' Miller said, without enthusiasm. Petty theft wasn't high on response priorities, but they'd been on the doorstep. And with a child missing you never knew.

She turned. Brightening, 'Yes. They feature in all the interiors magazines.'

'Take your word for it.'

'The professor isn't keen on it. That's why it ended up out here. Not that Harold's in a position to criticise. He's a hoarder,' she confided. 'Wants to hang onto things. "For the grandchildren", he says. They're toddlers. By the time they're old enough to use the stuff it will be obsolete.' Pointing, 'Take that wooden sledge, far too heavy for a child. Those lightweight plastic ones you can buy nowadays are far more...'

'Do you lock the garage when you go out?' Souter interrupted. The way things were going they'd be there all day.

'No. If we're only going to be a short while we don't even bother to shut the doors.'

'Don't you think that's...?'

'This is a very good area,' she said defensively.

Souter bit his lip. Sandwiched between the two deprived housing schemes of Seaton and Tillydrone, The Chanonry was an enclave of imposing detached period houses. Formerly occupied by the clergy of the 12th-century St Machar Cathedral, then the homes of university dons, they now sold for sums reaching in excess of a million pounds.

'Not much happens around here,' Mrs Pendreich ran on. 'And, besides, the grounds are protected by a high wall and strong double gates. We always secure them behind us.'

Swivelling his head, Souter took in the ivy-covered house, the terrace flanked by stone statuary, the sweeping lawns bordered by tall trees. His Shirley would give her right arm for such a home. In a spreading horse chestnut, a ramshackle tree house leaned perilously. He turned back. 'All the same.'

'It's such a hassle otherwise,' she continued. 'Harold's getting on. He's due to retire at the end of next semester.'

'There's nowhere safe nowadays,' Miller said dolefully. 'Opportunist theft, you wouldn't believe.'

'There's nothing of any great value,' Celia Pendreich continued. 'So I can't see it would be worth anybody's while. That notwithstanding, I have a strong personal attachment to that stool. It was given me by my godmother. An amazing woman. Sadly, long departed. She…'

Reaching for his pocketbook, Souter said, 'If you'll give me a description.'

'Oak,' she replied. 'Or maybe pine.'

He sighed inwardly.

'Held together by pegged joints.'

'An antique, would you say?'

'Certainly. Came down through the family since…'

'Dimensions?'

'No more than a foot across.'

Souter cast a chary look into the garage. 'Couldn't it have got knocked down the back?'

'You think I haven't looked?' said Mrs Pendreich, face heavy with affront.

'How about value?' he said quickly.

'Not much in monetary terms. Forty pounds, maybe. In sentimental value, priceless.'

'Any distinguishing features?'

'There's a hole in the seat.' Catching his horrified expression, she added, 'A handhold, I should say.'

'You wouldn't happen to have a photograph?'

'Sorry.'

He fished in his pocket. 'Here's my card. If you ring in to the station, they'll give you a reference number for any insurance claim.'

A Major Incident

The Incident Room was jam-packed, every seat occupied by plain-clothes, uniformed and support officers, a straggle of cops standing around the walls.

Conversation stopped and the company rose to its feet as DCI Melanie Coutts swept into the room, dark bob shining above a pristine collar. She took up position in front of the whiteboard. Once everyone had settled, she announced, 'As you're no doubt aware, this case has been escalated to a major incident, which I've been tasked to oversee.'

Standing alongside, Chisolm noted mixed reactions. They'd been expecting DCI Scrimgeour. Steady Eddie was known for his plodding thoroughness. Mel Coutts was a different story. Recently promoted from DI, she had a sharp mind, a quick tongue, and took no prisoners. Hence her soubriquet, Killer Coutts. Chisolm smiled inwardly. He speculated on what the troops called him. Supposed he'd find out in due course.

Scoping the expectant faces, the DCI said, 'As most of you know, an investigation of this type is governed by Standard Operating Procedures. Anyone unfamiliar will find the handbook online.' Turning, 'DI Chisolm will bring you up to speed on the investigation. Inspector,' she waved a hand, then sat down on a seat – hastily vacated – in the front row.

'Ma'am.' Chisolm turned to the whiteboard. Maps and photographs were inter-connected by coloured lines, actions numbered and listed, along with the detectives allocated to each. In the centre, Frankie Bain's small face stared gravely out. 'What do we know?' he began. 'Frances Bain – known as Frankie – left her home in...' He broke off as the door opened and several cops from other stations entered the room.

'Apologies,' the first announced, face flushed.

'Find yourselves a space,' Chisolm said. He waited until they had dispersed. 'As I was saying, Frances Bain – known as Frankie – left her home in Seaton Walk shortly before 9 a.m. this morning to walk the short distance to Seaton Primary School. She never arrived. An initial search of the vicinity by the Community Policing Team yielded no sightings, nor have response officers drafted in found any clues to her whereabouts.'

'Sir,' a voice called from the back of the room. 'Do you suspect foul play?'

'Not at this juncture. There are a number of innocent explanations why Frankie might never have reached school: she's at the home of a friend or neighbour. Has committed some misdemeanour and gone walkabout, afraid she'll get into trouble. However, we can't ignore the possibility she may have been taken – either by someone known to her or by a stranger – for nefarious ends. As was Scott Simpson, another nine-year-old, who was abducted from a park near his home in Powis Circle.'

A hand went up. 'What happened to the kid?'

'Strangled by a convicted sex offender. I don't want to put off time on the details. That's something you can look up. And there have been others: June Cruickshank, whose body was discovered only thirty yards from her home in Woodside, which she'd left on an errand to the corner shop. Pauline Whalley, who was abducted from Aberdeen Market. Might be useful to familiarise yourselves with the case files. These victims just happened to be in the wrong place at the wrong time. We don't want to add Frankie Bain to their number.'

His eyes scanned the assembled company. 'You've got your actions. Those of you on search detail, I want you to go out there. Look in every shed and outbuilding. Under every bush. Turn over every branch, twice if you have to.' Scanning the sea of upturned faces, 'The point I want to hammer home...' He paused to ensure he had everyone's full attention. '...Is because Scott Simpson's body took days to find and was discovered in an area that had already been searched by locals and by police, that little boy's family suffered the most horrific ordeal. We can't begin to imagine what was going through their minds.'

A hush descended in the room: bodies stilled, faces grave, everyone lost in their own thoughts.

'Don't forget,' Chisolm urged. 'Time is critical. That first golden hour of opportunity is long gone. We have a tight window before it gets dark. With every minute that passes, so too do our chances of finding Frankie Bain alive.'

Squaring his shoulders, 'Any further questions?'

When none were forthcoming, with a nod of acknowledgement to Mel Coutts, Chisolm wrapped up the briefing, 'Let's get to work. Stay focussed. Keep in the front of your minds, our top priority is preservation of life.'

The Inversnecky

Maggie pulled a wry face when she read the message chalked on the board outside the Inversnecky: 'Irony, the opposite of wrinkly'.

'Makes me feel like Methuselah,' she said, conscious of Lynsey Archibald's unlined skin.

She led the way into the cafe. Situated on the Esplanade in a parade of shops dominated by Codona's Rollercoaster and Wheel, the Inversnecky is famous for good, simple food and friendly service, with a reputation for one of the best breakfasts in the city. Add to that, manager Martin Vicca's pun-filled sandwich boards serve to brighten the dreichest day.

That day, dreich was an understatement. The sky was overcast, the sea a study in grey. The atmosphere in Seaton School had been fraught. The police had taken statements from members of staff (students couldn't be interviewed until parental permission had been sought and given). Maggie jumped at Lynsey's suggestion they have a restorative coffee after work.

Once they were seated in a quiet back corner and had been served, 'Did I need that!' Lynsey sighed, taking a mouthful of her Americano.

'You and me, both,' said Maggie, sipping her latte.

For a few minutes they sat in reflective silence. Then, 'I feel terrible sitting here,' Maggie fretted, 'when we could be joining in the search for Frankie.'

Lynsey wagged a finger. 'Leave that to the police.'

'Yes, but—' Memories came flooding back of the last Misper case she'd become embroiled in: Sam Clark, whose disfigured corpse had ended up in a Dundee builders' skip.

'Remember what I said about not getting involved.'

'Hear me out.'

Lynsey said, 'You've got two minutes.'

'Everyone seems to be working on the premise Frankie's been abducted. What if there's nobody else involved? What if her disappearance is a cry for help?'

'Because of the bullying at her last school, you mean? There's been no evidence of that here.'

'Frankie doesn't look like she's fitting in either, and we both know how cruel kids can be.'

'Give her time.'

'There might be trouble at home,' Maggie persisted.

'That wouldn't be new.' With a high proportion of single-parent households, Seaton was one of the most deprived communities in the region, one in three children living in poverty.

'I haven't seen her mum this week at all.'

'You're not here every day.'

'Is there a dad?'

Lynsey shrugged. 'If there is, she hasn't mentioned.'

'What I haven't told you is Frankie approached me in the playground last week. She looked miserable, poor kid. Said she wanted to tell me a secret.'

Sighing, Lynsey said, 'Now, we're getting to it.'

'As I told the police, the bell rang before Frankie could say any more. And I didn't see her again that day. And...' The words came out in a rush. '...The next day she was in class so we couldn't speak in private. And I've been thinking about it ever since.'

Lynsey banged down her cup. 'I've warned you already not to get involved.'

'I know. But this is different. I think Frankie might have gender issues.'

'That's a bit of a leap.'

'Think about it. The name, for starters.'

'Mebbe hates being called Frances. Doesn't think it's cool. When you consider the rest of the class: Chloe, Riley, Madison—'

'And that hair? Don't you think Frankie looks a bit, well, androgynous?'

'You're seeing a girl with gender issues,' Lynsey scoffed. 'I'm seeing a girl with a short haircut.' Tilting her head to one side, 'Wouldn't be the first who didn't fit in.'

'I suppose.'

'Gender stereotyping's got a lot to answer for. We've maybe got past the "pink for a girl and blue for a boy" thing, but toys are still directed at one sex or the other: dolls and craft for girls, construction and technology for boys.'

'You're so right,' Maggie allowed, with a frisson of guilt. She'd been as culpable as any with her own two.

'Directly influences the activities children take part in. Shapes their interests and skills. Downside is, it assumes all girls will be the same and like the same things. Ditto for boys. Leaves no room for the girl who likes to play with cars or climb trees or the sensitive, artistic boy.' Tilting her head to one side, 'I hope you didn't come out with that to the police.'

Maggie's eyes dropped to the table. 'No.'

'Just as well. Look, Frankie Bain's parents have split up. She's had problems at school. Moved away from everything that's familiar. Poor kid probably doesn't know whether she's coming or going.'

Glancing up, Maggie said, 'That day I had to take her to the toilet, she wouldn't let me near her.'

'So? There's nothing odd in wanting a bit of privacy, even if you're only nine. You know as well as I do, when children approach puberty they can become very self-conscious. And with good reason.' Taking another sip of her coffee, Lynsey chuckled, 'I can remember being mortified by the whole thing. Can't you?'

'Too long ago. Though I do recall you'd sort of smuggle your sanitary towels out the chemist. Changed days, when sanitary products are all over the television.' Maggie's expression darkened. 'I still think there's something we're not seeing.'

'I doubt it,' Lynsey said emphatically. 'Much more likely Frankie's snowed by all the changes in her life and not able to voice her concerns.' She checked the display on her phone. 'Look, you've had way more than your two minutes.'

'I know,' Maggie said. 'But…'

Lynsey looked her straight in the eye. 'Can we talk about something else?

Time to Get Serious

The helicopter hovered over the city like an angry bumblebee, black and yellow livery stark against the scudding clouds, engine drone persistent. Operational twenty-four hours a day, it can be called out from Police Scotland's Air Support Unit based at the Clyde heliport in Glasgow to attend a wide range of incidents: search and rescue missions, vehicle pursuits, firearms incidents, housebreakings. However, the majority of the unit's assignments involve looking for missing persons.

That day, as rain threatened and daylight leached from the sky, it had been called to assist in the search for Frankie Bain. In the front seat, alongside the civilian pilot, Police Air Observer PC Ross McCutcheon was charged with operating the equipment: a multi-sensor camera containing a daylight, low light, and thermal image camera, all in one housing. It is particularly good at searching large open areas, covering a square mile of open ground in about twelve minutes. Also in the same unit is GPS, which links in with the police computer system, a sophisticated moving map which can provide a computer-generated image that overlays streets and street names on to the video feed from the camera. This reduces the workload of the observer and makes the search more efficient.

'Full tank?' Ross joshed to the pilot, in a nervous attempt at black humour. On 29 November 2013, Police Scotland's only helicopter – a Eurocopter EC135 – crashed into The Clutha Vaults pub in Glasgow, killing ten people, including all three crew, and injuring another thirty-one. The findings of the resulting inquiry were that the pilot had ignored low fuel warnings.

Pilot Chris Dunlop made a show of checking his instruments. 'Not looking too good,' he replied, deadpan.

Ross's stomach hit his boots. Just days earlier, he'd completed the tough selection process: an interview and five-day evaluation to determine if he was suited to flying, followed by a week spent with crews, then a four-week training course and assessment flight. Not a strong swimmer, he'd congratulated himself on getting through the underwater escape training, but still felt the odd queasy twinge when they flew over open sea.

'If you could see the look on your face,' Chris said, with a mischievous grin.

The tension eased from Ross's body. 'Bastard,' he retorted.

Behind him, next to the empty seat reserved – if need be – for a passenger, PC Dave Kinnear was responsible for navigation, photography and visual searching. He would also maintain radio communications via both Airwave and VHF between the helicopter, officers on the ground and control rooms. Both officers were equipped with image-stabilising binoculars and digital cameras that are capable of taking more detailed shots of the ground if necessary.

'We've got something.' Dave's voice came from over his shoulder.

Ross snapped to attention, bringing the searchlight into play. Capable of lighting up an area half the size of a football field, it can direct officers on the ground to something spotted on the thermal image camera.

'Is it a body?'

He had a kid at home.

Was having a hard time keeping his dinner down as it was.

Dave re-focussed his binoculars.

'Hard to say. Can you take us in closer, Chris?'

'Do my best.'

With a cheeky wink at Ross, 'Hold tight.'

Ross retched as the chopper suddenly lost height. Then, straining forward, watched as the searchlight narrowed in on a small bundle.

Christ!

Feeling the vomit rise in his throat, he clapped a cupped hand to his mouth.

VIII

Generation Z

Maggie tensed as she indicated left from Dundee's Kingsway and turned onto Riverside Drive. She'd set off not long after six. Enjoyed the drive south, roads clear at this time in the morning. Swooping down the £1 billion bypass to Stonehaven, she'd felt a sense of liberation, despite the seriousness of her mission. The night before, she'd taken a call from Kirsty's flatmate, Sarah, telling her Kirsty had been skipping lectures, staying out till all hours. Before Maggie had the chance to ask questions, Sarah had rung off. Now, mind teeming with conflicting thoughts, she cursed herself for failing to get to the root of the matter.

At the slip road for Ninewells Hospital, she caught her first glimpse of the Tay. The rail bridge, scene of the 1879 disaster when it collapsed carrying a passenger train, stood starkly silhouetted against a patchwork sky. Passing the small local airport, she took another left at Barnetts' car dealership in the shadow of the bridge to reach her destination.

Maggie had always loved this corner of Dundee. Lying off the Perth Road, home to the campuses of Dundee University and Duncan of Jordanstone College of Art, Magdalen Green offered a verdant haven, despite being a vehicle rat run from the riverside. Elegant detached stone villas – many now institutional or subdivided for multiple occupation – lined the cobbled Magdalen Yard Road. In the centre of the green space, a Victorian bandstand offered live music in the summer months.

Her pulse quickened when she parked beside the red sandstone tenement that housed Kirsty's student flat. Memories flooded back: the day she and George had driven Kirsty down to matriculate. The day she'd come on her own, sick with anxiety, fearing Kirsty was pregnant. And now? She hadn't scrimped to put her only daughter through private school, only to see her future go up in smoke.

Maggie's heart was thumping as she pressed the buzzer.

No answer.

She hadn't called or texted to say she'd be coming. That was a mistake. Kirsty wouldn't take kindly to a surprise visit. Didn't take kindly to much Maggie did.

She tried again, more determined this time. There was always the chance Kirsty might not be at home, though Maggie had timed her arrival to minimise that likelihood.

Heart-sore, Maggie turned away, inwardly cursing her own stupidity. A morning wasted and for what? If she'd only stopped to think before jumping in the car. Picked up the phone.

She turned back. One more go and she'd call it a day. Angry with herself, she stabbed the door buzzer. Left her finger pressed hard against it.

The door burst open.

A young man stood on the threshold, wearing nothing but a pair of budgie smugglers. Shielding his eyes against the light, 'Yes?'

'I'm looking for Kirsty Laird,' Maggie stuttered, quite taken aback.

'She's still asleep.'

Collecting herself, 'Who are you?'

'Luke,' the young man said. 'Kirsty's boyfriend.'

*

'What were you thinking,' Kirsty demanded, outrage written all over her young face.

'I was worried about you,' said Maggie. Luke had been dispatched back to bed and they were sitting at the kitchen table. No sign of Sarah.

'We've spoken on the phone. Why didn't you say?'

'I know,' Maggie admitted, though in her mind that last phone call fell far short of a conversation.

Suspicious, 'Has Sarah been in touch?'

'Why would she?'

For a few moments there was silence, then, face like thunder, Kirsty asked, 'It's Cat, isn't it?'

'No,' said Maggie, compounding the lie.

'I thought that fat cow was after something,' she added with a sneer.

'If you're referring to Wilma…'

'Who else? Last time I was home, she stuck her head in when you were on the landline in the hall.'

'What did she say?'

'It's what she didn't say. Bitch must have been snooping, like she does the whole time. Sussed I was home. Would have been wetting her knickers to know who my 'friend' was?'

'Don't be so vulgar,' Maggie snapped.

'You can talk. Your pal Wilma wouldn't know 'vulgar' if it was staring her in the face. Bet she thought we're lesbians,' Kirsty added, a note of triumph in her voice.

Are you? Every fibre in Maggie's body was screaming. She'd travelled a long road from her sheltered background. Congratulated herself on her lack of bias. And yet, her maternal instincts were nagging, isn't life complicated enough?

'You're so fucking out of touch. Not everyone my age is attracted to the opposite sex, only about half.'

'I know.' Maggie had read that sixteen to twenty-four-year-olds – known as Generation Z – were moving away from categorical binary definitions of sexuality and identity even more than Millennials had.

'Women in particular,' Kirsty persisted. Rising, she crossed the room. 'Here,' she thrust a book under Maggie's nose.

Detransition, Baby.

'Read that. And tell your bosom buddy to eff off.'

'How are the studies going?' Maggie asked, strategically changing the subject.

'So-so.'

'Can I help? Are you managing on the money front? Eating properly?' She cast a sharp eye around the kitchen, where worktops were

166

littered with empty takeaway cartons, dishes piled high in the sink.

'I'm fine.' Softening a tad, 'I'd offer you a cup of tea, only the milk's gone off.'

'No problem. I'll grab a bite on the way up the road.' Maggie made to rise. 'I'm glad you have good friends,' she said, with a nod to the kitchen door.

'Yeah,' Kirsty concurred. 'Sarah, she's solid. Cat's a laugh a minute. Luke…' Her eyes misted. 'He's a total sweetheart.'

Meston Walk

'We've had a development on the missing from home,' Chisolm announced when his core team had gathered for an update. 'CCTV have identified a figure which might be Frankie Bain.'

Everyone snapped to attention. They'd been gutted when the object picked up by the police helicopter's thermal imaging camera the previous evening had turned out to be an injured sheep that had strayed onto the roadside.

Douglas asked, 'Where?'

'Old Aberdeen: High Street near Meston Walk.'

Brian said, 'That rings a bell. Isn't there a bus stop nearby?'

'Yup,' Bob Duffy answered. 'Serves the Number 20 from Hillhead of Seaton to Balnagask.'

'You suggesting Frankie may have headed back to Torry?'

'Think about it. Kid doesn't like her new house. Or she's had an upset at school. Wants to go back to her old stamping ground.'

Chisolm said, 'Wouldn't that have required a degree of planning?'

'It's not beyond the competence of a nine-year-old,' Lisa countered. 'Frankie would have been able to check out bus routes on her phone.'

'She doesn't have a phone,' Susan said, joining in.

'Computer, then. Tablet. Whatever.'

'Why that bus stop?' Douglas pondered. 'There are buses would have taken her from King Street.'

'She'd have had to change in town,' said Duffy. 'The number 20 would have taken her all the way to Tullos without getting off.'

Brian came in. 'What about her fare? If the mother is to be believed, Frankie didn't have any cash on her.'

'She could have been nicking small amounts,' Douglas offered. 'Got pocket money from her dad.'

'Check with whoever is co-ordinating the CCTV search,' Chisolm ordered. 'Obtain the time-stamp off those CCTV frames. Double-check we've retrieved footage from Frankie's last address and Tullos school. Susan, get onto First Bus. See if they have on-board cameras on that route.'

'Boss.'

'Brian, we'd better widen the search area. Phone around the outlying stations. Ask if they can spare us any extra bodies.'

'Will do.'

'Where are we at with the dad and the boyfriend?'

'There's a question mark over both. We've called them in for a follow-up interview, along with a registered sex offender who's gone off-piste: Lee Marshall, recently discharged from Peterhead.'

'What puts Marshall in the frame?'

'Member of the public reported seeing him buy alcohol in St Machar Drive Spar the night before Frankie disappeared.'

'How is that significant?'

'He's registered to an address in Kincorth.'

'Got you. For Lisa's benefit, child sexual abuse crime is one of our policing priorities. Nearly two thousand online child sex abuse crimes were logged by Police Scotland in 2020–2021, a rise of almost 6% on the previous year.'

'I'm up to speed on that,' she confirmed. 'Figures are near 25% higher than the five-year average. And rising. Online grooming is a major contributing factor. It is also generally accepted that there is under-reporting of all sexual crimes.'

Susan stole a glance at Douglas. Found him regarding Lisa, slit-eyed.

'Take that Glasgow case,' he trumpeted. 'Sean McCuaig pled guilty to blackmailing a number of schoolgirls, including causing them to look at nude images with their faces superimposed on them. And that was only what we could bring to court. I bet there would have been more victims.'

'Follows.' One eye on Chisolm, Lisa added, 'Kids are often

169

uncertain as to whether what has happened to them is a crime.'

'Quite so,' he said drily. 'To return to Lee Marshall, we need to establish his movements on the morning of Frankie Bain's disappearance. Might be a longshot. On the other hand—' He need say no more. There wasn't a member of his team hadn't prior knowledge of the abduction and sexual abuse of a child.

'It's not looking good,' Duffy said gloomily. 'Coming up twenty-four hours since the last confirmed and corroborated sighting of Frankie Bain alive and well.'

'We'll have to pull together,' Chisolm said. 'Hope for a positive outcome. Keep me in the picture. Make sure actions are properly recorded and signed off.'

'Speaking of which,' said Brian, 'anything new on our suicide?'

Around the table, heads were shaken.

Chisolm gathered his paperwork. 'That's it, for now. Thanks everyone. And don't forget to update HOLMES.'

A Souvenir

'Well,' Wilma said. 'How did you get on?'

Wayne looked to Kevin, who made a show of looking around the pub. The Bide a Wee was empty, save for a barman busily emptying the dishwasher and an old mannie reading a red top in the opposite corner.

Kevin cleared his throat. 'We went to the address like you said.'

'And?' Wilma strained forward, scarce able to contain her excitement.

'Subject wasn't in.' He sat back in his seat and folded his arms.

'You don't mean to tell me,' Wilma said, incredulous. 'You went all that way—'

Taking a slurp of his pint, he said, 'We called back a couple of times.'

'"A couple of times." What the fuck did you do in between?'

Kevin's eyes dropped to his lap. 'This and that.'

Wilma looked to Wayne.

'Went round the shops,' he said, setting down his glass. 'Weren't up to much. 'We hit on an ace cafe, mind. More of a greasy spoon, but they did whacking great…'

'God grant me patience,' she breathed, hand on heart. 'You two are up to more tricks than a car-load of monkeys.'

'We had to keep our strength up,' Kevin pleaded. 'Just in case.'

Drawing a calming breath, Wilma said, 'Then, what did you do?'

'Took us till after teatime to get somebody in. We wis expecting a looker: legs to her armpits, knockers you could…'

'Cut the crap.'

'It wis a bloke.'

'What sort of bloke?' Wilma croaked, heart pumping so hard she could barely get the words out.

Kevin piped up. 'Puny.'

'He's right,' Wayne said. 'You'd have thought some foreign low-life: Albanian heavy, Nigerian fraudster maybe. But this was a wee guy. Young, an' all. Looked about fifteen. Proper geek.'

'Did he admit to the scam?'

'Not right away. We'd have scared him,' he added, flexing his biceps. He looked for backup to Wayne, who re-arranged his features into what he hoped was a threatening expression.

'What was the upshot?'

'We put the frighteners on him, but the lad – Mark Entwhistle was his name – insisted he was skint, even when we...'

Wilma flapped her hands. 'Don't want to know. What I do want is to find out what he spent our client's money on?'

'Gaming add-ons,' Kevin replied. 'Loot boxes, container keys an' that. Totted up a big bill. Decided the easiest way out was to run a scam.'

'How did he get from there to dating fraud?'

'Same way they all do: social media; chat forums like Discover. You can get online codes for popular games like Counterstrike and Fortnite. Once you get involved in gaming cheat websites and game modification forums, you'll maybe get an approach offering free cheats. From there, a challenge to hack into a friend's computer, a request to set up a fake website—'

'Costs money, surely, to do that. I thought you said he was skint.'

'Nah. You can buy a domain name somewhere like Namecheap.'

'He didn't have a conscience?'

'If someone's stupid enough,' Wayne ventured.

Wilma silenced him with a glower. 'Does he have a girlfriend, this wee guy?'

Kevin said, 'Don't think so.'

'Then, how come,' she jabbed a finger, 'he managed to conduct a credible courtship?'

'Downloaded stuff off the net. Told us you can get 'love letter' templates translated from a foreign language into English.'

The bottom fell out of Wilma's stomach. She should have thought of that. Then, fraud's fraud. Doesn't matter who perpetrated it. 'How about the parents? If he's underage, they…'

'Tried that. Dad has gone AWOL. Mum was out. Works in a factory, minimum wage.'

Sensing defeat, Wilma asked, 'How did it end up?'

Shrugging, Kevin replied, 'We gave it our best shot.'

'Best shot?' Wilma shrieked. 'Pair of useless fuckers, that's what you are.'

Wayne thrust out a paper bag. 'Here.'

'What's this?' she asked, suspicious.

Bashful, he turned his head away, buried his chin on one shoulder. 'Souvenir,' he mumbled.

'Aww.' Her features softened, just a tad. Reaching out, 'You shouldn't have.'

Wilma opened the bag.

Dipping a hand in, she pulled out a squat, round canister.

Keep Calm and Carry On Survival Kit, she read.

A shadow crossed her face. 'This a joke?' She looked from Wayne to Kevin and back again.

Wayne lifted his head. 'Naw. Open it,' he urged. 'It's got a compass. And a magnifying glass. And a candle.'

'What would I be doing with an effing compass?'

'Thought it would come in handy in your line of work.' Then, seeing Wilma's expression, 'Couldna find a stick of rock.'

'Never you mind fucking rock,' she thundered. 'You two will be the death of me.'

Then reality hit home.

Forget Wayne and Kevin.

What in hell was she going to tell Maggie?

Lee

Lisa got straight to it. 'Please account for your movements yesterday morning.'

'Yesterday,' Lee Marshall repeated. 'Let me think.'

Of below average height and build, thinning hair receding over a hooked nose. Not a God! was Lisa's first thought when he'd been escorted into the interview room, having being traced to a tower block in Seaton.

For long moments they sat, Lisa mentally primed for her next question, Brian implacable beside her.

Finally, she spoke. 'Come on, Lee. We haven't got all day.'

'I'm thinking.' Lee Marshall regarded her with watery blue eyes. 'I've a busy social life, you understand.'

'That must be since you were released from Peterhead,' Lisa commented, referring to HMP Grampian. Last time she looked, 'A' Division had over a hundred registered sex offenders in custody and well over four hundred in the community. 'A week past...' She consulted her interview notes. '...Thursday.'

'You've done your homework.'

'Always,' she said, with a sideways glance. She hoped Brian took her response on board. 'Shame you're not as well-organised.'

'Don't know what you mean.'

'Under the terms of the Sexual Offences Act 2003, you are required to notify the police within three days if you spend seven days or more – whether consecutively or within a twelve-month period – at an address you have not already notified to the police.'

'So?'

Brian came in. 'According to information received, you've been resident at an address in Seaton since last Tuesday.'

'Not my fault,' he protested. 'When I got down the road, my place was reeking of damp, and I couldn't get anybody out from the Council.'

'That's a clear breach of your notification requirements.'

'Christ!' Lee exclaimed. 'Do you no have enough on me: name, address, date of birth, national insurance number, credit card, bank and passport details. You'll be wanting the shirt off my back.'

'It's so we can get hold of you,' Brian said, his voiced loaded with intent, 'should the need arise.'

Lisa asked, 'How come you ended up in Seaton?'

'Mate of mine.'

'That would be...' Checking her notes again, '...Malky White.'

'On the nail.'

'A person with whom you shared multiple images of under-age girls. Would I be correct in stating you were convicted for grooming, in a series of text messages, a young girl?'

Sniffing, Lee said, 'She wasn't that young.'

'Twelve? That's the age she stated explicitly early in your conversation.' Lisa's voice rose. 'A girl whom you subsequently arranged to meet.'

'That's not a crime.'

'I shouldn't have to remind you that, in Scotland, any person under the age of 16 is classified as a child.'

'As I said...' He gave a dismissive shrug. '...hooking up, it's no crime.'

'Even when you were found, when intercepted by police officers, to be carrying in your rucksack a vibrator and a tube of lubricating gel?'

'I was fitted up,' he protested. 'Those were for my own use.'

'Regardless. I put it to you, Lee, you know perfectly well sexual conversations with children or young people are classed as Child Sexual Abuse: any act that involves the child in any activity for the sexual gratification of another person, whether or not it is claimed that the child either consented or assented.' Reading from her notes, 'Sexual abuse involves forcing or enticing a child to take part in sexual activities, whether or not the child is aware of what is happening. The activities may involve physical contact, including

175

penetrative or non-penetrative acts. They may include non-contact activities, such as involving children in looking at, or in the production of, pornographic material or in watching sexual activities, using sexual language towards a child or encouraging children to behave in sexually inappropriate ways.' She looked up. 'Sound familiar?'

With the back of his hand, Lee brushed beads of sweat from his brow. 'I've done my time.'

'Which brings me back to my earlier question: where were you yesterday between the hours of 8 a.m. and 12 noon?'

'In bed. At Malky's place. Blootered. We wis in the boozer Sunday afternoon. Sunday night we got a carry-oot.'

'Can anyone vouch for you?'

'Malky.'

'Anyone else?'

He shook his head.

'That's unfortunate,' Brian said. 'Because yesterday morning a young girl went missing from Seaton Walk.'

'That right?'

'No distance from the multi-storey flat in Seaton's Northview Towers where you claim to have been sleeping.'

'I was sleeping,' Lee contested, one knee jiggling furiously. 'So would you have been if you'd drunk near on a dozen cans of Spar Cider.' His teeth bared in a grimace. 'Fuckin pish.'

'From where I'm sitting,' Brian said, 'it's a bit of a coincidence that you just happened to land up in Seaton on the very day a schoolgirl disappeared.' He paused to let his words sink in. 'Too much of a coincidence, I'd say.'

'Look, I hold my hands up to not telling you I was living there. I told Malky it would be just for the one night. But the Council—'

'We'll want to check out the address.'

Lee's eyes widened in fright. 'Do you have to? Malky'll go aff his heid.'

176

Ah, weel

'Good of you to come out,' Bill MacSorley said. 'Tell me to my face.'

'It's the least I could do,' Maggie responded. In truth, she'd rather enjoyed the drive. Port Elphinstone, Inveramsay, Chapel of Garioch, Aberdeenshire was rich in quirky place names. The rolling hills, the fields bounded by drystane dykes brought back memories of life on the farm: when life followed the seasons with a comforting certainty. What innocent times they were, when she'd wait at the end of the farm road for the bus that would take her to Methlick village school. It seemed frozen in her memory from that time when she was still carefree. Still unmarried. Still childless. Still unburdened by the cares of a forty-something single mother trying to juggle a part-time job with a struggling business.

Now, 'I'm only sorry I couldn't have recouped at least some of your money.'

'Ah, weel,' he said philosophically. 'Sounds like your people gave the guy a fright. Maybe I've saved somebody else a load of grief.'

'I hope so.' Maggie hadn't pressed Wilma for details of how her sons had extracted the information she'd relayed, but she could imagine. Not that Wayne and Kevin were criminals. From what Wilma had told her, they managed to stay just clear of the law. But they'd been brought up in a different culture, where reparation was swift and often violent. If the investigation was referred back to the police, the less she knew the better.

'Now you have the fraudster's details, will you pursue the matter?'

'I doubt it. More trouble than it's worth. Not to mention the loss of face,' he added with a grimace.

'Don't be too hard on yourself. It's tough being on your own.'

His expression softened. 'You sound like you've been there.'

'My husband died some time ago.'

'I'm sorry.'

'Don't be,' she said, all business again.

With a curt nod, he acknowledged her discomfort. 'Best put the whole episode down to experience. If you'd care to send me your invoice, I'll settle by return.'

'There's no need,' Maggie said quickly. Too quickly. The agency couldn't afford to be distributing largesse.

'Kind of you,' Bill MacSorley protested. 'But you must have incurred significant expense: sending two agents all that way, not to mention your own time.'

Agents?

'Mmm,' she murmured, not trusting herself to look him in the eye. 'I'm only sorry we didn't get the result we were looking for.'

'Tell you what, why don't you bill me for your outlays. And...' He hesitated, then the words came in a rush. '...let me take you out for dinner sometime.'

'Thanks,' she murmured. 'But in the circumstances...'

Nice man. But not a patch on Allan Chisolm.

She conjured a mental picture: the dark good looks, the chiselled jaw, the—'

'I understand.'

'Now, I really must go.' And with that, Maggie gathered her things and fled.

Ancient History

'With regard to your previous convictions—' Brian opened the interview.

'Don't give me that,' Jason sneered, 'It's ancient history.' Straining forward in his seat, he added, 'And it's got fuck all to do with that kid's disappearance, so don't even go there.'

Brian looked to Lisa, who quirked an eyebrow in response.

'Last time we spoke,' she said sweetly, 'You told us you were employed as a builders' labourer on a site at Bridge of Don.'

'That's right.'

'Only your account doesn't tally with what your employer told us: that you were dismissed a fortnight ago.'

Above his hoodie, Jason's face flushed scarlet.

'As a result of a serious assault on a fellow employee.'

'They've no proof.'

'Do you have a temper, Jason?'

Leaning back, he yawned extravagantly. 'No more than most.'

'Can you explain to me how Isla Bain came by that bruise on her face?'

Shrugging, 'Why don't you ask her?"

'I put it to you,' Lisa persisted, 'that when you hooked up with Isla, you found her nine-year-old daughter an inconvenience, to the extent that...'

His pupils flared. 'That's a load if shite. I hardly saw the kid. She was either in her room or at her dad's.'

'Coming back to last Saturday, what time did you arrive at Isla Bain's flat in Seaton Walk?'

'Can't remember.'

Smiling, Lisa said, 'Let me help you out. You arrived at around 9 p.m.'

'Yeah,' he said. 'I remember, now.'

'How did you spend the evening?'

'Necked a few beers. Watched the telly.'

'Can you tell me what was on?'

'Usual Saturday night rubbish.'

'Like what, for example?'

'Can't remember. Not off the top of my head.'

'Try.'

Jason's eyes slid sideways. 'I'd most likely have spent the time jumping between Netflix and Amazon.'

'Where was Frankie?'

'In her room.'

'Doing what?'

'What most kids would be doing at that time of night: sleeping, I guess.'

'She could have been up to anything,' Brian said, the razor blade and bloodied knickers uppermost in his mind. 'Did either of you get up and go to check on her.'

Shrugging, he answered, 'Not my problem.'

'How about her mum?'

'She might have. Can't remember. As I said before, me and Isla had sunk some beers.'

'You married, Jason?'

'Was.'

'Do you have children?'

'Two.'

'How do you get on with your ex?'

'What has that got to do with anything?'

'Just trying to get a picture.'

With an exaggerated yawn, he said, 'Haven't seen her in yonks.'

'How about your children?'

'Them neither.'

Tullos School

'Tug of the sleeve,' the head teacher said. 'Tap on the back and run away. That was about the extent of it.'

'Oh,' Susan said, deflated. She'd been hoping for more. 'There was no physical assault?'

'Not as such. But there was social bullying, that's for sure.'

'Perpetrated by?'

'Girls in her year group. Always the same two or three.'

'This social bullying, can you elaborate?'

'From what I've gleaned, it started – as it often does – in the classroom: faces pulled, notes passed. Spread to the playground. Name-calling: dirty dyke, that sort of thing. Fake rumours. Circulating gossip. Constantly leaving Frankie out and encouraging others to do the same.'

'Over what period of time?'

Consulting his records, he replied, 'Six months or thereabouts. Frankie came back to school after the holiday break with a new, very short haircut. She's very much an individual: strong, determined, happy in her own company. But this set her even further apart.'

'Did she report the incidents?'

'No. Her mother rang me up to complain. It was at that point I called the girls' parents in to a meeting.'

'What was the outcome?'

'Behaviours changed, but only for a week or two, I'm sorry to say. The parents were asked to attend again. Advised in the strongest terms the consequences if this bullying were to persist. That seemed to do the trick. The playground activity ceased.'

Douglas asked, 'How about outside school?'

'Nothing I'm aware of.'

'Social media?'

'Ah.' Passing a weary hand across his brow, the head teacher said, 'That's another story. Kids constantly use the internet – mobile phones, texting, Snapchat – to send cruel, untrue or hurtful messages.'

'You think Frankie Bain was a victim?'

'I'm sure of it.'

'What action did you take?'

'I spoke to the girls concerned. They denied it. And it's hard to prove. The perpetrators can set up temporary accounts.' Sighing, he added, 'Kids are so tech-savvy these days.'

Susan said, 'You think the bullying was all down to Frankie's perceived sexuality?'

'It's hard to tell. On the one hand, she was upset, certainly, by her parents' split. And that could have manifested itself in a bout of rebelliousness. On the other, there's such pressure on social media to conform to certain stereotypes. Girls are especially vulnerable to believing they are valued more for their appearance than their character or achievements.'

'Tell me about it!'

'They put selfies up and judge their self-worth from the amount of 'likes' they have. And it only takes a single ill-judged post to unleash a torrent of criticism. Worse, downright abuse. I've had parents in this room at their wits' end. Kids not eating. Refusing to go to school. Self-harming, they're so terrified of the repercussions. As you're no doubt aware, online bullying is a contributing factor for many young people having thoughts of suicide.'

'You don't think gender dysphoria has had any bearing on this?'

'Hard to tell. As I say, girls in particular feel under pressure, and it's a confusing age anyway.'

Susan nodded acknowledgement. 'That's so true. It's all very well saying you can be whoever you want, putting the pronouns on your bio, and everything's cool, but it takes a pretty strong individual to feel sure of themselves at that age, let alone assert themselves.'

'Over 200 schoolchildren die by suicide every year in the UK.

What can you do?' He looked to the detectives for understanding. 'So, to return to your original question: was Frankie Bain the victim of an assault? Not that I have established. Was she persecuted in other ways? Most certainly. And it wasn't so much the severity of the bullying as the sheer volume.'

No Angel

'Do you know why you're here?' Lisa asked.

With a shrug, Stuart Bain replied. 'It's to do with Frankie, I assume. That sighting, have you—?'

She shook her head.

'So you're no further forward?'

'We're committing all possible resources into finding your daughter,' Brian responded. Alive, was what he thought.

'There are a couple of things we would like to clarify,' Lisa said. 'We've verified your account of your movements at the time Frankie went missing.'

'It's not for want of witnesses,' said Stuart. 'We were packed in that chopper like bloody sardines.'

'Do you have a girlfriend?'

'You kidding? I've been keeping my nose clean, waiting for Isla to cool down.'

'And if she doesn't?' asked Brian, joining the conversation.

'She only chucked me out to give me a fright. And it worked. All I want is for us to be a family again. Deep down, I know that's what Isla wants, too.'

'What if you're wrong? If your wife were to file for divorce, it's more than likely she'll be awarded custody of Frankie, especially given the nature of your employment.'

Stuart said, 'I'll get a job onshore.'

'You'd do that?'

He nodded. 'And fight for custody. But I don't know why you're going down that road. It might not come to that.'

Lisa said, 'Would you also be willing to pre-empt such an outcome by taking matters into your own hands?'

'Hang on,' he said, his voice rising. 'I thought I came in here voluntarily to answer a few questions. Are you accusing me of something?'

'I'm suggesting,' Lisa said evenly, 'you might think removing Frankie from her mother's house a good idea, given there's a new boyfriend you don't approve of.'

'I wouldn't do that,' he protested. 'I'm no angel, but I'm not a complete idiot.' Registering the scepticism in her eyes, he added, 'And, besides, where would I put her? You've seen where I live. There isn't room to swing a cat.'

'You've told us relations with your wife are strained.'

'Correct.'

'To the extent you argue. Do you ever come to blows?"

With a sigh, Stuart answered, 'I get where you're coming from. If you think I'm a wife-beater you've the wrong end of the stick. In all the time we've been together, I've never laid a finger on Isla. Ask her if you don't believe me.'

'How about Frankie? Have you ever laid hands on her?'

'Hit her, do you mean?'

'Either that, or…' The sentence hung, unfinished.

'No way.'

Brian asked, 'Would you be willing to surrender your laptop?'

'What do you need that for?'

'It might help progress the investigation.'

'I suppose,' Stuart said, with obvious reluctance. 'Depends on how long you'd want it. When she stays at my place, Frankie uses it to play games, so it would be an inconvenience. But I'll do anything…' His voice broke. 'Anything at all that will help bring her back.'

A Power Walk

IX

A Power Walk

'Keep up,' Wilma urged, looking over her shoulder. She'd forsaken the Day-glo and was kitted out head to toe in Nike.

'I'm doing my best,' Maggie puffed, incongruous in Primark leggings and an outgrown hoodie of Colin's. 'It's alright for you. Your legs are longer than mine.'

'I'm carrying more weight,' Wilma countered, elbows churning like pistons.

They were on their early morning power-walk, a practice that had morphed out of Wilma's banishment from the boxing gym. Most days, they'd drive to the Esplanade, where they'd join joggers and dog walkers taking the sea air. When time was tight, they stuck to their own neighbourhood.

It was a sharp late-autumn day, leaves still on the trees, birds tweeting valiantly in the branches. A watery sun struggled to burst through the clouds as they passed the sleeping semis in Auchinyell Gardens.

'Anything new?'

'They haven't found Frankie Bain,' replied Maggie. 'Not as of this morning's news bulletin.'

Wilma grumped, 'She'll turn up. I meant on the agency front.'

'Don't ask. We can't compete with the big players. They have the manpower and technical resources to leave us standing. There must be a dozen private investigation firms, now, in Aberdeen: Bluemoon, Insight, RPI, to name just a few.'

'Och,' said Wilma, 'we don't need to bother our backsides about them.'

'I don't agree. They're often manned by ex-military or security personnel with skills we lack. And the competition is growing.'

'Keep us on our toes.'

'Some of them offer a nationwide network of agents,' Maggie expanded. 'Every client assigned their own personal Case Manager. An online portal to manage the investigation and view results in real time.'

'Small is beautiful,' countered Wilma. 'Plus, we're the only detective agency owned and staffed by women.'

'How about Harriet Bond?'

'I bet the name's made up. Plus, they're based in bloody Nottingham.'

'That's as may be, but from what I've gathered off the website their Live Chat call handlers look to be exclusively female. Accept it, we're on a hiding to nothing.'

'Bollocks!'

'Our market share is dwindling by the day. Yet, despite hard evidence, you refuse to accept there's potential in pet thefts.'

'Bottle it,' muttered Wilma.

'Romance fraud is dead in the water.'

She stopped short. 'I don't accept that.' Then, tugging at the waistband of her jogging pants, 'These control knickers are killing me.'

'Might help to buy the right size,' Maggie retorted. Wilma was in the habit of purchasing a size down, in the happy expectation whatever diet she was currently on would work.

'Size isn't the problem.' Stretching her knickers as far as they would go, Wilma contemplated the red ring around her midriff. 'It's the style. Waistband's too tight.' Snapping the elastic back in place, she set off again at top speed. 'Romance fraud. I don't accept it's a dead duck.'

'How can you possibly argue that, when Bill MacSorley...'

'Remember that case, good while back: Helen somebody-or-other?'

'Cruickshank.'

'Needed us to vet a guy she met on a dating site.'

'I don't know why you're bringing that up,' said Maggie. 'I would have thought, after the Woking business, you might have learned something.'

'You going to keep throwing that in my face?'

'All I'm saying is, we've got to accept our limitations.'

Wilma's jaw dropped. 'That's rich, coming from somebody not that long ago was up a hill trying to tell one sheep from the effing other.'

'Okay,' Maggie allowed, as they reached Garthdee Road. 'Rural theft is not our bag.'

'We never made a brass farthing out that case,' Wilma groused.

'That was a mistake, I'll admit. But it was you who sent me chasing out to Inverurie.'

'Nobody strong-armed you to take the case on.'

'And nobody asked you to send those two lads on a fool's errand. You're lucky they came back in one piece. They could be dead and buried at the hands of some criminal gang.'

For a few minutes they walked in step, then, 'We were mebbe a wee bittie ambitious with that one,' Wilma conceded. 'But the Cruickshank case was different.'

'I don't see how.'

'For one, we got a result.'

'Achieved by running a background check, as I recall.' Panting, Maggie added, 'Online. But as I said from the start, we don't have the resources to mount that sort of investigation.'

Wilma paused to jiggle her breasts in their sports bra. 'Instead of trying to shut the door when the horse has bolted, why don't we tackle the problem from the other end: offer a background report service on dating site matches – like we did with Cruickshank – before the client gets in too deep?'

'I can see there might be a market,' Maggie grudged. 'Now you mention it, I had a call along those lines just the other day.'

Wilma set off again at the toot. 'Trust me, it could be mega. Even folk don't go as far as pretending to be someone they're not, photo editing is so common people often don't look like their Instagram profile in real life. Either they use filters or manipulate their profile some other way.'

'I hear what you're saying,' Maggie wheezed, trying her best to keep pace. 'What I don't get is why you'd want to go down that road. All you'd be doing is sitting in front of a computer.'

'The online search would only be a small part of the investigation,' Wilma argued, as they passed Robert Gordon's Sports Centre. 'Most of our work would be outside: meetings with the client, surveillance of the subject and his or her associates. We'd see life in the raw. If you think back, Helen Cruickshank's fancy man had a wife and four kids.'

'I thought we were done with infidelity.'

'This is different. Niche. I tell you, mature women like us, we're made for it. We could corner the market.'

'The way I see it,' Maggie sniffed, 'we'd be nothing more than proxy relationship counsellors.'

'Think of the sport we'd have.'

'There you go again. How many times do I have to tell you this isn't a game?'

'Never said it was,' Wilma mumbled, chin on chest.

'Maybe not. But I tell you this: the way things are going, if we don't pull in new business, we might as well call it quits.'

Wilma's head came up. Pink-cheeked, she protested, 'I'm only trying to help.'

'You'd be more help if you concentrated on the job in hand,' Maggie said. 'That, and stay within the confines of the law.'

Wilma stopped, mid-stride. 'Well, if that's the way you feel.' She set off again at a trot.

Striving to keep up, Maggie followed.

Gray's School of Art flashed past on their left.

Looking neither right nor left, Wilma shot across Garthdee Road.

Helpless, Maggie watched her dwindling figure loop around the bend onto Morrison Drive and out of sight.

Persons of Interest

'Persons of Interest?' Chisolm prompted, when they'd gathered in the Incident Room for the latest update.

'Three,' Brian replied: 'Frankie's dad, Stuart Bain. Her mother's boyfriend, Jason Eadie, and the RSO, Lee Marshall.'

'Before we go into detail, who'll bring me up to speed on the Meston Walk sighting?'

'Nothing useful from CCTV,' Douglas answered. 'Nor from the bus company.'

'Isla Bain's old neighbours in Tullos didn't give us much either,' Susan added. 'Seems the family lived pretty quietly. They didn't see much of Stuart, him being offshore for weeks at a time, and Isla kept herself to herself.'

Douglas said, 'The school was more forthcoming. Seems Frankie was the subject of an extensive and sustained cyberbullying campaign. There's been speculation about either her sexuality or gender identity at the root of it.'

'That would fit with what we got from the statements at Seaton School,' Susan supplied. 'Plus, the items that were found in her bedroom. Doesn't follow Frankie would self-harm, but there may be a link. Might be worth another chat with her mum. Isla could be in denial.'

'Have another word, by all means. But, remember, we have no concrete evidence to substantiate this hypothesis, so tread carefully. By all accounts, Frankie is a bit of an outsider. But a girl suffering gender dysphoria is completely different from a girl who some people might describe as a tomboy. And keep the distinction between sex and gender at the forefront of your minds.' Chisolm looked, pointedly, at Bob Duffy, the dinosaur in the room.

Rolling his eyes, Duffy said, 'Doesn't happen at that age, surely?'

'It's a fact children become sexually aware from a much earlier age. The internet is a major factor: the increasingly easy access children have to pornography and explicit information. They want to replicate or experiment with what they've viewed. It's also a fact that with improved awareness of trans identities, an increasing number of young people are 'coming out' as transgender in primary school settings.'

'What next?' Duffy exclaimed. 'If it's not #MeToo, it's…'

'This isn't a new phenomenon,' Brian said. 'It was just not talked about.'

'Unlike now,' Chisolm observed. 'It's non-stop heated debate: on the one hand, the trans lobby. On the other, radical feminists.'

Susan said, 'Don't get me started. We're hardly even allowed to say the word "woman" any more.'

'Where will it bloody end,' muttered Duffy. 'That's what I want to know.'

Chisolm held up a hand. 'As I said, it's a contentious subject, but not one we should be prioritising right now. Moving on, 'What's the story on Stuart Bain?'

Lisa said, 'He seems devoted to Frankie. But if Isla Bain goes ahead with divorce proceedings, and he fights her for custody, as he says he will… It wouldn't be the first time a desperate dad has abducted his children.'

'Safi case springs to mind,' Susan volunteered, with a deprecating glance at Lisa. No way was she going to let her hog the briefing.

'What case?'

Smirking, Susan said, 'Go and look it up.'

Lisa waved a manicured hand to catch Chisolm's attention. 'Something I didn't mention: when Frankie goes to stay at her dad's, the sleeping arrangements are less than satisfactory.'

Chisolm looked to Brian. 'Interview Stuart Bain again. Under caution this time.'

'Boss.'

'Which brings us to the boyfriend.'

Lisa spoke up. 'Hostile, uncooperative. Plus, he lied about his employment history.'

'Haven't we all?' Duffy said, looking her straight in the eye.

Colour drained from her face. 'Don't know what you're getting at.'

'There's previous,' Brian chipped in. 'Might explain his attitude.'

'It's something more than that. I can smell it.'

'That's not a lot of use,' said Douglas.

Lisa's eyes flashed. 'Who asked for your opinion?'

Chisolm intervened. 'Have another chat. See what more you can get out of Jason Eadie. And do another sweep on his background. You never know what you might turn up. Establish if he or Stuart Bain owns a vehicle. Run a ANPR check.' He turned to Brian. 'Has someone managed to pin down the errant RSO?'

'He was interviewed this morning. We can place him in Seaton at the time of Frankie's disappearance. He claims to have been sleeping at a pal's house in one of the high-rises, but we've no corroboration.'

'Make sure that's followed up. Anything else?'

'I've a report in from response,' Duffy volunteered. 'Theft of camping equipment from the garage of a house in Old Aberdeen.'

'Who were the response officers?'

'Souter and Miller.'

Wiping a tired hand across his brow, Chisolm sighed, 'God save us.'

Douglas said, 'Probably some druggie from Tillydrone.'

'Waste of police time,' said Duffy, 'when we've a fast-moving Misper case on our hands.'

'Still, keep a watching eye. These petty thefts often come in clusters. But don't waste too much time on it. Finding Frankie Bain has to be our number one priority.'

Duffy raised a hand in mock salute. 'Whatever you say, boss.'

Chisolm acknowledged him with a tight smile. 'The clock's running down, the odds of recovering that little girl alive and in good shape lengthening with every minute that passes.' Shuffling his paperwork, he rose to his feet. 'Thanks everyone. Now, get out there and find that child.'

Malky

Brian had forgotten how small he was: no more than five foot six, he judged, when – finally – Malky White came to the door. Barrel chest over the shortest legs Brian had ever seen on an adult male. Close-set eyes. Tight mouth.

The two detectives showed their warrant cards.

'We need a word,' Brian said.

A panicked expression crossed Malky's face, swiftly followed by one of sullen malevolence. He spread both arms, biceps bulging under a black Lycra T-shirt, hands like hams supporting the door-jamb. 'I'm no' in the mood.'

'Not a problem,' said Lisa, plastering a fake smile on her face. 'We can come back. We'll keep coming back until you're in a better frame of mind.'

Beneath his bald pate, Malky's monobrow quivered.

'This isn't about you,' Brian said.

He squinted. 'It's that cunt Marshall. Fucking knew I should never have let him in.'

'Is Lee here?'

'Why are you asking me? Was it no you bastards sent him hot-footing back to Kincorth.'

*

'What is your relationship with Lee Marshall?' Lisa asked, once they'd managed to gain entry.

'Whaddya mean, "relationship"?' Malky growled. 'Lee's a mate, is all.' Then, seeing her disbelieving expression, 'He's no my arse bandit, if that's what you're getting at.'

'How long have you known him?'

'Couple years. We wis banged up together.'

'Meaning Peterhead prison?'

He stripped her with his eyes. 'Aren't you the clever one?'

'Then you'll be aware Lee Marshall is on the Sex Offenders Register, and required to remain at his home address, unless…'

'Fuck all to do with me,' Malky broke in, blood rushing to his face. 'Far as I'm concerned, he's a free agent.'

'There are good reasons,' Lisa began.

Veins stood out on his temples. 'Did you no' hear me?'

Brian stepped in. 'Are you aware a child has gone missing in this locality?'

Running a meaty hand over his forehead, Malky said, 'I get it. You're trying to fit him up.'

'We're trying to satisfy ourselves,' Brian said, 'as to Lee's whereabouts on Monday morning.'

Malky jerked his head towards the living-room door. 'He was through there. In his kip.'

'All morning?'

'All fucking day.'

'Mind if we have a look?'

'You got a warrant?'

'No.'

With a leer, Malky replied, 'There's your answer.'

'We'll leave that, for now,' Brian said. Turning to Malky, 'Where were you?'

'In my bed.'

'You're not telling me you were in bed all day Monday too?'

'Naw. Just till about 2 o'clock. Me an Lee wis on the booze all weekend.'

Brian bet booze was just for starters. Malky White was known to the police: a string of convictions for the supply of Class B drugs. 'Catching up, were you?

Malky stared him out. 'Something like that.'

A Quiet Pint

Allan Chisolm took a long draught of his pint and relaxed into his seat. Situated across from Marischal College, the BrewDog pub in the city's Gallowgate, though only a couple of blocks from Police HQ, was not somewhere he'd patronised more than a couple of times since he'd arrived in the city.

That was about to change. During the course of 2021, Aberdeen HQ was to be vacated as part of Police Scotland's estates strategy to develop greater integration by co-locating with partner organisations. The Queen Street building was due to be demolished in order to make way for Aberdeen City Council's civic quarter project as part of the City Centre Masterplan, and staff distributed between the local authority's headquarters at Marischal College, Aberdeenshire Council's Woodhill House, and the existing police buildings across the city.

'Didn't expect to see you here.'

Chisolm looked up to find Lisa Haldane standing over him.

His spirits sank. When she'd first appeared in DCI Scrimgeour's office, he'd taken the trouble to get the lowdown from Bell Street. Didn't like what he heard. Now, 'Fancied a change.'

'Trying to get away from us?' she teased.

'Would I do that?' In truth, he'd determined to give the Old Blackfriars and Illicit Still a body-swerve – too many fellow cops – in favour of a quiet pint alone with his thoughts.

'Mind if I join you?'

'Well—' He was still fumbling for a convincing excuse when she slid into the booth.

Chisolm made a show of shifting along the bench seat. 'What brings you here?'

'Same as you, I expect.' Shrugging out of her jacket, she deposited it alongside. 'Taking time out. I was having a wander, actually.' She fixed him with an innocent look. 'Still trying to get my bearings. Thought this place looked cool.'

Deconstructed, he would have said. A traditionalist at heart, the pub's industrial-chic decor didn't do a lot for him, though Brewdog offered dozens of craft beers, supplemented by interesting limited editions. What's more, alongside pizzas, the food menu listed platters, including some of his favourite cheeses from George Mellis. Save him cooking a meal, an enticing thought after the day he'd just had: a day burdened with duty rosters and shift allowance forms and cost projections and progress reports, all crammed into gaps between meetings.

'You never did give me the city tour,' Lisa was saying, now.

'There's a tour bus,' he informed her. It sounded churlish, even to him. 'Sorry. Long day.'

'I get it,' Lisa said, edging closer. 'Takes a fellow cop to really understand.' Tossing her blonde bob, 'This is cosy.'

Chisolm leapt to his feet. 'What can I get you to drink?'

*

He was waiting to be served when he spotted the lad, standing further down the bar. 'Colin?' he'd called out, before he stopped to think.

The boy turned, colour rising from his collar to suffuse his face.

Chisolm moved to his side. 'Wasn't sure if it was you. Been a while.'

'Yup.'

The barman slid a glass across the counter. 'Pint of IPA.'

With a furtive glance over his shoulder, Colin urged, 'Don't tell Mum.'

Chisolm clocked the school shirt, just visible under the North Face jacket. The absent tie. Probably rolled up in his pocket.

Poor sod. Colin must be under-age, still. Not that Chisolm could blame the bar staff. Even with the keenly-priced RGU Students Union around the corner on Schoolhill, the venue must attract a fair amount of student custom. It was easy enough to fake ID, and Colin looked eighteen, at the very least.

'Won't tell a soul,' he said.

'Likewise.'

Chisolm followed his eyes to where Lisa was sitting, frowning prettily as she thumbed her phone.

Damnation!

Feeling his gaze upon her, she looked up.

Gave him a little wave, accompanied by a coy smile.

Serves You Right

It's so dark. Darker than my bedroom, even when I pull my duvet over my head. I wish I had my duvet now, soft and warm and smelling of Mum's washing liquid. Not like this old thing I'm lying on. It's damp and smelly, and the floor is so hard and bumpy, I'm sore whichever way I turn.

My teeth are sounding rat-a-tat-tat.

My fingers are stiff and raw.

I bunch them up.

Put them in my mouth and blow.

That helps a bit, though my nose is dripping onto my chin.

"Serves you right", I can hear Mum say.

She's always on at me to wrap up, wear a hat and gloves.

Not going to happen. Not in the knitted stuff she bought in some sale. Pink. And mittens with flaps, like I was four. The other kids would laugh at me. They do already. Don't want to make it worse.

My tummy is rumbling. Hasn't stopped. Another thing Mum nags me about. "If you'd eat a good breakfast, you wouldn't be looking for snack money". Another thing I got wrong. If I'd grabbed something from the fridge, or even taken a few coins from Mum's purse, I could have bought something at the shop. I looked in a couple of wheelie bins, but all I found was a Fanta bottle with some left in the bottom. I made that last a while.

But that was before the man asked if I was okay.

I know not to talk to strangers. Mum's dinned it into me since I was in Primary 1. And you get it at school. We even had a policeman came and gave us a talk about it.

But this man had a dog.

And it wanted to make friends.

There's a noise at my feet: a rustling, then a scratching of small claws.

I clamp my hands over my ears.

Squeeze my eyes tight shut.

I'm cold.

And my teeth are chattering.

And I'm scared.

So scared, my heart is thumping under my jacket like it's trying to escape.

Then it all goes black.

Mitchell's Hospital

In a quiet corner of The Chanonry, Bruce Anderson exited the patrol car and pulled on his uniform cap.

Vish Patel followed.

The single-storey building was laid out in the shape of a letter H, the wings bridged by a central refectory crowned by a bell-cote.

The two constables ambled up the path of the pretty cottage garden to a courtyard in whose centre sat a stone sundial.

Jerking a thumb over his shoulder at the nearby St Machar kirkyard, Anderson quipped, 'One step from the grave.'

A memorial plaque set into the wall informed them Mitchell's Hospital, founded in 1801 by the philanthropist David Mitchell, was endowed as an alms house to lodge, clothe and maintain five widows and five unmarried daughters of Old Aberdeen merchants. Now owned and managed by the University of Aberdeen, Aberdeen City Council and the Cathedral Church of St Machar, the early Victorian building had been modified to provide four self-contained flats for elderly ladies.

'Where do you want to start?'

'Take your pick.'

Tentatively, Vish tapped on the nearest door.

No answer.

'You'll need to knock louder than that,' said Anderson. 'The old buggers will be deaf.'

Vish knocked again, more forcefully this time.

Still no answer.

Moving to a window, he shaded his eyes and peered inside. 'Looks empty.'

Frustrated, they moved onto the next door.

And the next.

Elicited no response.

Anderson asked, 'Want to cut and run?'

'Better not,' Patel replied. 'Give me a mo.'

But before he could knock, the fourth door opened.

An elderly lady stood on the threshold.

Taking in the uniforms, she exclaimed, 'You've found him.'

'Who?'

'Macavity.' She raised rheumy eyes to the sky, 'The Lord be praised.'

Patel looked to Anderson for succour.

Found none.

'We're looking for information,' he said, 'with regard to a missing child.'

'"Child?"' The old lady eyed the two constables accusingly. 'I thought you'd come about my cat.'

*

'What d'you reckon?' Vish asked when they were back in the car.

'Lost her marbles,' Anderson replied. 'Couldn't tell you the time of day.'

'I'm with you there. All that stuff about losing her cat. Bet if we run a check she hasn't even reported it missing. Died, most like.'

'Aye. In nineteen o dot.'

'As for someone nicking its dinner, if the old biddie was daft enough to leave food out, the seagulls would have scoffed it. They'd eat a fish supper out your hand.'

'Right enough.'

Patel said, 'Stray dog, my best guess.'

'Could be a fox.'

'No way.'

'I'm telling you, red foxes are common in cities these days. More like domestic dogs. Not much fear of humans. And we're near enough Seaton Park.' Anderson pointed to the open gates.

'I suppose,' Patel said doubtfully.

'Did you not see that video on social media last summer? A

woman just had a baby at the Maternity Hospital. And she's sitting on the grass outside, eating a sandwich in the fresh air. And this fox appears – casual as you like – and snaffles the sandwich wrapper, then has a roll on the picnic rug.'

'That for real?'

'Hundred percent. Brings to mind thon woman in Australia: Lindy Chamberlain. Ayer's Rock.'

'What did she do?"

'Claimed a dingo ate her baby. Got tried for murder.'

'Not her. I meant the woman up Foresterhill.'

'Dunno. Probably ran screaming back into the hospital.'

For a while they sat without speaking, then Patel asked, 'What are we going to tell Sarge?'

'Tell the truth,' Anderson said. 'We could only run down one resident and she was bloody havering.'

All I Ever Wanted

'All I ever wanted in this world,' Isla Bain wept, 'is for Frankie to be happy.'

'And she will be,' Brenda said, patting Isla's knee as they sat together on the sofa. 'Just as soon as...' Seeing Susan's worried expression, she stopped.

Isla wiped her nose with the back of her hand. 'If I ever get her back.'

'What would help,' Susan offered, 'is if I could ask you just a few more questions.'

Isla turned. 'I thought you'd come to give me some news.'

'I'll leave you to it.' Brenda said tactfully. She rose and walked through to the kitchen.

'What do you want to know?' Isla said. 'More about my love life?'

'Nothing like that,' Susan responded, with a sideways glance at Douglas. 'It's to do with the trouble at Tullos school.'

'Do you have to bring that up again? I thought it was over and done with.'

Douglas looked up from inspecting his fingernails. 'It's alleged other children were calling Frankie a dyke. Is that true?'

Susan's shoulders slumped. So much for treading carefully.

Nodding, Isla replied, 'That's the least of it.'

'The reason we ask,' Susan said, eyes flashing warning signals. 'Is Stuart mentioned her wanting to be called Frankie is quite a recent thing. And what with that and the haircut— '

'You think she's queer? Don't you think I'd know, her own mother?'

'I think she may be going through quite a troubling period in her life.'

'Aren't we all?'

'How is she at home?'

'How do you mean?'

Choosing her words with care, Susan said, 'How does she present herself?'

'If you're asking does she dress up in my clothes, nick my make-up, the answer's no. She's never been a girly girl, but that doesn't make her...' Isla stopped, pink-faced. 'Then, you're right, the Frankie thing is new. She was called after my mum. Don't know what gave her the idea to change it. Something she saw on social media, most likely. As for the hair, she took a pair of scissors to it right after Stuart and I split up. Nail scissors and all. Cost me a fortune at the hairdressers to get it fixed.'

Susan asked, 'Are Stuart and Frankie close?'

'As close as anyone. Frankie's her own person. Doesn't give much away.'

'When you were together, did Frankie ever share your bed?'

'When she was wee.'

'And since?'

'If she's feeling poorly, she'll come in for a cuddle.'

'When Frankie stays at her dad's, where does she sleep?'

'In a sleeping bag, she says.'

'And you believe her?'

'Of course. She thinks it's a big deal. You would at that age, wouldn't you?' Seeing the doubt in Susan's eyes, she asked, 'You don't think there's anything going on?' Then, getting no reaction, 'Stuart might be a cheating bastard, but he wouldn't do a thing like that.'

*

'How is she doing?' Susan whispered.

'Not great,' Brenda replied.

They were in Isla Bain's kitchen on the pretext of washing up yet another round of tea and coffee mugs.

'She's been glued to the television,' the FLO continued. 'Every news bulletin, she gets herself up to high doh. Ends up in tears. Either that or she'll take to her bed.'

'Do you think she'd be up for a press conference?'

'Nae chance. What with her medication, and…'

'Pity,' Susan interrupted. 'We've drawn a blank with that last sighting. A TV appeal might generate some productive leads.'

'Give it a couple more days,' Brenda said. Then, seeing Susan's concerned expression, 'We don't have that amount of time?'

Wordlessly, Susan shook her head.

A Misunderstanding

Maggie was in the bathroom when the doorbell rang.

'Dammit!' she swore under her breath. She'd confronted Colin when he'd come home late, smelling of beer. Felt heartsick at his admission he'd bumped into Allan Chisolm in company with a young woman. Torn between rage and disappointment, she'd treated herself to a rare half hour of pamper time. Had painstakingly plucked her eyebrows, was in the middle of painting her toenails.

Hastily replacing the cap on the bottle of nail varnish, she set it on the shelf and gingerly made her way down the hall.

Allan Chisolm stood on the doorstep. 'I should explain.'

'There's no need,' she said loftily.

'May I come in?'

'Sorry,' she managed, from between gritted teeth. 'I'm busy.'

He gave a wry smile. 'So I see.'

Maggie looked down at her bare feet. On one, five shell-pink nails shone alluringly. On the other, a mint green foam toe separator – a trick she'd learned from Wilma – spread her digits at all angles.

Feeling like a five-year-old, 'Now, if you'll forgive me.' She made to shut the door.

Chisolm took a step forward. 'Maggie.'

Instinctively, she recoiled.

'Please.'

Her heart melted. 'I'll give you five minutes.'

*

Maggie said, 'Colin never could keep a secret.'

They were in the sitting room, Chisolm on the sofa, she – legs curled under – in the big chair in the bay window. She'd quickly removed the toe separator and stuffed it in the pocket of her housecoat.

On the other side of the room, the empty mantelpiece stared accusingly. The day after she'd invited Allan Chisolm into her bed, Maggie had swiped the photograph of her and George from its cherished place and secreted it in the sideboard drawer.

'I don't know who was more surprised,' Chisolm was saying, now. 'Him or me. Poor lad.'

'Poor lad, nothing. Colin thinks I don't know he drinks. Smokes weed occasionally. But he should know better than to chance his arm in a pub a stone's throw from school. On a weekday, too. He got the third degree, I can tell you, when he came home.

Chisolm smiled his understanding.

'I thought he'd put all that behind: bunking off from school, nicking wheel badges, pushing the boundaries. He has a steady girlfriend, and he's working with a tutor to help him catch up.'

'I know, from experience, it's hard to achieve a balance.'

'From policing?' Maggie fished. 'Or...' She left the sentence open, hoping he might share something of his private life.

'Speaking in general terms,' he responded, his expression bland.

'Okay.'

'He'll be fine. You've two good kids.'

Maggie's resolve wobbled. George would be so proud.

An uncomfortable silence ensued.

Maggie could contain herself no longer. 'Colin mentioned you were with a friend,' she ventured, in what she hoped was a casual tone.

'Colleague,' Chisolm corrected.

Maggie's mind ran riot. Colin had been characteristically vague. 'Young,' he'd said. 'Blonde.' She'd quizzed him as to how attractive. He'd said he couldn't tell.

'DC. Joined the team from Bell Street.'

'That must be a help,' she said unconvincingly.

Chisolm's lips thinned. 'That's to be seen.'

'What's her name?' Maggie asked, despite herself.

'Lisa Haldane.'

In her imagination. Maggie conjured up a willowy blonde. Wondered how many drinks she'd shared with Allan Chisolm?

'Bit of a coincidence,' he added. 'Her showing up at the same time in the same place. Then, again, maybe I shouldn't be so cynical. That's what policing does to you.'

Seizing her opportunity, Maggie said, 'Now you mention it, is there any news on Frankie Bain?'

Stiffening, Chisolm replied, 'Nothing I'm at liberty to share.'

'In that case,' said Maggie, rising, 'You've had your five minutes.'

Going-forward

X

Going Forward

Maggie got straight down to business. 'Going forward.'

'Hold your horses,' Wilma objected, wiggling her bum cheeks to get comfortable. She reached for her glass and took a mouthful of Diet Pepsi. With a nod, 'On you go.'

They were in Di Maggio's Bon Accord restaurant. After their contretemps on Garthdee Road, Maggie had deemed it prudent to meet on neutral ground.

'I've given your proposal careful thought. The online dating market is huge, as you say, but in my considered opinion, online dating is a young person's game.'

'Old folk do it, an all, thon MacSorley for one.'

'And look how that ended up.'

Wilma's lower lip jutted. 'You're such a party-pooper. If I'd had any idea we were going to end up like this, I'd never have…'

'And before you talked me into this business,' Maggie shot back. 'You might have stopped long enough to consider the implications. You've good intentions, but I'm sick to death of your extra-curricular activities.'

'And I've had a bellyful of your moralising.'

Maggie drew a steadying breath. 'Before we go any further, I think it would be useful to re-state operational parameters.'

Digging into a stack of American pancakes slathered in Nutella, Wilma said, 'Dinna dress it up. Give it to me straight.'

'What's legal and what's not. Let's start with the basics: background checks. May I remind you they must be carried out using only sources in the public domain: telephone directory, electoral roll, Companies House, Land Registry…'

'…Court verdicts, Birth, Marriage and Death Records,' Wilma rattled off. 'Websites such as Google, Facebook, Linkedin. Not forgetting press cuttings and Freedom of Information.' Stifling a huge yawn, she added, 'That do you?'

Maggie's lips thinned. 'It's the illegal searches that give me cause for concern: the ex-directory telephone numbers obtained by stealth. The bank statements sourced from the workplace or gym membership. The medical records accessed by subterfuge'.

'You didn't complain when I brought you intel on Sheena Struthers,' Wilma beefed, referencing a previous domestic abuse case. 'Or the lowdown on laundering cash through Fixed Odds Betting Terminals.'

'As to the Data Protection Act, ' Maggie ran on full tilt. 'You know perfectly well it's okay to check out a person's school, friends, marital status or job history. Quite another to bribe insiders to access benefits or other databases.' She paused for breath. 'And while we're on the subject, you've turned blagging into an art form. You can't ring someone up and pretend to be somebody else.'

'Gets results,' said Wilma, rubbing at a smear of chocolate on her front. 'Give as much detail as you can, you'll likely be believed.'

'Don't want to know.'

'You've a brass neck. Weren't you the one sweet-talked Brian Burnett into giving us chapter and verse on more than one police investigation?'

Maggie ignored this. 'If you had your way, we'd be out half the night shadowing low-lifes, like we did on that last Misper case.'

'And if you had yours, we'd be sitting at a computer till we're square-eyed.'

Wilma rose from the table, 'Give us a mo. I'm going to nip to the ladies and get this shite off my shirt.'

*

'Fieldwork still has a place,' said Wilma, when she resumed her seat. 'Speaking of which, I managed to get another stock shrinkage case in the bag.'

'Well done!' Maggie exclaimed, teacup halfway to her mouth.

'How did you manage that?'

Modestly, Wilma dipped her chin. She wasn't planning to go into detail, and there's no way Maggie would ever find out.

'You didn't do anything dodgy?'

'Not as such.'

'For heaven's sake,' Maggie exclaimed. 'How often do I have to tell you—'

'If there's no other way.'

'There's always another way. You just have to exercise your mind until you find it, not go breaking into property, putting trackers on vehicles, pretending to be someone you're not.'

'Pfft.' Wilma took a slug of her Pepsi.

'That time you burgled the cannabis factory, for instance. I didn't sleep for a week worrying about us being put under witness protection. When you pepper-sprayed the vandals of that Chinese takeaway, I had their dads threaten me with extreme violence. And those are only two of the incidents you've admitted to.'

'Proof of the pudding: I got a result.'

'Fieldwork does have a role to play,' Maggie conceded. 'It lets us gather evidence in divorce and child custody cases. Helps re-locate missing persons and lost family in adoptions, or trace assets for child and spousal support. And it's something you're good at, I'll grant you. But…' she steeled herself, determined to address Wilma's off-the-books capers once and for all, 'the extra-curricular activity has to stop.'

So she did know.

Wilma looked away.

'As for what you so coyly refer to as "tools of the trade", tracking someone else's car without their consent is illegal. Added to which, The Data Protection Act 1998 defines the information gathered by GPS trackers as personal data.'

'Right,' said Wilma, not looking the least bit sorry. She ran a mental inventory of her online purchases, safely stowed at the foot of her wardrobe. In a recent search, a well-priced range of mini-cameras hidden in air fresheners, mobile phone chargers, clocks had piqued her interest.

Maggie's voice broke her train of thought. 'The nub of the matter is we put out too much time and effort chasing too little money. The bread and butter stuff – process serving, taking depositions, acting as professional witnesses – forms the bedrock of the business, but we need to augment our income from that with more weighty investigations.'

'Dinna use one word,' Wilma grumbled, 'when you can use the whole dictionary. Don't know why you didn't stick to being a legal secretary. Suits you down to the ground.'

'It might come to that, if we can't pull in new business. How about we try to sign another couple of corporate clients?'

'Nah,' Wilma pooh-pooed, wiping the last of the Nutella off her plate with her little finger. 'Boring.'

'Do you have a better suggestion?'

'That call you took about the dating match might be worth following up.'

'I doubt it.'

'Give it a go,' Wilma urged. 'It's not as if we've anything much else on the cards.'

'I'll think about it.'

'There's the Sellars' business.'

Maggie said, 'Drop it, will you?'

'There could be money involved.'

'I doubt it. Keith Williams had a substantial win on the People's Lottery not six months ago.'

It was Wilma's turn to look put out.

Operation Eco-Warrior

In the incident room, phones rang, keyboards clacked. In one corner a photocopier cranked out paper. Operation Eco-Warrior – the codename the investigation had been tagged with – topped the once pristine whiteboard in neat capital letters. Below the heading it was a mess: a cat's cradle of coloured lines criss-crossing one another; maps and diagrams and photographs pinned alongside lists of actions, completed and outstanding.

Allan Chisolm called the assembled company to order. 'We'll start with the nominals.' Pointing to Stuart Bain's photograph, 'Where are we at with Frankie's dad?'

'He's voluntarily surrendered his laptop,' Brian replied. 'Tech Support are working on it as we speak.'

Moving along the whiteboard, 'How about Jason Eadie?'

Lisa answered. 'One of Isla Bain's new neighbours has rung in. Says the boyfriend stayed over a lot more nights than either of them are admitting to.'

Duffy muttered. 'They could have done that kid in.'

His words were drowned by the ringtone of Chisolm's phone.

'Give me a moment,' he said, turning away.

Head bent, he listened for a few minutes. Then, switching his phone to silent, turned to face them. 'That was one of the Marischal CCTV operators.'

Working as part of one of five teams currently monitoring Aberdeen City Centre Public Space CCTV System at Divisional Headquarters, operators monitor a bank of CCTV screens and respond to developing incidents as they unfold, whilst simultaneously communicating on Police Airwave Radio and other partner radio networks.

'They've picked up a male who fits Malky White's description in a shop doorway at the junction of King Street and School Road.'

'What's unusual about that?' asked Duffy. 'Doesn't he live in one of the high-rises?'

'The time-stamp is showing 8.27 a.m. on Monday morning.'

Brian said, 'Got you. If we can establish the figure is Malky, it proves he was lying about being at home in bed until lunchtime.'

'And blows Lee Marshall's alibi clean out the water,' Lisa added.

'Apparently, White was in the company of another person,' said Chisolm.

'Male or female?'

'Hard to say.'

Duffy stroked his chin. 'So it's possible Lee could have been implicated in Frankie Bain's disappearance.'

'As could Malky,' said Brian.

Douglas came in. 'You reckon they could have been in it together? That's pushing it, don't you think?'

'I don't know. They were thick in Peterhead. Then – by their own admission – drinking all weekend. Most probably taking drugs. Who know what they might have hatched up.'

'Raise a warrant,' Chisolm instructed. 'Make a thorough search of Malky White's house: drinking vessels, food, items of clothing. Bloodstains, obviously. Anything to indicate a child's presence. And don't forget to check the washing machine for items that have been recently laundered. Pull White in for interview. Either he may be assisting an offender or he's up to his old tricks.'

'Boss.'

'And see if you can get anything out of Malky's neighbours.'

'Zero chance of that,' Duffy grumbled. 'Not in the high-rises. Even someone saw something, a head-banger like him, there's no way they're going to shoot their mouth.'

Chisolm's jaw set. 'We can but try. Ask the CCTV unit to retrieve any relevant footage from outside Northview Towers. We might get lucky, like we did in the Robertson case.'

In 2019, forty-two-year-old Norman Duncan was filmed by

CCTV cameras going into and leaving Promenade Court, where he was accused of – and later convicted for – sexually assaulting grandmother Margaret Robertson before stabbing her to death.

'There might be CCTV installed in the lifts,' Susan suggested. 'Some of the tower blocks got them a few years back. Reduced vandalism dramatically, according to residents, so that might work in our favour.'

Chisolm nodded. 'Good thinking. Get someone back out to Kincorth. Establish Lee Marshall is where he should be, then pull him in for another chat.'

'Boss.'

'And stick with Stuart Bain and Jason Eadie. I want you to pick over every aspect of those two individuals' lives. There's no way Frankie Bain could have survived this long on her own. She's far more likely to be in the company of an adult – or adults.'

He didn't put into words what they were all thinking:

If she's still alive.

A Whole Different Ballgame

'Are you done with my laptop?' Stuart Bain asked, when Lisa had run through the formalities.

'There's a few more details I'd like to clear up first.'

In the seat opposite, Stuart's shoulders sagged, his face tight with anxiety. 'Like what?'

'You said you don't currently have a girlfriend.'

'Look, this is the second time you've had me in here. I've answered all your questions. Can I go now? I'd like to join the search for my wee girl. If you've no objections.' He eyeballed each of the detectives in turn.

Lisa said, 'One more thing: do you have an interest in under-age girls?'

He sat forward in his seat. 'What?' he challenged. 'No way.'

'Then, why,' she asked, sliding a production across the table, 'do you have images like this on your laptop?'

Stuart peered at the photo in its transparent sleeve. 'Never seen it before.'

'You sure?'

'Hundred percent.'

'How would you react if I told you it was obtained from your device?'

'I'd say you were lying?'

Lisa eyed him levelly. 'Why would I do that?'

With a shrug, he replied, 'Set me up. It's pretty obvious your investigation is going nowhere.'

Brian intervened. 'Now, look here…'

'It wouldn't be the first time,' Stuart insisted. 'If you think back to Madeleine McCann, when the cops couldn't find anyone to pin it on, the parents were next in the firing line.'

'Returning to your laptop,' said Lisa. 'This...' She indicated the production. '...is just one of a number of images lifted from your device: a 'naughty schoolgirl' movie, in which the participants are clearly under-age. Pre-pubescent girls. Girls like your daughter, Frances.'

Stuart jumped to his feet. 'What are you suggesting?'

'Sit down.'

He slumped in his seat. Then, head buried in his hands, 'You can't seriously think...'

'I'm sure you'll accept,' Lisa said smoothly. 'We have to explore every avenue that presents itself.'

Brian stole a sideways glance. He had to admire her composure.

'We're talking hard-core porn,' she continued. 'Double penetration, and that's just for starters.'

Slowly, Stuart raised his head. 'If – and it's a big if – you found that stuff on my laptop, it must be years old. There can't be a man on that rig hasn't looked at porn of some sort, and I'm no exception. Time hangs heavy. You can be on call for twelve hours at a time. If you're not using the recreational facilities, there's not a lot to do other than sit in your cabin waiting for your next shift.'

Brian said, 'Adult porn I can understand. But this is a whole different ballgame.'

'You think I don't know that?' Stuart shouted. 'I've a kid of my own. A kid you should be out searching for, instead of wasting my time. As I said, if there's stuff on my laptop it's years old. Plus, I probably opened it by accident. I suppose you've never done that?'

He looked Brian in the eye. Then, lip curled. 'No, maybe not.'

A Dating Match

In the high-end kitchen/diner of her Bieldside villa, Flo Carruthers leaned forward, face expectant.

'If you could flesh out,' Maggie began, 'what you told me on the telephone.'

'Of course,' Flo said eagerly. 'What would you like to know?'

First off, 'How did you come to post your profile picture on a dating site?'

'Long story.'

Blast! Maggie thought with a sinking heart. For all Wilma's protestations, she feared a rerun of the MacSorley affair. Having politely declined the offer of tea or coffee, she was hell-bent on getting in and out as fast as possible.

'One you've probably heard before,' said Flo. 'So I'll be brief. My husband, Daniel, died eighteen months ago. I thought I was getting by. But these past few months…'

Maggie shifted in her seat. Too close to home.

'A member of my book group suggested I try online dating. She helped me put my profile together and guided me through the registration process. If it hadn't been for her, I probably would never have gone ahead.'

'What was the upshot?'

'I had a flurry of interest at first. Poor souls they were, too. I'm not that desperate.'

Maggie acknowledged this with a smile. Short and plump, with a pretty face and good skin, Flo exuded not only femininity, but resolve.

'More than a week passed before John Gibson got in touch. By that time, I'd given up on the idea, so it came as a pleasant surprise. More than pleasant. To be honest, Mrs Laird, I was skittish as a kitten.'

'Understandable.'

'It has been too long since I experienced any degree of intimacy. And that's important. When one suffers a bereavement, people are, on the whole, sympathetic. They offer practical support. But what they don't really grasp is how devastating the loss of companionship: to have someone on the other side of the table at mealtimes, a comforting presence in your bed.'

You don't have to tell me.

'Not that sex isn't important,' Flo qualified. 'I can't say I was instantly attracted. John's profile photo is pretty average. I'll bring it up for you once we're done talking. He's no god. But he has a good job. He's in marketing.'

'Mmm,' Maggie murmured, trying her best to look impressed.

'And a kind face. That's what persuaded me. The only fly in the ointment is,' knitting her brows, 'he keeps dropping off the radar.'

'Can you be more specific?'

'He'll message me non-stop, then he'll disappear, sometimes for days on end.'

Bigamist, Maggie judged. 'Have you asked him for an explanation?'

'Puts it down to pressure of work. It was when he started to probe my background – did I have close family, had I been left comfortable – alarm bells really began to ring. That's when I decided to call on your services.'

'You haven't actually met this man?'

'No. We've only chatted online. He's pressing for an assignation. But you read so many warnings about staying safe, I've been nervous about taking the plunge.' Hands fidgeting in her lap, 'My husband and I decided to put off having children, which is a matter, now, of deep regret. But I'm not too old, and I'm looking for a partner who is, above all, reliable.'

'Before we go any further,' Maggie said, drawing a sheet of paper from her bag and passing it across. 'I should make you aware of our fees: hourly rates for research, surveillance and so on, flat fees for things like a neighbourhood check, should that prove necessary, plus mileage and expenses as incurred.'

Flo Carruthers glanced at it briefly, then set it down on a side table. 'Dan was killed in an industrial accident,' she confided. 'I've been awarded a substantial settlement, hence my caution. Whatever your fee, it will be small price to pay for peace of mind.'

*

Maggie was on her way home when Wilma rang.

'How did you get on?'

'Waste of time.'

Wilma said, 'Client's got the dosh, hasn't she?'

'And plenty of it.'

'Well, then.'

'Where are we supposed to start?' Maggie complained. 'We've nothing to go on but a name – John Gibson – and a few sketchy background details, none of which may be true.'

'Did you take a note of Gibson's user name?'

'No. Should I have?'

'Could come in useful. If it's distinctive enough, we might be able to bring it up on other sites like Twitter. Verify if he's posting under his real name.'

'Dammit,' said Maggie. 'I wouldn't have thought of that.'

'You'll have seen his profile pic?'

'Yes, but how we're supposed to trace the guy when we don't have an address or telephone number...'

'Do a reverse image search like we did in the MacSorley case.'

'And look how that ended.'

Sighing, Wilma said, 'That old chestnut.'

'I knew from the get-go romance fraud was a waste of time, and I'm sure – deep down – so do you.'

'How would you know what I'm thinking?'

'Okay,' Maggie conceded. 'What do you suggest?'

'Give Flo Carruthers a ring. Ask her to save John Gibson's profile pic.'

223

'Will the website let you do that?'

'If not, get her to take a screenshot and send it over.'

'What if…?' Maggie began.

But Wilma had already hung up.

Give Me Time

Lisa opened the interview. 'You are here under caution to answer questions in connection with the disappearance of Frances Bain. Do you understand?'

Jason Eadie looked for guidance to the solicitor who sat alongside.

He was rewarded with a world-weary nod.

Then, with a careless shrug, 'Yes,' he replied.

'My client will answer no further questions,' stated the duty solicitor, an angular, pallid woman in a shapeless polyester suit.

Lisa and Brian exchanged resigned looks. Going 'no comment' was par for the course.

Jotting a note in the folder in front of her, Lisa continued, 'When we spoke last, you told me your wife "moved away" with the children, is that correct?'

Sprawled in his seat, one foot in its Nike trainer akimbo on his other knee, Jason drawled, 'No comment.'

'Wouldn't it be more accurate to say she was moved?' Lisa challenged.

Unblinking, Jason held her gaze.

'According to information received, police attended your address on a number of occasions in response to 999 calls. Calls which arose from incidences of domestic abuse.'

The solicitor held up her hand. 'Let me stop you there. My client was never charged in connection with these alleged incidents, so I fail to see the relevance of this line of questioning.'

'I'll tell you why it's relevant,' said Lisa, trying to contain her irritation. 'Following a particularly brutal assault, Mrs Eadie and her children were removed to a place of safety and later rehoused.'

It was the solicitor's turn to scribble a note.

Brian came in. 'Would it be fair to say this, taken together with the recent allegation of assault at your workplace and your prior convictions, points to a pattern of behaviour?'

'No comment,' Jason replied, blank-faced. His knee was jiggling, now, in its white trackie bottoms.

'I'll ask you, again,' said Lisa. 'Where were you on Monday last between the hours of 8 a.m. and 12 noon?'

'No comment.'

'Have you ever laid hands on Frances Bain?'

'No comment.'

'Interfered with her in any way?'

For a few moments there was total silence, Brian and Lisa alert to Jason's reaction, the solicitor wary.

Jason was sitting upright, now, both feet planted on the floor.

He leaned forward across the table.

Face inches from Lisa's, he fixed her with a venomous look.

'No comment,' he said, spittle flying from his contorted mouth.

Lisa didn't react, but sat eyes locked on Jason until he turned his head away.

He broke the silence. 'If you've something else to say, get on with it. Otherwise...' He made a show of looking at the clock. '...you're wasting my time.'

'More pressing business, have we?' Lisa asked. 'Job interview perhaps? Am I right in saying you lost the last job after assaulting a colleague?'

'He started it.'

'Does the name Vincent Sellars mean anything to you?'

Lisa had been less than thrilled when Brian dropped this nugget into their interview prep at the very last moment.

Getting no response, 'Let me refresh your memory: site agent at Bridge of Don.'

'So what?'

'Would I be correct in stating he was responsible for giving you your books?'

With a shrug, Jason said, 'Wouldn't be the first time. Building trade has a high turnover. Folk come and go.'

'I can imagine,' said Lisa sweetly. 'There must be a lot of pressure, tempers running high.'

Jason nodded his agreement.

'So high, I put it to you, you perpetrated a serious assault on Vincent Sellars' person and then proceeded to write graffiti on his van as a parting shot.'

'Could have been anyone.'

'But it wasn't, was it, Jason?'

He looked in desperation to his solicitor. 'You can't prove it.'

Smiling, Lisa said, 'Give me time.'

The Sand Dollar

Lynsey raised her glass in a toast. 'Cheers!'

'Cheers!' Maggie mirrored the gesture. She'd felt an unaccustomed glow of pleasure when her colleague had mooted a glass of wine on the seafront after work. Closely followed by a stab of guilt. She couldn't spare the time. There would be telephone enquiries to deal with, paperwork to address, a meal to prepare.

Sod it! Since she'd taken on the detective agency, Maggie's social life had been limited to the occasional night out with Wilma, supplemented by an infrequent – and usually disastrous – date. Friends from her life with George had melted away. Neighbours she rarely saw. The few hours she worked at Seaton weren't conducive to forming relationships.

Now, she and Lynsey were installed at a window table of the bistro cafe, two glasses of chilled Pinot Blanc in front of them.

'Ooft,' Lynsey said, brushing a hand across her brow. 'What a day.' She took a gulp of her wine.

'Day like today, I'm thankful I only work part-time. But being in school, I can't but think on Frankie. Do you think she's still—?'

Lynsey put a finger to her lips. 'Didn't we agree not to go there?'

'Yes, but I can't get her out of my head. The secret she wanted to share, I've been racking my brains. What if Frankie's trans?'

Sighing, Lynsey said, 'If that's the case, you know as well as I do we have clear gender dysphoria guidance protocols: teacher e-learning course, toolkit of teaching resources, dedicated information website. We'd start by helping support her in understanding her gender identity: how she wants to present or be treated, and the name she wants to be known by.'

'Which Frankie has done.'

'Pronoun use, too. Something Frankie hasn't raised. Which is why I think you're making something out of nothing.' Narrowing her eyes, 'You sure you didn't float these ideas in front of the police?'

'No,' said Maggie. 'I was scared they'd think me delusional.'

'They'd be right.'

'Plus, I've read the guidance issued to schools by local authorities breaches parental rights and equality laws. There was a case in Wales last year: the parents weren't told by the school…'

Lynsey cut her short. 'Don't take this the wrong way, but the age difference probably comes into play. Without being rude, sex and gender, do you actually know the difference?'

'I've teenagers, so I know the facts. Sex relates to biology: chromosomes, hormones and reproductive organs. Gender relates to how one identifies. But to tell the truth, the labels leave me cold. Plus, there has been so much noise on the trans issue I'm finding it hard to keep up: trans activists, anti-trans, clinicians, all with a different viewpoint. And the argument has become so polarised: on the one hand Stonewall lobbying for change, radical feminists arguing against.'

'I'm with you there.'

'As a mother, my heart goes out to these young people. As a parent, I'm less than thrilled about the message this sends. I wouldn't be happy for a school to decide it knows better than me what's best for my child. And it's normal, surely, for youngsters to question, to experiment.'

With a grimace, Lynsey said, 'Too true.'

'Plus,' Maggie went on, 'there are so many grey areas: children on the autistic spectrum, for example, who are highly suggestible. I can't help thinking they're being pressured down the wrong path, some of them, and who knows how that will end. Take puberty blockers. Is there enough known about the long-term side-effects? There was that Tavistock Clinic case.'

'That was about consent. There are other options: antidepressants, for example, or talking therapies. But not all transgender young people seek assistance, and teachers shouldn't assume young people want it.' Lynsey wagged a cautionary finger. 'You're treading dangerous ground. I've told you umpteen times not to get involved.'

A young waitress approached their table. 'Can I get you anything else?'

'Not for me, thanks.' Maggie looked enquiringly to Lynsey.

'I'm good. But we didn't come here to talk shop. How are your kids?'

'Fine. Colin's gone up to sixth year.'

'Clever lad.'

Maggie pulled a wry face. 'He's got the brains, if he would only apply himself. Kirsty's the opposite: workaholic. Not that I see much of her. And when she's home, she does nothing but put me down. If it's not my clothes, it's my hair. And as for being a private investigator—'

Lynsey laughed. 'Mothers and daughters. I bet we were exactly the same at that age.'

'Probably.'

'I don't know how you do it: teaching support and running a business to boot. It's a whole lot different for me. I'm hoping to progress up the salary scale. Plus, I'm not qualified to do anything else.'

Maggie said, 'It's amazing what you can turn your hand to when you're up against it.'

'You don't talk about the detective business, but it must be fascinating. I'm intrigued to know more.'

'Discretion is all.' Changing the subject, 'How's life with you?'

Lynsey said, 'I broke up with Jack a couple of months back. Or, rather, he broke up with me.'

Maggie extended a comforting hand. 'I'm sorry.'

'Thanks. I've been a bit of a hermit this past while. Thrown myself into the job. Won't do me any harm. Not if I want to get on.'

'There isn't a new man in your life, then?'

'Haven't had the time. And, besides, the older you get, the less you can be bothered. Dating's such an effort.'

'I quite agree.'

'How about you?'

Maggie took a pacifying swallow of wine, 'I should be so lucky,' she lied. The recent misunderstanding with Allan Chisolm had only served to underscore the strength of her feelings.

Lynsey drained her glass. 'You up for a refill?'

Maggie sneaked a peek at her watch. 'I'd better be heading. Colin's late home tonight. He'll be famished when he gets in.'

'Shame. I've enjoyed your company. Maybe we could do this again.'

Raising her glass to her lips, 'I'll drink to that,' Maggie said.

*

She was barely through the front door when Maggie heard someone tapping on the kitchen window. Thinking Colin had forgotten his keys, she hurried down the hall.

Wilma's face was framed in the glass.

Her spirits sank. She'd been buoyed by her unexpected break from routine. Anticipated a whizz through her chores and a quiet evening.

Impatiently, Wilma rat-tatted on the pane, gesturing for Maggie to open the door.

Reluctantly, she turned the key in the lock.

Wilma stormed in. 'You're late on the road. Something come up?'

'No,' Maggie replied. 'Went for a coffee with Lynsey after work.' She wasn't going to admit to alcohol.

'Lynsey, is it?' Wilma said, looking distinctly put out. 'I thought you'd been away touting for new business.'

'I have,' Maggie protested. 'I did. Only, I've been frantic with worry over Frankie Bain. Welcomed the chance to air my concerns.' Then, 'You got something to tell me?' she asked pointedly. 'Only I'm dog-tired and Colin's due back any minute.'

'I get you.' Mouth turned down, Wilma made to leave. 'Hope you had a good time,' she threw over her shoulder.

Maggie's body sagged.

'It was only a coffee,' she said.

But Wilma was already out the door.

Back to Square One

Chisolm asked, 'What's the story on Malky White?'

'A search of his Northview Towers flat turned up nothing of interest,' Brian replied, 'other than a small quantity of skunk, which he maintained was for his own use. There was evidence another person had slept there, but that doesn't move us forward. When we pulled Malky in for interview, he went "no comment".'

'How about Lee Marshall?'

'He's back at his own place in Kincorth.'

'Didn't he claim it was unfit for habitation?'

'I gather he bigged that up. It's not Buckingham Palace, from what uniform have told us, but his accommodation is basically sound. I suspect he landed back there and fancied a bit of company, hence his visit to Malky.'

'Any more on CCTV from the King Street shops?'

Duffy responded, 'We've a fair chance of putting Malky in the frame, so to speak. Height and build tally. Clothing matches items found in his flat. Problem is the second figure. On close examination, we've had to rule out Lee Marshall. There appears to be an exchange taking place. Best guess is Malky White was dealing drugs with some local bawbag.'

'Who's not going to come forward,' said Brian.

'So Malky could have nipped out to do a trade,' Lisa posited. 'And left Lee sleeping in his flat.'

'Or he could have chucked Lee out before he left,' Douglas argued. 'And Lee's on a bus to Kincorth.'

'Or Lee could be in Spar buying fags,' Susan suggested. 'That would place both him and Malky close to where Frankie Bain was last seen.'

With a long whoosh of breath, Chisolm said, 'How about Stuart

Bain?'

'There's the porn on Stuart's laptop. Historic it may be, but we can't completely discount it.'

'You're right,' Chisolm acknowledged. 'In most cases, people don't suddenly wake up one day and decide they are going to abuse a child. What seems to happen, particularly those looking at online sexual images of children, is there is a drift towards that behaviour. They become bored and desensitised by legal online pornography and go looking for more extreme material.'

'That New Byth case is a prime example,' said Brian. 'Kevin Robertson admitted possessing hours of video footage showing children as young as six being abused.' He looked to the DCs. 'Worth checking out.'

'Doesn't come as a surprise,' Duffy grouched. 'If the tech bosses don't make their sites safe, offenders will use them as a playground.'

Lisa spoke up. 'Instagram in particular.'

Nodding, Chisolm said, 'Hence the dedicated Sex Offender Policing Unit established, now, in every one of Police Scotland's Divisions. But, getting back to the material found on Stuart Bain's device, we'd struggle to build a case around that.' Drawing a statement from his file, 'Jason Eadie. Where are we at with him?'

Douglas answered his question. 'Lot more luck on that front, Susan managed to collar Eadie for the grafitti on Vinnie Sellars van.'

'News to me.'

Brian said, 'Sorry, boss. You were in meetings back-to-back.'

Turning to Susan, Chisolm asked, 'How did you manage that?'

'Took me a while to join the dots. The outfit where Eadie worked didn't go under the same name as the one we spoke to about Sellars. Turned out it was the parent company and has a number of subsidiaries.'

'Well done, you.'

Douglas added, 'Records show our officers responded to a number of incidents at Eadie's previous address: neighbours reporting a disturbance; allegations of domestic abuse.'

'Anger management issues, then?'

'Taken together with the pre-cons, that's for sure. Jason has admitted to being in Frankie's home the evening before she went missing. Who's to say he left? He could as easily have spent the night, and during the course of that night assaulted Frankie.'

'With or without collusion from Isla Bain,' Brian contributed.

'Throw into the mix, Malky White,' said Duffy, re-joining the conversation.

'You think he's a player?' Chisolm asked. 'There's no evidence Malky White has an interest in children.'

'Maybe not. But taken together with Lee. We all know how manipulative sex offenders can be.'

'Lee told the response officers he'd been in contact with Stop It Now!' argued Lisa. 'Getting in touch with an agency that offers a confidential support service for offenders doesn't sound like someone hell-bent on picking up where he left off.'

Duffy said, 'I don't buy this "reformed character" line. These individuals are sick in the head till the day they die. Take that Michael Taylor. Bastard was 71 when he was convicted for assaulting kids after enticing them with sweets and money. He filmed his rape of a young boy and instructed another victim to video him abusing a girl in Aberdeen. Claimed his victims "enjoyed" his sexual abuse.'

Chisolm again. 'Who's our best bet?'

'I'd rule out Stuart Bain,' Susan replied. 'He seems to be a loving father to Frankie. Plus, divorce proceedings haven't progressed to the degree that custody has become an issue.'

Brian said, 'I reckon Jason Eadie is out the picture. Admitted, he's an unsavoury character, but if something happened in that flat Isla Bain would have known. Even if she was implicated, a neighbour would have called it in.'

'Not necessarily,' Lisa countered. 'Didn't you say there were students upstairs? They probably wouldn't notice. Or care.'

Duffy spoke. 'My money's on Lee and Malky. They both have previous. They've been banged up together. Who knows what Lee could have put in Malky's head?'

'So to recap,' Chisolm said. 'We have a missing child. No witnesses. No direction of travel. We have three suspects, all of whom claim to have either been in bed, asleep, or in transit, at the time Frankie Bain went missing. No independent corroboration. On the contrary, we have evidence all three lied: Stuart Bain as to the porn on his laptop; Jason Eadie as to when he left Isla Bain's house; Lee Marshall as to how long he'd been dossing on the other side of town to where he was registered.'

Duffy's mouth turned down. 'Looks like we're back to square one.'

'We've been here before,' Chisolm argued. 'A case such as this often kicks off with a burst of activity, followed by days – or weeks – when nothing much happens.'

'Except,' said Susan. 'When a child's safety is at stake, time isn't on our side.'

Brian said, 'Speaking of time, boss, have you had any word back from forensics?'

'Not a peep.'

'Would it be worth retrieving Frankie's old phone?' Douglas suggested. 'If it's just the screen that's cracked, the techies might be able to get into it. Use a USB OTG cable, maybe, to connect to the phone and a mouse. Use the mouse to unlock it. Transfer the Android files to another device. Then…'

Chisolm cut in. 'Anything's worth a try.' When Douglas got in geek mode, his enthusiasm tended to run away with him. 'What we have to accept is our chances of finding Frankie alive and well are diminishing by the minute. With no means of communication and no money, a child that age is unlikely to survive.'

'Not in the open,' Brian concurred. 'Not unless she has managed to find shelter somewhere.'

'Or been hidden,' Duffy muttered.

'I'm asking each of you to redouble our efforts. Have another look at those CCTV images. Chase down those alibis. Ensure every single call from the public is followed up.' Loosening his shoulders,

Chisolm added, 'Any questions?'

Around the table, tired heads drooped.

'Thanks, all, for your hard work thus far. Now let's give it one last push, see if we can recover Frankie Bain alive.'

XI

Super-sleuth

Wilma sang along to Claire & Craig's Big Breakfast on the car radio as she drove around North Anderson Drive. On days like this the job was a breeze.

Despite Maggie's strictures, the Sellars' suicide was still bugging her. Following the bombshell about the lottery win, Wilma had grudgingly accepted that, as motive for murder, Jean's affair with Keith was a non-starter. Lauren she'd ruled out of the equation. Aside from absence of motive, the timeline was wrong. Wilma had confirmed Vincent Sellars' daughter was on duty at ARI on the afternoon of his death.

That left the son. Wilma racked her brains. What did she know? Damn all, except what she'd gleaned from the internet, that and newspaper reports. An enquiry to Harvey Sellars' Head Office had elicited little other than the usual Data Protection caveat. "If she wished to leave her details", the stuck-up receptionist had said, "a representative would be in touch".

Wilma stole a glance at the dashboard clock. 10.41. The subject was out on a call. She'd taken the precaution of phoning his office again on a flimsy pretext, withholding her number before hanging up.

The property the Satnav directed her to was situated at the top of a cul-de-sac behind the now defunct Treetops Hotel in Springfield Road. A detached two-storey home with pebbledash render, it would have been built in the 1960s on the former Craigiebuckler estate, where in 1826 the grand Craigiebuckler House had been built by James Blaikie, first Lord Provost of Aberdeen.

Wilma parked at the kerbside. No time to waste. And, besides, who would suspect a fat wifie in a Fiesta? Nonetheless, after Ian left for work that morning, she'd retrieved a set of fake stick-on number plates from her stash in the wardrobe, just in case.

She made a show of ringing the doorbell.

No answer.

Walked around the side of the house.

Shielding her eyes with cupped hands, Wilma peered in the kitchen window.

The room was sterile: walls, work surfaces, table bare of decoration. No evidence of a female presence.

Figures. Harvey Sellars' entry on the voter's roll listed a single occupant at the address.

With mixed feelings – after the ding-dongs she'd had with Maggie, Wilma was gagging for a juicy outcome – she was making her way back to the front of the house when the next-door neighbour came out of her garage carrying gardening gloves and a trowel.

'Can I help?'

'Thought I might catch him,' Wilma ad-libbed. 'I'm sure he said he was off work.'

'You must be thinking of last week,' said the woman, seventy-something in shapeless jumper and slacks.

Alarm bells rang in Wilma's head. She could have sworn the papers said Harvey Sellars was away on business. 'What day?'

'The day his dad died. Dreadful losing a parent like that. I expect you heard.'

'What time?'

'Mid-afternoon. Said hello in passing.'

'You sure?'

'Absolutely. I had the chiropodist at 2.30 and she'd just gone. Such a difference it makes. Afterwards, you feel you're walking on cloud nine.' Head on one side, she asked, 'What's your connection to Harvey? You're not the new girlfriend, are you?'

'Just a friend,' said Wilma, hopping impatiently from one foot to the other. 'I've been abroad,' she fibbed. 'Never got to meet his partner. She still around?'

'Far as I know. Runs a florist in Thistle Street. Petals, I think it's called. If you give me a minute, I can check.'

'Got to run.' Wilma said, making a dash for her car.

*

'Anne Cromar?' Wilma enquired. She'd checked out Petals' website and Facebook page.

The woman looked up from arranging cut flowers in a block of oasis. 'How can I help?'

Wilma cut to the chase. 'I was hoping you could give me some information on Harvey Sellars.'

Putting down a pair of secateurs, 'Why do you want to know?'

'Asking for a friend.' Then, seeing Ms Cromar's dubious expression, Wilma clapped a hand to her breast. 'God's honest truth. I've a friend interested in him.'

'Romantically?'

'You got it.'

'Why ask me?'

'There's only so much you can learn from a person's online profile.'

'I'll say,' Anne acknowledged.

'So?' said Wilma.

'Typical salesman. Has all the moves. Don't get me wrong, Harvey's a nice enough guy, but look behind the patter, he's a mess.'

'In what way?'

'He's insecure.'

'That all?'

'It's all I'm willing to say.'

'Fair dos,' said Wilma. 'Can I leave you my number? If you think of anything else...'

'Why don't you speak to him yourself?' I'll give you his mobile number.' Turning, Anne drew open a drawer, rummaged for a few moments, then, 'Here.' She handed over a business card.

'Thanks.'

The florist looked over her shoulder.

There was no one else in the shop.

'One thing he won't tell you...' Leaning close, she whispered in

Wilma's ear.

'No!' Wilma exclaimed, eyes like saucers.

'Trust me,' Anne Cromar said.

Dancing in the Dark

DCI Coutts responded to Chisolm's knock with a peremptory nod. 'Take a seat. I'll be with you in a mo.'

Chisolm did as he was bid. Mel Coutts had leap-frogged him on the promotion ladder. As he watched her, head bent over a laptop, he couldn't help but speculate on his own career prospects. When he'd first moved to Aberdeen, he'd been happy enough to put the past behind him, settle for the status quo. Now, Brain Burnett was nipping at his heels, a constant reminder he should be moving on. But to what?

Snapping the lid of her laptop shut, Mel raised her head. 'Sorry about that. A report I needed to finish.' She offered a rueful smile. 'The joys of admin.'

Chisolm reciprocated with a grimace. 'It's never-ending. Policing never used to be like this.'

Life never used to be like this. An image of his old home came to mind: solid red sandstone in Glasgow's West End, the polar opposite of his Aberdeen bachelor flat. Clare and his two girls—

'Operation Eco-Warrior.' Mel's voice brought him back to the present. 'What's the state of play?'

'Not promising,' he confessed. 'With no direction of travel and no witnesses coming forward, we're dancing in the dark.'

'That's not good enough. The press pack is pushing for information. There's only so much "following several leads of inquiry" I can fob them off with. The Executive is getting antsy.'

'I understand you're under pressure,' Chisolm said. 'We all are. The investigative team are working their balls off, but any leads we've had to date have proved unproductive.'

'What's the story on your suspects?'

'We've called them back in. My officers are checking out every last detail in their statements. But it's a slow process and, lacking independent witnesses, basically it's our word against theirs.'

'In short, you're nowhere near finding Frankie Bain, nor putting a case together.'

'That's the nub of it.'

'Where are we at with the public?'

'Control are handling a large volume of calls, but as happens, a significant proportion are without foundation.'

'Make sure they're followed up.'

'We've put out an appeal for webcam and doorbell footage.'

'What about the child's mother? Last news I had, she was too distressed to take part in a televised appeal.'

'That's correct. I'll have someone check with the FLO and get back to you.'

Tight-lipped, Mel said, 'Might be after the event.'

Chisolm was saved by the telephone.

'I'd better take this.' Reaching for the handset, 'DCI Coutts.'

A return to the central belt was out, Chisolm decided, the telephone conversation playing in the background. Not unless something tempting came up at Gartcosh. Eight miles from central Glasgow, the Scottish Crime Campus brings together a number of anti-crime agencies under one roof. Chisolm couldn't see himself in what was for all intents and purposes a corporate setting. Bad enough the job had become as deskbound as it had. But he missed his girls desperately. Saw them little enough, Aberdeen an extra leg on an already long journey. His thoughts turned to Maggie Laird, another aspect of his life that was going nowhere fast.

'Understood, sir. Bye.' Mel Coutts replaced the handset in its cradle with a clatter.

One thing Allan Chisolm did know: in a long-term lesbian relationship, DCI Coutts kept her private life close to her chest. Something, at least, they had in common.

Fixing Chisolm with a hard look, she said, 'Good or bad. I need a result. And fast.'

The Kings Links

Chisolm entered the room. 'Morning all.'

'Morning, boss,' came the dispirited response.

'That includes you, Douglas.'

'Boss,' he replied, desperately chewing a bacon roll.

'Have you had anything back from Tech Support on Frankie Bain's phone?'

'Not so far.'

'Chase them up. I've had Control on the line. A call has come in: member of the public reported seeing a child fitting Frankie's description around 9 o'clock on Monday morning.'

'Whereabouts?' Duffy asked, brushing crumbs from his chin.

'Edge of the golf course.'

Brian said, 'That's promising.'

'And not before time. We could do with some good news.'

'Don't get your hopes up,' said Chisolm. 'The caller reported the child was in the company of a man.'

'The Kings Links are no distance from where Frankie Bain was last seen,' Susan volunteered. 'If she'd turned left instead of right at the school into Seaton Crescent and past Aulton Court—'

Douglas voiced what everyone was thinking. 'Lee Marshall.'

Susan clamped a hand to her mouth. Speaking through her fingers, 'If he was shacked up in Northview Towers, he could have intercepted her.'

'Classic,' Duffy said morosely. 'We've been looking in the wrong bloody place.'

'That's not the case,' Chisolm snapped. 'Search teams, supported by the police helicopter, have scoured the area within a wide radius of Frankie Bain's home address. Every possible CCTV opportunity has been investigated.'

'Plus,' Susan added, 'there's nothing on the Links to attract a nine-year-old. I can't see the Auldmill Links football ground being a draw. Same goes for the golf clubhouses or the driving range. It's not unreasonable for us to have worked on the premise Frankie would have headed for the King Street shops or caught a bus somewhere.'

Chisolm said, 'We'll need to obtain a full statement from this caller. Establish if they're a credible witness.' He looked to Brian and Lisa. 'See to it, you two.'

'Boss,' Brian acknowledged.

'I'm on it,' Lisa added, with a knowing smile.

Catching Douglas's eye, Susan clutched a hand to her throat in a vomiting action.

He reciprocated by blowing a silent raspberry.

'Report back to me ASAP,' Chisolm said. 'If there's substance to this, and Frankie has headed in the direction of the Links or the beach, we'll need to further extend the search area. Notify the coastguard, too.' He turned to Duffy. 'Bob, get the CCTV unit to re-run everything they've got from those tower blocks. See if they can identify Lee Marshall, in company or otherwise.'

'Maybe best prioritise the blocks directly on Seaton Crescent,' Douglas suggested. 'If Frankie took that route, she'd have needed to make a detour to pass the others before reaching Golf Road.'

Chisolm nodded approvingly. 'Good thinking. Before you head out, is there anything further on Stuart Bain or Jason Eadie?'

'Where Eadie is concerned,' said Brian. 'We can testify to bad character, but that's about it. Stuart Bain we've little more than historic child porn.'

'How about the mother?'

'When questioned about the disparity in their accounts,' Susan replied. 'Isla Bain said she lied about how often Jason stayed the night because she was scared it would affect her benefits.'

'That's credible.'

Douglas spoke. 'My money's on Jason Eadie.'

With a scathing expression, Lisa said, 'Give us one good reason.'

Stirring it. Susan threw her a venomous look.

'Time is of the essence,' Chisolm said firmly. 'Let's concentrate on following up this latest sighting and take it from there.'

*

'Who does she think she is?' Duffy said, when they came out of the briefing.

'Probably still thinks she's sergeant material,' Brian said gloomily. He'd quite enjoyed pairing with a good-looking young woman when Lisa had first arrived. Now, what with his failed attempts at making it in front of the promotion board, and Lisa's in-your-face attitude, the novelty had well and truly worn off. 'She's acting above her station, that's for sure.'

'What gets my goat,' Duffy grumbled, 'is the way the boss just sits there and takes it.' Head cocked, he added, 'Maybe he fancies her.'

'I doubt it,' said Brian, a picture of Maggie Laird popping into his head. Younger Lisa Haldane might be. Blonder, more outgoing. But Maggie was a one-off. His pulse raced at the very thought. 'We better look smart,' he added, jolting back to the here and now.

Duffy quickened his pace. 'She'll get her come-uppance,' he said. 'You mark my words.'

Blaikie's Quay

The Coastguard Rescue helicopter in its distinctive red and white livery flew overhead, its crew scanning the coastline. Operated since 2015 by Bristow's on a contract previously provided by the RAF and Royal Navy, it provides the 999 helicopter SAR service to HM Coastguard, responding to incidents overland, around the coast and at sea.

In the control room of the Maritime Rescue Coordination Centre on the 4th Floor of Marine House on Blaikie's Quay, Steve Fiddes sat on a high-backed scarlet desk chair. In front of him, a bank of four screens bore the HM Coastguard logo, one proclaiming "I'm a dispatcher" on a bright yellow background.

That day, the helicopter had been paged to assist Police Scotland with their search for missing schoolgirl, Frankie Bain. With a patch – or guard – that stretches from Balmedie in the north to Doonie Point, near Muchalls, in the south, Aberdeen Coastguard rescue team's remit covers some twenty-five miles of coastline, which varies from sandy beaches to sheer granite cliffs. The area also includes Aberdeen Harbour and the helicopter landing site at Aberdeen Royal infirmary.

'What are the chances?' asked Ken Muir, from his seat at a second desk, on which another four monitors sat back to back.

'Could be lucky, like the wee Duthie lad couple years back. Came off with nothing worse than a fractured skull after plunging thirty feet down a cliff near Buchan Ness Lighthouse, trying to save his bike.'

'Or not,' Ken remarked. 'Think on that teacher.'

'Who was that?' Missing persons was a large part of the coastguard's remit. In 2018, 3,494 people were reported missing in the North East.

'The one up Bullars of Buchan.'

In August 2020, coastguard participated in a huge multi-agency search for a missing rock climber who fell into the North Sea near south of Peterhead. Tragically, the body of the victim, Robert Gordon's head of biology, Owain Bristow, was swept out to sea and a recovery operation mounted.

'Is the Bon Accord out?' Ken continued.

'Affirmative.'

That day, Aberdeen's all-weather lifeboat, the Bon Accord, had been launched in support. Their activities encompass rescuing people from inshore and tidal waters or people threatening to jump from bridges, searching for missing persons, guiding other rescue services to a casualty's position, and setting up and manning emergency helicopter landing sites. In May 2021, the Moray Inshore Rescue Organisation (MIRO) lifeboat, with a helicopter also standing by, assisted police carrying out searches for a man who had been reported missing. The body of 25-year old James Thomson was later discovered in the Burghead area.

'Drone?'

'No,' Steve replied. 'Police will put it up if it's needed.'

'Okay,' Ken acknowledged, bending back to his screens. 'Fingers crossed.'

Join the Club

'It's not easy being a mother,' said Netta McBain, turning from her place at the kitchen sink.

Maggie shrugged. 'Join the club.'

She'd just got back from submitting the agency's proposals for a major corporate job. Work she knew in her gut the business was unlikely to win. Wilma had gone quiet. Maggie hoped that wasn't a bad sign. To cap it all, she'd learned the agency's biggest client, Harlaw Insurance, was undergoing a management shake-up. If they opted to follow the competition by taking investigations in house, it would be the end of Harcus & Laird.

'There's no need to be sarcastic. You never used to be like that.' Turning back, Netta fished a carrot from a basin of water.

'I never used to be lots of things: forty-something, a single parent, skint.'

Resolutely scraping the carrot, 'If you'd only find yourself a decent job.'

'Such as? And don't say legal secretary. I wouldn't last five minutes.'

'I'm sure that's not the case.' Picking up a sharp knife, her mum began to dice the carrot on a chopping board. 'Surely there's something you could do. Something that doesn't involve...'

'...Wilma Harcus.'

Her head swivelled. 'That's not what I said.'

'It's what you meant, isn't it?' Maggie thrust her face up close. 'Isn't it?' she repeated.

Still clutching the knife, she let out a slow breath. 'I'll make no bones: that neighbour of yours isn't someone I'd want as a friend.'

'I wonder why? Probably because you're so narrow-minded.'

Lips compressed, Netta said, 'There's nothing wrong with having old-fashioned values.'

'I quite agree, just as long as you don't foist them on other people. I'm sick to death being the butt of so much criticism. If it's not Kirsty, it's you. And if it's not you—' It was on the tip of Maggie's tongue to say Wilma. She stopped just in time. No point giving her mum more ammunition.

A wounded expression on her face, Netta's eyes dropped to the floor.

'Sorry, Mum,' Maggie said, throwing an arm around her mother's thin shoulders. 'Didn't sleep well last night.'

'Me neither.'

'Can we start again?'

Netta wiped her hands on her apron. 'I suppose.'

*

'Your dad and me,' Netta said, once they were settled in the front room. 'We're getting on. You need to make allowances.'

I bloody do, Maggie thought mutinously. Her folks' visitations had crept up from one day a fortnight, as they'd agreed, to once a week. Twice, sometimes, the day they'd surprised her with Allan Chisolm a case in point.

'Your whole married life you're looking out for your children and – overnight it seems – they don't need you anymore.'

Maggie nodded her understanding. Already, she had the same feeling: that she was clinging to Kirsty and Colin by a thread.

'Your world shrinks,' her mother went on. 'Friends die off, or they're not up to doing what they used to.'

Maggie let her eyelids droop. She'd been at odds with her mum since ever she could recall. Hadn't had the courage to go against her wishes. Not until she met George. And now? If her relationship with Allan Chisolm was to go anywhere, she couldn't have her parents turning up on a whim. She'd have to nail the visits on the head.

'We might look old.' Her mother's voice jolted her back to reality. 'But we don't feel old. Inside, you're exactly the same person you were for as long as you can remember.'

She couldn't argue with that.

'All you want is to hang onto your independence. Feel useful. That's why we were so pleased when you asked us to help with the housekeeping.'

'I'm glad you brought that up,' Maggie said. 'Because…'

'Gives us a sense of purpose,' her mother interrupted. 'Your dad especially.'

'Where is he?'

'Away to the shop for Windolene. Your windows are a disgrace.'

'Window cleaner's due next week.'

'Well, if you're happy to be seen with dirty windows—' Hearing the back door open, she stopped short.

Maggie said a silent prayer it wasn't Wilma. Another few minutes and she could wrap this up.

Her dad entered the room. 'How's my girl?' he asked, a smile creasing his face.

'Fine,' Maggie fibbed.

'I was just telling her,' said Netta, 'how much good it does us, helping out. Lends a framework to the week.'

'Pleased to hear it,' Maggie said. 'But there's really no need for you to trail into town more often than every other week. As we agreed,' she added pointedly.

'Oh, but we want to. Don't we, Rab?' Netta looked to her husband for backup.

Maggie's eyes flitted from one to the other.

Her dad just stood there, looking bemused.

'Like I said,' Maggie persisted. 'There's no need. Less to do, especially now it's coming to the end of the gardening season,'

No reaction.

'And winter will be coming on soon,' she added, in desperation. 'The roads will be dangerous. I don't want you to risk having an accident.'

'Ever since your dad's heart scare,' her mother said in a tremulous voice, 'helping you out has given him a new lease of life.' She turned to her husband. 'Hasn't it, pet?'

What do I have to do?

Shoulders slumped, Maggie turned away.

Up the Swannee

'What's bugging you?' asked Susan, spooning yogurt from a plastic tub. 'You've a face on you like a wet weekend.'

Douglas broke off from chewing a buttered rowie. 'The job,' he muttered into his chest. 'It's getting on my wick.'

They'd grabbed a short break in the police canteen before heading out.

'It's all right for some,' he went on. 'Where the boss is concerned, you can do no wrong.'

'That's not true.'

'It bloody is. If it's not the boss, it's Sarge. And if it's not Brian—' He took a long draught of his tea. 'Don't get me started on Haldane.'

Susan raised her eyes to the ceiling. 'She's a pain right enough.'

'Pain doesn't start to describe it. Did you see the way she sooked up to the DI this morning? Gives me the boak.'

'I wouldn't worry about that. The boss isn't fooled.'

'You reckon?' Then, 'Fuckit!' He swore as melted butter dripped down the front of his shirt.

'That's what you get for eating stuff like that,' Susan chided. Leaning across the table, 'Here.' She passed him a clean napkin.

'Just you wait,' Douglas said as, head bent, he dabbed at the stain. 'I've seen dames like her in action. She'll get in Brian's good books, then turn her attention to the boss.'

'So what if she does? If we do our jobs…' Susan stopped, mid-sentence, as Lisa Haldane materialised at Douglas's side.

'What are you two up to?'

Douglas leaned back on his perforated wooden chair. Plastering a smile on his face, 'Just grabbing a bite before we head back to the coalface.'

Lisa uttered a brittle laugh. 'The way you two were sitting, I could have sworn you were hatching something.'

'Chance would be a fine thing.'

'Mind if I join you?'

'We're just going.'

'Shame,' Lisa said coquettishly. 'And me the bearer of good news. That last sighting,' she confided, bending his ear. 'We got an excellent witness. Gave us a lot of detail. We've managed to trace the man and the child.'

Susan said, 'That's great.'

'Sorry to get your hopes up. Turns out the child in question is an eight-year-old boy.'

'Fucks sake,' Douglas grumbled. 'How did they manage that?'

'Easy done. Child was similar in build to Frankie. Short, dark hair. Same clothing: black puffa jacket. jogging bottoms, black shoes.'

Susan asked, 'Has the coastguard been stood down?'

'Too right.'

Douglas screwed up his face. 'What a bloody waste of money.'

'Better safe than sorry,' Susan argued. 'In their line of work, they're used to false alarms.'

'Still,' said Lisa. 'Where does that leave us?'

'Up the Swannee without a paddle,' Douglas muttered. 'There's no way a nine-year-old could have survived, not in the open. The weather may be good for this time of year, but the average temperature overnight can fall to as low as 6C.'

'Someone must be holding her.

'Either that, or she's dead in a ditch.'

Susan said. 'We've had cases before now, where missing kids have turned up safe and well.'

'Like when?'

'Can't think off the top of my head.'

Douglas stuck out his tongue. 'See.'

'I thought you said you were just leaving,' Lisa said petulantly.

Dabbing her lips with her napkin, Susan said, 'We are.'

But before she could gather her things, a uniformed officer dashed through the door. 'Have you seen DI Chisolm?'

'No. Something up?'

'There's been a body found on the beach at Fittie,' he said, visibly agitated. 'He's needed in the incident room right now.'

Footdee

The body lay, face down.

Chisolm took one look. 'Has the police surgeon attended?'

'Yes, sir. Death pronounced. He's just this minute away.'

'Get this tented up.' Chisolm barked. 'And the scene secured.'

'Sir.' The uniformed officer, who had been keeping a watching brief, scurried off in the direction of the patrol car parked by his fellow officer on the far side of the sea wall. Minutes later, the two PCs returned with a roll of blue and white tape and set to work delineating the primary scene boundary.

A veil of haar hung over the North Sea, the air sharp, redolent of ammonia and tar. The beach was deserted, having already been cleared of dog walkers and joggers, and surfers called back to dry land.

Chisolm gazed down at the small figure, cropped dark hair stark against the bleached shingle. The sea had done its work. The shoes and most of the clothing had gone. The torso was more bloated than the head or limbs. He noted damage to the fingers. Not that this came as a surprise. With an average depth of 95m, and a water temperature range of 5°C to 12°C, the North Sea didn't treat its victims kindly.

This wouldn't be the first drowning he'd seen since he moved north. In 2019, the body of twenty-five-year-old Alastair Done was found at Balmedie Beach. He was believed to have travelled to Aberdeen from his home in Malpas, Cheshire. A similar incident occurred in 2020, when Ellon Police Station received a report of a man's body on the same beach, and in December of that same year a woman's body had been found on the beach at Footdee. Police investigations confirmed all three deaths to be non-suspicious. Chisolm wondered how this scrap of humanity had met its end.

His attention was drawn back up the beach as a SOCO van drew up behind the patrol car. One by one, it discharged its occupants:

photographers, evidence recovery personnel, specialist operatives.

Weighed down by equipment, a couple of SOCOs approached,

'Morning, sir,' said the first, unrecognisable in white coveralls and hood. 'Duty pathologist been called?'

'On his way.'

'At least it's not raining,' the officer said cheerily. 'Plus...' He gestured to the ribbon of beach. '...we've plenty space to work.'

'Makes a change,' the second grumbled. 'You guys have no idea what we're up against: working at heights, in confined spaces, being outdoors in all weather conditions.'

'What are the chances of obtaining ID?' Chisolm asked the Team Leader. A tight knot formed in his stomach. If – as he suspected – the body was that of missing Frankie Bain, the child's parents would be devastated. And not only the parents. His thoughts turned – momentarily – to Maggie Laird.

The SOCO eyed the remains. 'Not great.' He bent to take a closer look. Straightening, he added, 'This one isn't too bad, mind. Mebbe hasn't been in the water that long.'

'Doesn't hold a candle to that Arbroath murder,' his colleague chipped in.

In 2008, police were called when a woman's head was found by children playing on Seagate beachfront in Arbroath. A human hand lay nearby. Forensic teams failed to establish the identity of the woman using fingerprints and dental records. Recognising that the quality of dental work was not in line with British standards, they called on specialists at Dundee University to create a computer generated image of the victim's face. A police officer recognised it as belonging to Lithuanian migrant worker, Jolanta Bledaite.

'First up, we'll want to determine if the recovery location is the primary death scene,' the Team Leader continued. 'The presumed circumstances that would have placed that body in the water environment. For example, a death may occur on land and the body subsequently placed in the water as a means of disposal. We'll pay particular attention to anything weighting the body down: external wrappings like blankets, curtains or sheets, clothing on the body.'

The tent had been erected and the scene boundary cordoned off. On the far side of the tape, a knot of curious onlookers – some in jogging gear, others with dogs straining at the leash – craned their necks. A generator was up and running, its engine noise striking a discordant note. Arc lights had been set up. The photographers were already at work. Evidence would be recorded using photography, video, and specialist pano photography: a series of sequential photographs taken by a fish-eye camera. R2S (Return to Scene) technology allows the Senior Investigating Officer and Procurator Fiscal to later 'walk through' the scene.

Chisolm stuck his head inside the tent. The SOCOs were bent to their tasks, white-suited figures in a variety of poses forming a macabre tableau around the small body. When their work was done, they would write up reports, process recovered evidence and prepare statements at a police station.

As he turned to go, Chisolm offered a silent prayer they'd get the result Mel Coutts was pushing for.

And soon.

*

Before her boss even had time to take his seat, 'Is it Frankie?' Susan asked, anxiety written all over her face.

'Can't say,' Chisolm replied. 'Given the way the body was positioned, together with its condition, scene investigators wouldn't even commit as to whether male or female.'

Douglas asked, 'Wasn't the clothing a giveaway?'

'We don't know what items are missing, and what's left isn't in good nick. What's more, there may be a significant post-mortem interval before any of these remains are found.'

'Fittie's a fair distance from where Frankie was last seen.'

Duffy said, 'Not if you've got all day. And the weather was dry. If she did take that direction, there's plenty to engage her: Codona's on the Esplanade; the Beach Boulevard Retail Park.'

Brian added his contribution. 'She might have been to Fittie at some point. Fancied another look. It's a quaint wee place, and we know she's an adventurous kid.'

'There's a playpark,' Douglas expanded. 'And the pier. And a lighthouse.'

'The playpark isn't up to much,' Brian observed. 'So I doubt that would have been a draw.'

'Plus,' Duffy growled, 'There's no access to the pier. It's all fenced off.'

'She could have gone in the water,' Susan suggested, 'and the tide carried her to where she was found.'

'Gone in, how?' sniped Douglas. 'Accident? Murder? Suicide?'

Joining in, Lisa asked, 'How about witnesses?'

'Response officers have taken statements, but I'm not hopeful. That part of the beach, there weren't many people about."

'Is the locus within sight of the houses?'

'Those that have had skylights or dormers added. The sea wall would inhibit sight-lines from the rest. Uniform are going door-to-door in the immediate vicinity as we speak.'

Brian said, 'Problem is, many of these cottages are holiday homes, unoccupied for much of the year.'

'We'll extend the house-to-house and put out a press appeal for witnesses. But until that happens,' Chisolm eyeballed his team, 'we're playing a waiting game.'

Goldfinger

'Ta-da!' Wilma bounced into the kitchen. Arms flung wide, she struck a sexy pose.

Maggie's jaw dropped.

'Well,' said Wilma, 'What do you think?'

'Breathtaking,' Maggie replied, hoarse all of a sudden.

Patting her peroxide up-do, 'Suits my colouring, don't you think?' She nudged the door shut. 'Bought it online. Wasn't sure about the sizing, but it fits like a glove.'

'You can say that again,' Maggie stuttered.

Talk about sprayed on!

The gold lame sheath clung to Wilma's curves. Like Shirley Eaton in the James Bond movie, Goldfinger. Only not. The plunging neckline exposed more breast than a maternity bra. The hemline covered Wilma's privates. But only if she didn't move.

Maggie caught a flash of black knickers, a canyon of cellulite. 'Bit short, maybe?' she ventured.

'It's got long sleeves.'

As if that makes a difference.

'Do they accept returns?'

'Does it matter?'

Maggie commanded, 'Do a twirl.'

Teetering on vertiginous heels, Wilma executed a tight pirouette. Came to rest with a wobble.

'It's not so much the fit,' said Maggie, 'as the fabric.' Clutching the hem, she scrunched a handful of material in her fist. 'Polyester tends to give off static. Wouldn't want you to electrocute yourself.'

'As if,' Wilma sniffed. 'You telling me you don't like it?'

'I do. Only... doesn't Wayne have a girlfriend?'

'What's that got to do with it?'

'It's his party. You wouldn't want to upstage anyone.'

'His party?' Wilma snorted. 'It's me that's footing the bill. I can upstage who I want.'

'Just saying.'

Wilma thrust out her chest. 'If we weren't pals, I'd tell you where to get off.'

'Sorry,' Maggie said. 'But you did ask for my opinion.'

Mouth turned down, Wilma began, 'More fool...'

Her words were drowned by the door bursting open, almost knocking her off her feet.

'Wow!' Colin gasped. 'You look amazing, Wilma.'

'You think?'

Behind her back, Maggie made frantic eye signals.

'What's it in aid of?'

'Wayne's 21st.'

Maggie held her breath.

For a beat nobody spoke.

Then the penny dropped. Colour flooding his face, Colin said, 'Right.' Eyes popping, he re-appraised the outfit. 'Well, in that case...' His mouth opened and closed. Then he said, 'I don't suppose there's anything to eat.'

XII

The Police Mortuary

The small body lay naked, its chest cavity gaping. The chest bones had already been removed, the organs pulled out to be examined and weighed.

Around one of two stainless-steel cutting tables, the procurator fiscal and two pathologists stood alongside the Exhibits Officer and Allan Chisolm, who had called a favour: asked Pathology to prioritise the post mortem. Instructed Lisa Haldane to join him as a familiarisation exercise. In the background, Junior Anatomical Pathology Technician, Tracey, hovered attentively. Her role would involve passing instruments to the pathologist, helping to retrieve and initially labelling samples, specimens and organs and reconstructing the deceased after examination.

A diminutive figure in rubber apron and welly boots, lead pathologist, Alec Gourlay, turned to Chisolm. 'I can confirm the deceased is female, and likely ethnically Chinese or Vietnamese. Further examination of the anthropomorphic features – skull and facial bones – should give a clearer picture.'

'Age?'

'You'll have to wait for my report.' Brown eyes twinkling below the protective cap that hid all but a few strands of sandy hair, Gourlay added, 'I expect next you're going to ask me the cause of death.'

'That, and whether criminality is involved.'

'Criminality is your field, inspector. As to mine, determining the cause and manner of death for bodies recovered from water can be challenging, more so as the post-mortem interval increases. The progression of decomposition changes in a liquid environment is altered by temperature, current, interaction between the remains and the physical environment, and marine fauna predation.'

Making her presence known, Lisa – shapeless in protective

clothing – asked, 'How does that manifest itself?'

'In addition to the usual post-mortem signs – vascular marbling, dark discolouration of the skin, bloating and putrefaction – weeds, rocks, silt and sand exacerbate the water damage. Fish and chips, we call it.' He bent to the task, deep perforated channels either side of the table catching the blood and entrails. 'Once a body is removed from the water, putrefaction will likely be accelerated. Gases will be produced, primarily in the chest and gut, that will inflate a corpse like a balloon.'

Chisolm asked, 'Found anything interesting so far?'

Gourlay replied. 'What I can say is the deceased didn't die from drowning in sea water.'

'How can you be sure?'

'Death by drowning occurs after the lungs take in water. This water intake then interferes with breathing. The lungs become heavy, and oxygen stops being delivered to the heart. Without the supply of oxygen, the body shuts down.' He resumed his work.

'Is the position of the deceased when found significant?'

'If a body is "washed up" on the beach, how it floated when in a depth of water greater than the girth of the body becomes irrelevant, as the body will be in shallower water before it is deposited. That deposition may be due to the body being cast up by waves or left as the wave or tide retreat. Whichever way it lands on the beach, there is likely to be some turbulence, tossing the body around from whatever position it started.'

Lisa said, 'I thought women always floated face up.'

'The majority of drowned bodies initially float face down,' Gourlay explained, 'due to the weight of the arms and legs. However, people with excess fat in the breasts or stomach may float face up, as do bodies with shorter limbs. Most drowned corpses of both sexes will eventually flip face up, as the decomposing body fills with gases and becomes more buoyant.'

Chisolm again. 'Are you saying this body hadn't been in the water very long?'

'Impossible to tell, not at this stage. Post-mortem changes are not only affected by water temperature, however. It is not unusual for small fish and crustaceans to gain access to the interior of the body through skin and soft tissue defects or even normal body orifices.'

'Gross!' exclaimed Lisa.

Gourlay acknowledged this with a grunt. 'What's more, putrefaction and scavenging creatures will dismember the corpse in a week or two and the bones will sink to the seabed. Small crustaceans and shrimp-like organisms prey on soft tissue. Given the opportunity, they can completely de-flesh exposed parts of the body. Last example I saw was at the base of an oil rig. Less than twenty-four hours was all it took.'

'How about injuries?'

'That's a tricky one. You'll note abrasions to the hands and feet. Here,' he pointed. 'And here. Some damage to finger extremities.'

Lisa strained forward.

'From the fish, there is loss of circular pieces of exposed skin,' he indicated. 'Often with a slightly crenated border. There are also widespread, superficial abrasions – particularly on the face – where the body has been rumbled over sand or shingle. Establishing cause and manner of death for bodies recovered from a liquid environment is difficult enough without the additional complexity of interpreting post-mortem changes—' He stopped abruptly, as Lisa lurched against him.

Chisolm's arm shot out to break her fall.

'Here,' Tracey moved to Lisa's side, and between them they led her through to the small office and lowered her onto a chair.

'You carry on,' said Tracey. 'I'll get her a drink of water.'

Gratefully, Chisolm returned, past the big fridge with its sliding trays, to the dissection room.

'Is she okay?' the second pathologist enquired.

'She'll be fine,' Chisolm said irritably, rolling his eyes at the PF. He couldn't blame the woman. A post-mortem – even of an adult – was not a pretty site. Add to that, the sight of the instruments lining the walls – drills and saws and scalpels – was enough to make anyone nauseous.

Beneath the extractor fans labouring overhead, Alec Gourlay hadn't deviated from the task in hand. Taking a brief shufti over one shoulder to acknowledge Chisolm's presence, he continued, 'Forensic pathologists must be familiar with the expected post-mortem changes that occur in immersed and submerged bodies as well as post-mortem artifacts such as predation by marine fauna that may be misinterpreted as ante-mortem injuries.'

At the same time, Chisolm mused, it wasn't as if Lisa Haldane was a rookie. She must have attended dozens of post-mortems, and known not to look at the face, He wondered if her fainting fit was an act.

'Large fish and large crustaceans will cause tissue damage,' Gourlay kept up his running commentary, 'that in some cases may mimic injuries and should be interpreted with care. Moreover, in a strong current or rough sea state, the remains may strike rocks or brush with enough force to create the appearance of significant external trauma to the body. And that's before you factor in injuries from harbours or shipping. I've seen amputations, decapitations and dismemberment caused by hulls and propellers.'

Chisolm asked, 'What are the chances of retrieving DNA?'

'Depends on how long the body has been in the water. Exposure to long periods of immersion makes DNA analysis difficult. In the absence of viable soft tissue, we'd look to get something from muscle, deep tissue or bones. The new DNA profiling facility at Gartcosh enables us to identify twenty-four individual DNA markers, where previously we could only identify eleven. This dramatically increases the odds of obtaining a result from smaller or lower-grade samples. But it all takes time.'

And costs money, Chisolm thought, conscious of the overtime figures that sat, awaiting his attention.

'Sorry, folks,' Lisa said, materialising at Chisolm's side. 'Hope I haven't missed anything.'

Her face was pale, he noted, her eyes sharp as ever.

The Fittie Squares

PC Bruce Anderson rapped on the door of the terraced cottage, PC Vish Patel standing at his side.

Dating from 1809, the fishing village of Footdee – pronounced locally as Fittie – was purpose-built to re-home the city's fishermen, who were living in poor quality accommodation around the harbour. Adjacent to the coastguard tower at the mouth of Aberdeen Harbour, the Fittie Squares – single-storey thatched cottages, inward-facing to protect them from the sea – sit around a central drying green. Originally single-storey, the two-roomed cottages with outside toilet were often occupied by more than one family, ramshackle outhouses built to store fishing equipment. Now a conservation area, the houses are tiled and gentrified with primary-coloured paint, planted window boxes and nautical artefacts, the squares filled with rows of brightly coloured outhouses or 'tarry sheds'.

'Widna be the first,' the old man said, when he opened his door and the officers had outlined the reason for their call. 'I mind there was another body. Last Hogmanay it was.' Scratching his bald patch, 'No, Hogmanay fell on the Thursday. Must have been the Wednesday. Or mebbe…'

'Do you mind if we come in?' Anderson interrupted. He understood, now, why the village had been laid out the way it was. The wind could have cut you in two.

'Nae bother.' The man – identified from the front door's brass nameplate as Mr Tait – led them into a living room crammed with heavy furniture. 'Sit yourselves down.'

Anderson lowered himself onto an ancient moquette couch, raising a cloud of stoor.

Patel squeezed in beside him.

'Cops got me oot o' bed,' the old man continued, creakily sinking into a matching armchair. 'Hammering on ma door at eight in the morning. Ah've nae need tae rise that early,' he confided. 'Not nowadays. Hours they were on the beach. Sealed it off from here to Burger King.'

Anderson had a vague recollection of the incident: a woman's body found on the foreshore.

'Loon is it this time?'

'Too early to say.'

'Ah'll put money on it's one o' them surfers,' Tait grunted. 'Lads, nooadays, they've nae respect for the sea. It's no' Bondi Beach we're talkin, where the temperature is a whole lot different an' there's a lifeguard station every few hundred yards. Me, ah've been at the fish ma whole life, an'...'

Patel pointed to the telescope mounted on a tripod by the front window. 'That's an impressive piece of kit.'

Mr Tait looked him up, down and sideways. 'Aye.'

Vish took this in good part. Given Asians comprise only four per-cent of the Aberdeen population, he was accustomed to being an object of curiosity among its older denizens. Add to that, in 2020 only 253 of Police Scotland's 17,693 serving officers came from ethnic minority backgrounds, and none of the executive team. 'Have you spotted anything out of the ordinary?'

'Ye kiddin me?' Tait's rheumy eyes danced with merriment. 'Jist keep the thing for auld times' sake. I've macular degeneration. Canna see twa feet in front o' ma face.'

So much for witnesses.

Vish looked to Anderson, who responded with a resigned shrug.

A New Investigation

In the Incident Room, detectives, uniformed officers and ancillary staff waited, suits crumpled, complexions grey, deep lines etched into foreheads.

Allan Chisolm strode into the room. 'Sorry to keep you all waiting.' He took up position in front of the whiteboard. Waving a sheaf of paper, he announced, 'I've just come from the mortuary.'

You could have heard a pin drop, every officer lost in his – or her – own thoughts. They'd have heard the news – either on the jungle or on social media – of the body washed up at Fittie. Anticipation mixed with dread. They were all desperate to know if the body had been identified as Frankie Bain. And at the same time in denial. Of all the outcomes, nobody would have wished for that.

'I won't keep you in suspense. The body found at Fittie early this morning is not Frankie Bain.'

This was met by a collective release of breath.

'If it's not Frankie,' a voice spoke up from the back of the room. 'Who is it?'

'We've no ID as yet. There was nothing found on the body: phone, wallet, bank cards. No labels attached to the clothing.'

A uniformed officer said, 'We've been told the deceased is female. Has Pathology established how old?'

'Early teens: twelve or thirteen.'

'How come we thought it might be Frankie? She's only nine.'

'From her description, Frankie Bain is tall for her age. The Footdee body is correspondingly small. And there's a reason for that.' Chisolm waited until he had everyone's full attention. 'The Footdee victim is IC4: of South-east Asian extraction.'

A ripple of consternation ran around the room.

'Why couldn't they have told us that straight off?' someone

protested. 'Saved wasting time.'

There were murmurs of support. The clock was running down on the search for Frankie Bain. If it hadn't already run out.

'The condition of the body precluded it,' Chisolm responded. 'Preliminary findings point to a female child – small woman perhaps. We're looking at a range of possibilities: Filipino domestic or care worker, trafficked Vietnamese.'

Lisa asked, 'Could it be a Thai bride? We had a case last year in Dundee: Bennylynn Burke and her two-year-old daughter Jellica were reported missing and later found bludgeoned with a hammer.'

'It's a possibility,' Chisolm said. 'Best guess is Vietnamese. But with no recourse to UK DNA or fingerprint databases or dental records, we're heavily reliant on lab work to take our investigation forward.'

Brian joined in. 'That and intel. What do you reckon to our chances, boss?'

'Better than they were. Vietnamese are now the most commonly detected victims of trafficking in Scotland. If you read up on the subject, you'll find forced labour is the most common form of exploitation, followed by sex work for underage girls. Cannabis cultivation is one of the biggest forms of employment, and the proliferation of nail bars has also provided cover for the traffickers. North-east nail bars are hoatching with under-age girls.'

'Not only girls,' said Douglas. 'There was a case few years back: teenage boy trafficked by an organised crime gang? Kid didn't speak a word of English. He'd no ID or work permit. Only the clothes on his back. When he was picked up, poor bugger didn't even know what town he was in.'

'Where was he?'

'Bathgate. Las Vegas Nail Spa, if I remember right.'

'Christ,' said Duffy. 'You couldn't make it up.'

'Gartcosh reckon, because nail bars are a cash business, OCGs are using them as fronts to launder drug money.'

'Are you all aware,' Lisa added, putting her oar in, 'that in 2020 Police Scotland recruited two Vietnamese officers to assist with cultural and language difficulties in response to a surge in trafficking cases?'

Susan rolled her eyes at Douglas, who responded with an exaggerated sigh.

'Sadly,' said Chisolm. 'More than half the victims are children, as we suspect is the case here. Cheap, disposable commodities.'

Another uniform spoke up. 'Does the report say how long the body had been in the water?'

'Days. They couldn't accurately establish how many. What I can tell you is this young girl was not the victim of seawater drowning, accidental or otherwise. So we have a new investigation on our hands.'

'Are you saying she was murdered?'

'She suffered trauma, certainly, before her body went in the water. Plus, her underclothing was disturbed, which may point to sexual interference. Then again, it may have been caused by the action of the water.'

'She might have run away,' Lisa volunteered.

'That's less likely. Child victims are often brainwashed to want to flee back to their traffickers, even after being rescued.'

'There have even been cases,' Lisa said, 'where trafficked children have mobile phone SIM cards stitched into their clothing so they can contact traffickers when rescued.' Clutching a dramatic hand to her breast, 'Wouldn't that break your heart?'

Chisolm ignored her. 'For now, that's of secondary importance.' He turned to the whiteboard, where so many items had been crossed out it looked like a pop art installation. 'Getting back to Operation Eco-Warrior, where are we at?'

'Battling on,' some wit replied.

Sighing, Brian said, 'We're at a standstill. The phone lines have stopped ringing. We're below the evidence threshold by a country mile on all three of our suspects. And time isn't on our side.'

'Doubt it will make a difference,' Duffy complained. 'Let's face it, if that kid wasn't dead by Monday night, she's sure as hell dead by now.'

Justice or Love?

'I've cracked it,' whooped Wilma, crashing into Maggie's kitchen. She'd been itching to share the outcome of her expedition to Craigiebuckler. Decided against. She still had work to do.

Maggie turned from peeling potatoes at the sink. 'Cracked what?'

'The Sellars suicide. I was right all along.' Hands on hips, she paused for maximum effect. 'Vincent Sellars was murdered.'

Wiping her hands on a tea towel, Maggie asked, 'Who by?'

'The son.'

'How did you arrive at this conclusion?'

'Can we grab a seat?' Steering Maggie by the elbow, Wilma propelled her through to the dining room. Once they were seated, 'It was your Carruthers case that did it.'

'How?' Maggie demanded. 'Why?'

'Once I ruled out the wife and her lover…'

'You ruled them out?' she gasped.

'…it could only have been him.'

'Wasn't there a daughter?'

'Couldn't have done it. She was at work at the time.'

'But…'

'I had no joy with the user name. But when Flo Carruthers finally sent John Gibson's profile picture, a reverse image search took me straight to Harvey Sellars' Facebook page.'

Maggie said. 'And you didn't think to tell me?'

'Client took her time.'

'She's not computer-savvy. Probably have needed help taking the screenshot.'

'You had your folks in an all. Plus, I was stymied by Sellars' advanced privacy settings. But a check of the phone book and voter's roll cross-checked with an address in Craigiebuckler I'd thrown up previously.'

'So Harvey Sellars and John Gibson are...'

'...one and the same.' Beaming from one ear to the other, Wilma sat back with a resounding thud.

'But,' said Maggie, 'Using a false name, isn't that a bit underhand? I'm sure Flo Carruthers will think so.'

'There's the thing: the name was kosher. I'd have been none the wiser had I not come by this.' Palming a business card, Wilma flicked it across.

'Harvey J.G. Sellars, Sales Representative', she read, frowning. 'But I still don't see...'

'There was something bugging me the minute I laid eyes on it it, but it took me time to work out: Harvey Sellars' middle names are John Gibson.'

'Oh,' said Maggie, mouth agape. 'You didn't get Harvey Sellars to admit to trying to dupe a grieving widow?'

'Not exactly.'

Then, portentously, 'You haven't used those two loons of yours to press-gang him into confessing to murder?'

'No, but I've tracked down a witness can poke a gaping hole in his story about being in Dumfries at the time of his dad's suicide. It's well known they didn't get on, the timeline fits, and we've a credible witness.' Triumphant, 'We've hit the jackpot, like I said we would.'

Head in hands, Maggie said, 'I don't believe it! We're dealing with people's lives here, not competing in some fantasy TV show.'

'Now you mention it, have you watched Catfishing?'

Maggie silenced her with a withering look. 'If – and it's a big if – you have obtained worthwhile evidence, by lawful means, I will take it to Inspector Chisolm and let him decide what to do with it.'

'But,' Wilma protested, 'that's not fair.'

'You're a fine one to talk about fairness. You've an angle on every damn thing.'

'If you think I've knocked my pan out, spending hours on surveillance, cleaning bedpans, wangling my way into...'

Maggie put her hands to her ears. 'Don't want to know.'

'You've another think coming.'

Hands dropping to her sides, 'Is that a threat?'

Jaw set, Wilma said, 'It's for the good of the business.'

Maggie said, 'Only you could flagrantly break the law and argue it was in a good cause. What would Ian have to say if he knew what you'd been up to?'

'Leave Ian out of this. It's nothing to do with him.'

'On the contrary, it has everything to do with him if, as may well happen, we not only lose our licence, but are sent to jail.'

'Don't exaggerate. Ian says we're not real PIs, anyhow. We're nothing but contact tracers and debt recovery agents.'

'Is that so?'

'Can't you see,' Wilma pleaded, 'this would prove him wrong. Prove them all wrong, solving a murder case.'

Maggie's lips thinned. 'Didn't you hear me the first time?'

'You're the one has been screaming justice since ever we met. Do you want to see a murderer get off scot-free?'

'Of course not.'

'There's been nothing in the paper, so the police can't have wrapped it up. Think of the kudos if we beat them to it.'

'Think of the consequences if we're charged with interfering with a live police investigation.'

Not to mention the fallout with Allan Chisolm.

'It would put the agency on the map.'

Maggie squeezed her eyes tight shut. Taking Wilma's information to the police meant sanction, ridicule at best should her claims prove unfounded. Either way, it would mark the end of her relationship with Allan Chisolm. Their romance wouldn't survive another crisis.

Thinking back to their conversation at Banchory Lodge, Maggie felt sick to her stomach.

Justice or love? The decision was hers, and hers alone.

Opening her eyes, she fixed them on Wilma. 'The answer's still the same.'

'My way or the highway, is that it?' Jabbing a finger, 'You've no imagination, that's your problem. Canna see past the end of your nose.'

'And yours is, you never know where to draw the line. Here's what's going to happen. You'll write down everything you've just told me. Then we'll put the facts in order and take them to the police.'

'If you do that, pal, it's curtains for us.'

Maggie said, 'You don't mean that.'

'Try me,' said Wilma.

A Can of Worms

'I've had news just in,' Chisolm began.

Everyone caught their breath. They'd been summoned at short notice: Duffy from a fly cup in the canteen, Brian from changing his shirt in the locker room. Susan had run from the toilet where, having overslept, she had been hastily applying makeup. Douglas had been collared negotiating a space in the Rear Podium Car Park, Lisa halfway up the stairs.

She was first to speak. 'Frankie Bain?'

He shook his head.

'Fittie?' Susan queried.

'There's been nothing further from the lab. What I can tell you is there was a call to emergency services early this morning: a resident of Old Aberdeen rang the ambulance service after finding a child lying injured on her lawn.'

Brian said, 'What's the story?'

'I haven't had the details.'

'Bloody typical,' Duffy grumbled.

In 2017, the controversial decision to close Aberdeen's police control room and service centre had been approved by the Scottish Police Authority. Emergency calls were now passed via central service centre responders to the North Area Control Room in Dundee for dispatch, with non-emergency calls handled at centres in Glasgow, Motherwell and Midlothian.

'First responders?'

Chisolm looked down at his notes. 'Esson and Elrick.'

'Christ,' Duffy groaned. 'That pair couldn't batter a fish supper. Between Elrick's stutter and Esson's IQ, we'll be lucky to get any feedback before lunchtime.'

'Remember that theft report?' said Susan. 'Could there be a link:

some wee toe-rag from Tillydrone, perhaps, back to have another go?'

'Quite possibly,' Chisolm said.

'It could as soon be Frankie,' suggested Douglas.

Lisa disagreed. 'In somebody's garden for the best part of a week? I don't think so. That whole area has been thoroughly searched.'

'Who said how long the kid had been there?' he snapped. 'Fact is, we don't know.'

Susan spoke up in support. 'Nor if the emergency call was made by the same person who reported the theft.'

'Alleged theft,' Brian emphasised, with a sideways glance at Duffy, who was giving Lisa the evils.

Chisolm said, 'There's one way to find out. Douglas and Susan, get yourselves up to ARI. Phone me in a full update. Bob, get a transcript of that 999 call. See if it gives any more information. Brian, familiarise yourself with the theft report. Then you and Lisa get over there. Speak to the householder. Face-to-face. I don't want any cock-ups.'

'Yes, boss.'

'And, Lisa, when we're done here, I want a word.'

*

When the team had dispersed, 'Well,' Lisa said, striking a pose, 'I'm all yours.'

Chisolm took a deep breath. 'That wasn't the only phone call I took this morning.'

'Okay.'

'An old pal gave me a bell. Well, when I say 'pal' he's more of a sparring partner: Harry Geddes.'

'Harry?' she repeated, colouring. 'I had a drink with him a couple of nights ago. He didn't mention you.'

'Known him long?'

'As a matter of fact, we've only just met. Bumped into one another in Revolution last Saturday. He asked me out on the Sunday.'

'Ah,' said Chisolm. 'He always was a fast worker.'

'And I'm a single woman.'

'Didn't mention his line of work by any chance?'

'Marketing,' Lisa replied.

'I suppose marketing does come into it. You see, I know Harry by his nickname.' Seeing Lisa's bemused expression, 'Snoop,' he expanded. 'Harry Geddes is a senior reporter with the Press & Journal.'

The colour drained from Lisa's face. 'I thought...'

'I'm more interested in what was said. According to my pal Harry, you not only divulged details of Operation Eco-Warrior, but also of the Fittie case.'

'Nothing that isn't common knowledge.' Lisa blustered.

'On the contrary, Harry Geddes is in possession of information which is not in the public domain. What's more, he is planning to run a story – perhaps more than one – which may compromise a potential people-trafficking operation.'

Lisa's knees buckled and she sank onto a chair. Head bowed, 'I don't know what to say.'

'You're fortunate Harry rang me and not DCI Coutts.'

'What are you going to do?'

Chisolm said, 'Leave it with me. In the meantime, I suggest you keep your head down and your mouth shut. Now get out of here.'

What a fucking can of worms!

He watched as Lisa made a dash for the door.

Aberdeen Royal Infirmary

'Frances Bain,' the staff nurse said in answer to Douglas's question.

'You sure?' he queried. He and Susan were in the Royal Aberdeen Children's Hospital within the ARI site at Foresterhill.

'That's the name on the jacket the patient was wearing when she was brought in.'

Susan asked, 'It's definitely a girl?'

'You think we don't know the difference?' the nurse said. Only half in jest, if the affronted look on her face was anything to go by.

'Her injuries,' said Douglas. 'Are they serious?'

'Frances – if Frances it is – has suffered a broken leg and multiple fractures. She may also be concussed.'

'Any idea how those injuries were sustained?'

'You'll need to speak to the registrar.'

'Is he or she available?'

'He's in a meeting. If you'd like to come back this afternoon...'

Susan cut her short. 'Where is your patient now?'

'Last I heard, she was in the Fracture Clinic.'

'How long before she's fit to be interviewed?'

With a sigh, the staff nurse said, 'I've already had cops here asking questions, and we've a line of injured kids as long as your arm. So, if you'll excuse me, I've work to do.' Walking away, she threw over her shoulder, 'As I said, come back this afternoon.'

*

'What are we going to tell the boss?' Susan asked, when they'd repaired to the Aroma Coffee Bar on the main concourse.

'More than we've got,' Douglas mumbled through a mouthful of jam doughnut. 'That's for sure.' Yanking his head in the direction of a bank of lifts, 'Kid might not even be Frankie.'

Susan put down her coffee. 'Everything points to it.'

'You reckon? If your theory of thieving toe-rags is right, they could as easily have nicked that jacket.'

Susan's shoulders drooped. 'I hadn't thought of that.' She deliberated for a few moments, then, 'But, surely, Frankie wouldn't have let it go easily, knowing her mum's tight for cash.'

'She could have been abducted, and lost the jacket in a struggle. Or the perp could have chucked it. Not only that, there's no way she'd have survived in the open without it.'

'Who said she was outside?'

'Dispatch.'

'According to the boss, they said she'd been found outside. There's a distinction.'

'Okay. But if Frankie Bain was desperate enough to do a runner, do you think she'd have nipped around the corner and holed up in somebody's garden? No way. She'd want to put distance between herself and whatever the problem was. Take the case of those two boys went missing from Tillydrone. They were found in Warrington, four hundred miles away.'

'They were fifteen.'

'Granted. But it's an established fact,' Susan said with a cheeky grin, 'girls mature earlier.'

'You win,' Douglas conceded. 'What's the plan?'

'Chance our arm at the Fracture Clinic. Check if the kid is conscious and lucid. Establish ID. If we manage that, whether the hospital have notified the parents. We can't sit here half the day, that's for sure. Boss will go ballistic.'

A Glasgow Kiss

The first floor function room of the Bide-A-Wee wouldn't have looked out of place in Guangdong. The walls were lined with crimson flock wallpaper punctuated at intervals by cranberry glass sconces, the circular tables overhung by fringed pendants.

On the buffet table, scotch eggs were heaped alongside sausage rolls and chicken wings. But the action was at the bar, where a scrum of twenty-somethings necked beer and exchanged intimacies, whilst assiduously thumbing their phones.

'Look at you!' Darren marvelled, eyes roving Wilma's body.

'Eff off!'

He sidled up. 'Don't be like that.'

'You've a brass neck. I'm still paying off the debt you landed me with.'

'Sorry,' he responded with a weak smile.

'Who invited you, anyhow?'

'Wayne.' He nodded in the direction of their younger son.

Wilma's eyebrows shot up. 'Since when have you and him been talking?'

'While back,' Darren said, not meeting her hard stare.

'Loon always was a bit soft in the head.' Her eyes narrowed. 'How about Kevin?'

He shrugged. 'Won't give me the time of day.'

'Him and me both. Now, eff off. Didn't you hear me the first time?'

'Can we not be friends?' he wheedled.

'Friends?' she mouthed. 'After leaving me with two bairns and not a stick of furniture to call my own?'

'Just for tonight,' Darren persisted. 'Special occasion.'

She waved a dismissive hand. 'In yer dreams.'

'Let me buy you a drink, at least. Raise a toast to Wayne's

twenty-first.'

'You treat me?' Wilma shrilled. 'That'll be a first. I've had to work nights downstairs ever since we split up, and that's on top of the day job.'

'I'm serious,' he said, reaching into his back pocket.

Wilma clocked the chunky gold jewellery, the Gucci trainers. 'Robbed a bank? No, don't tell me. You're still sponging off other folk. Talk about a waste of space.'

'Who are you calling a waste of space?' A figure materialised by Darren's side. Dressed head to toe in white – boob tube, skinny jeans, stilettos – with shoulder-length black hair tonged in corkscrew curls, she attached herself to one tattooed arm.

Wilma jerked her head. 'Who's yer pal?'

Smirking, Darren said, 'Chantelle, meet my ex.'

Wilma gave her the once-over. Skin the colour of a Seville orange, texture to match. Pillow lips that had seen too much filler. False eyelashes that wouldn't have looked out of place on a giraffe.

'Fit ur you lookin at?' Chantelle challenged.

Wilma may have given up the boxing gym, but she still had the moves. Adopting her fiercest expression, 'Fancy yer chances?' She threw a pretend 1–2 to the body.

The smack on her cheek came out of nowhere.

Wilma reeled sideways.

Stumbled.

Recovered sufficiently to land one on Chantelle's chin.

She was gathering herself when a kick caught her kneecap. Howling in pain, she doubled up, clasping the throbbing knee with one hand, the other clawing at Chantelle's ankle.

Her adversary toppled over, landing heavily.

'You okay?' Darren stooped to help Chantelle up.

'Bastard.' He was spreadeagled by Wilma's well-aimed kick on the backside.

'Mum?' Kevin yelled, dashing across the room. He squared up to Darren. 'Get the hell out.'

'No way,' Darren retorted. 'I've as much right as—'

His words were obliterated by a forceful head-butt, otherwise known as a Glasgow kiss.

XIII

Alice

Startled from sleep by an insistent buzz, Allan Chisolm groped for his phone. The display read 03.17. Nothing unusual there. In the course of his long police service, he'd had more disturbed nights than he cared to remember.

'Chisolm,' he rasped.

'It's Clare.'

His heart turned a somersault at the sound of his wife's voice. 'You alright?'

'Yes. At least, I was until...' Her voice wavered. 'It's Alice. There's been an accident.'

Chisolm jolted upright. 'What sort of accident?'

'She was knocked down by a car. Hit and run. Don't have many details.'

His training kicked in. 'The police?'

'On the scene within minutes. Ambulance wasn't far behind.'

Throwing back the duvet, he leapt out of bed. 'Have you booked a flight?' Crossing to the wardrobe, he started pulling clothes from hangers.

'No need. She's here, in Glasgow.'

'But...' Chisolm's mind went into overdrive. Since graduating, his younger daughter had been working in London as an accountant.

Had she packed in the job?

Was she paying a social visit?

If so, why hadn't she bothered to contact him?

'It was meant to be a flying visit,' Clare explained. 'A friend from uni Alice hadn't seen since she moved south: Rachel. You might remember.'

'Vaguely.' He grabbed his overnight bag and began stuffing things in.

'She got a bunch of the girls together. "Our posse", Alice calls them. Booked a booth at some nightclub. They were walking to a taxi rank when…' Clare broke down.

Chisolm headed to the bathroom. 'Where is Alice now?'

'At the QE.'

Opened in 2015, Glasgow's Queen Elizabeth University Hospital, located in Govan, south of the river Clyde, is one of the largest acute hospitals in the UK, and home to major specialist services. Known locally as The Death Star, due to its distinctive shape, Chisolm had joked about it many a time when he worked in Dumbarton Road.

Now, 'What are they saying about her condition?'

'Critical,' said Clare, her voice scarce more than a whisper. 'Head injuries. One arm broken. They can't say, yet, if there's internal damage. I'm calling from the hospital. Alice is in theatre now.'

'Christ,' Chisolm said, throwing toiletries into a sponge bag. Every day of his working life he had to deal with stuff like this, but you never thought it would happen to you. 'I can be there by…' he checked his watch, 'best guess, seven o'clock.'

'Thanks,' Clare said. 'I appreciate it.'

Her formal tone brought him up short. 'Alice is my daughter, too.'

'I know.'

The silence hung heavy between them.

Then, 'Oh, Allan,' she sobbed, 'if you could only see that poor girl's parents.'

'What girl?' Chisolm puzzled. 'Was someone else hurt?'

'Rachel,' Clare replied. 'She's dead.'

A Piece of Liver

'What happened to you?'

Touching a tentative finger to the leopard-print patch that covered one eye, Wilma answered, 'Wayne's twenty-first. Heavy night.'

'I'm sorry,' Maggie said, crestfallen. 'I've had so much on my plate, I completely forgot.'

The two were in Wilma's front room, its silver-patterned feature wall and glass chandelier a riot of excess compared with Maggie's own faded decor. She was relieved to note the purple cowhide rug had vanished, in its stead a vibrant zebra print.

'No probs.' From her supine position on the oversized black leather settee, Wilma turned a wounded face. 'It's not as if you were invited.'

'No.' The celebration was to have been low-key: only close family and friends. 'Still,' said Maggie. 'I'd bought him a present.'

'You didn't have to do that.'

'Wanted to. You are my best... mate.' Feebly, she completed the sentence. Allan Chisolm hadn't returned her calls. It was on the tip of Maggie's tongue to say she was still determined to take Wilma's intel on Harvey Sellars to the police, but she balked at picking a fight when her opponent was down. Instead, 'I'll run and fetch it if you like. It's not much: just a card and a voucher.'

'Good of you,' Wilma mumbled, her voice shaky. 'It's more than you can afford.'

Maggie threw her a sharp look. Could that be a tear glistening in the corner of one eye?

'Don't rush off,' Wilma added. 'It can wait.' Changing tack, 'What do you think to the eye-patch? Makes me look like thon war reporter, don't you think?' Chewing on a fingernail, she expanded, 'Marie somebody or other.'

'Colvin,' Maggie suppled. 'Foreign correspondent for The Sunday Times. And you don't look a bit like her.'

Thrusting out her boobs, 'She's a sexy piece'

'She's dead. Ten years back. She was killed in Syria.'

Wilma's face fell. 'Okay.'

'Let's have a look.'

Lifting the patch onto her forehead, Wilma squinted in the strong light.

Maggie started in shock. 'We've a big presentation at the end of this week. You can't go looking like that.'

'No worries,' Wilma breezed, putting the patch back in place. 'I've sent Ian to the butcher for a piece of liver.'

'Where was he when this happened?'

'Working a late shift. He'd have come, only he wasn't that keen on the idea, to tell the truth. Him and the boys don't see eye-to-eye. And, besides, Torry folk—'

Maggie could imagine. Although resettled by hard-working Polish families, Torry remained in the bottom twenty percent of the region's deprived areas with high levels of unemployment. Those in work were mainly in low-skilled jobs such as fish processing. Torry's main employer, Pelagia, was held responsible for the 'Torry pong'. Even the pubs were shutting down. Historic Campbell's Bar in Greyhope Road had been closed for several years, with plans to turn it into a community hub.

'Oh, well,' she said, 'I'm relieved it wasn't anything more serious. When I first laid eyes on you, I thought you'd been winging it again.'

'Would I do that?' Wilma asked, feigning innocence.

'As for the presentation, we'll have to rethink.'

'Can't I go like this?'

'Not on your life.'

'Why not? I mebbe don't look the spit of thon Colvin woman, but...'

She was brought up short by the sound of the front door banging shut.

'That'll be Ian, now.'

Maggie said, 'I better get back.'

'There's no rush. Stay and have a cup of tea. Or we could open a bottle, me being under the weather and all.'

'You want to stay off the booze,' said Ian, walking in on the conversation. 'Isn't one black eye enough?'

'Put the kettle on, and the liver in the fridge,' Wilma instructed. When Ian had gone, 'There's days like this I wish I'd stayed single.' Brightening, 'Now, about that wine…'

'Thanks,' Maggie said, weighed by the responsibility of what she had to do. 'But, no,' she replied. 'See you!' She made a beeline for the door.

The Chanonry

'I told him,' Celia Pendreich said. 'Told him time and again, "That thing's dangerous. One of these days it's going to fall down and kill somebody". I wanted to get people in to dismantle it. Harold wouldn't hear of it. Said he'd do it himself. Old men.' She looked to Lisa for backup. 'They're so obdurate.'

'It was your husband who called the emergency services?' Brian enquired, somewhat guardedly. He'd got a flea in his ear when Mrs Pendreich answered their knock.

'My stool!' she'd exclaimed. 'You've recovered it.'

When he'd disabused her of the notion, she'd been none too pleased. Now, they were standing on the terrace, a random heap of planks and old doors scarring an otherwise manicured lawn.

'Correct. I spotted the debris the minute I drew the bedroom curtains.' Pointing to an upper window, 'That's our bedroom. As you can see, it has a splendid view of the garden.'

Brian nodded his agreement. In common with other properties on the Chanonry, the main entrance gave almost directly onto the street, the rear facade enjoying uninterrupted views of the grounds.

Celia sniffed loudly. 'Did. Until…'

'What did you do next?'

'Called down to Harold. He was eating his breakfast in the kitchen. Porridge. Makes it every day.'

'So it was your husband who went out to the garden and came upon the little girl?'

'That's right.'

'Did you follow?'

With a snort, Mrs Pendreich answered, 'I did not.' Seeing Brian and Lisa exchange concerned looks, she added, 'To be frank, I was livid. It was a mess entirely of Harold's own making. I left him to it and went to run a bath.'

'You didn't actually see the child?'

'How would I? By the time I came downstairs, the ambulance had been and gone.' She looked from one to the other. 'And before anyone mentions liability, I'd like to know what that child was doing in our garden. How did she get in? That wall must be eight feet high, and as I told your officers, we're scrupulous about shutting the double gates.'

Gesturing to a narrow side entrance, Brian said, 'She could have walked in there.'

Mrs Pendreich drew herself up. 'Not without being spotted,' she said sharply. 'We spend most of our day in the morning room. As you can see,' she pointed to another window, 'it has a clear view.'

'Perhaps we could have a word with Mr Pendreich,' Lisa suggested.

'The professor,' Celia Pendreich said, with heavy emphasis, 'won't tell you any different.'

'All the same,' said Brian. 'We'll need his account.'

'Very well.' Turning, 'If you'd care to follow me,' she led the way past the front of the house and around the corner, where a door faced the side entrance.

On the threshold she paused.

Lowering her voice, 'Before you speak to my husband, I should warn you, Harold has been forgetting things, so don't expect too much.'

A Present

Maggie bent low over the supine figure. 'Frankie?' she said softly. 'It's me, Mrs Laird.'

The head teacher had given Maggie the news the minute she arrived at Seaton, and she'd headed to the hospital as soon as she was free, stopping only to buy a gift at Blackwell's bookshop in the High Street.

Frankie's eyelids fluttered.

'Do you want me to stay?'

She nodded, lips forming the ghost of a smile.

With a backwards glance – by rights she shouldn't have been there, but the nurses' station had been unmanned and she'd stolen in, unseen – Maggie manoeuvred the heavy orthopaedic chair face-on to the bed. 'I've brought you a present,' she said.

Frankie's eyes blinked open.

Dipping into the bag she'd dumped on the floor, Maggie extracted a brightly-coloured package and laid it on the bedcover.

'Can I open it?'

'Go ahead.'

Frankie tore at the wrapping paper, discarding it in ragged shreds. Reading the book cover, 'All – The – Way – Down,' she enunciated carefully. 'Am-az-on – Rain – For-est.' Eyes shining, 'Banging! How did you know?'

Smiling, Maggie said, 'I know a lot of stuff.'

'Because you're a detective?'

'Who told you that?'

'Someone at school.'

'Playground gossip,' Maggie scoffed. 'Bet they didn't tell you in 2020, 120 seedlings were planted in the school garden to help its carbon footprint?'

Frankie looked suitably impressed. 'But you are a detective?' she persisted.

'I am. Not a police detective, though.'

'So you'd be allowed to keep a secret?'

The door flew open.

Heart thudding, Maggie turned, expecting to see Frankie's parents, the police perhaps.

'Stay where you are,' a young nurse said. She unhooked a chart from the foot of the bed. 'Just checking.'

When she had gone, Maggie said, 'That secret...'

Frankie laid the book to one side. Lifting her head from the bank of pillows, 'Promise you won't tell.'

'Promise,' Maggie said, one finger pressed to her lips.

Frankie's head sank back. 'Saturday night,' she confided, in a voice scarce more than a whisper. 'I got up for a drink of water. The living room door was open. Jason and Mum were lying on the settee. They were having sex,' she said matter-of-factly. 'Only his hands were around her neck, and Mum was saying, "No, no," in this weird voice.'

'What did you do?'

Frankie's eyes slid away. 'Nothing.'

Mind racing, Maggie said, 'Okay.'

'I must have made a noise,' Frankie continued, 'because Jason turned and saw me. I ran back to bed and snuggled down under the covers. Next thing someone yanked the duvet off. It was Jason. He shouted if I told anyone he'd do the same to me.'

Maggie said, 'Where was your mum when all this happened?'

'In the living room, I suppose.'

'Did you speak to either of them again that night?'

Frankie shook her head. 'They had a row. I could hear them. Then Jason left.'

'How about your mum?'

'She came into my bedroom, but...' Her eyes brimmed with tears. '...I pretended to be asleep.' Brushing the wetness away with the back of her hand, she added, 'Mum's been mad at me since I cut my hair. I didn't want to make things any worse.'

'And the next day?'

'She never mentioned it. I didn't either. Her and Jason row all the time, so there's no point.'

Maggie hazarded a guess. 'So you decided to run away.'

'I was going to go to school on Monday,' Frankie said. 'I was,' she insisted. 'I was going to tell you. Then I remembered you only work part-time.'

'That day in the playground,' Maggie began cautiously. 'Was that what you wanted to tell me: that you saw Jason hurting your mum?'

Frankie nodded.

'Had you seen him hurt her before?'

'Not like that. Usually, he'll pretend-fight: give her lots of little slaps. Then, Boom! He'll clobber her really hard.'

'How does your mum react?'

'Sometimes she throws him out. Then we won't see him for a few days. But she always let him back.'

'You could have told someone else: Miss Archibald, Mrs Shirreffs.'

Frankie shook her head, 'They would have phoned the social, and I'd have been put in care.'

'That wouldn't happen,' Maggie argued.

'Jason wouldn't have happened,' Frankie said stubbornly. 'Not if my dad was still around.'

'Is that the only thing that's been upsetting you?'

'School. I'm worried they don't like me.' Pulling a long face, Frankie added, 'The haircut doesn't help.'

'You don't like it?'

'Hate it,' she said vehemently, touching a hand to her shorn head. 'Hairdresser said it was the best she could do.'

'What is your mum saying?'

'That I'll have to put up with it till it grows.'

'Anything else?' Maggie pressed. 'Something you don't want to share with your mum, perhaps?'

'Loads of things.' Frankie mumbled, not meeting her eyes.

Maggie said, 'You could always tell me.'

But before she could say another word, Frankie had tugged the sheet up over her head.

Something to Tell You

'Brian!' Maggie exclaimed when she opened the door.

Looking sheepish, he said, 'I've news of DI Chisolm. Thought you'd want to know.'

Her heart soared. Then, just as quickly, sank. Allan Chisolm still hadn't returned her calls. Could it be someone else had got to him first: spelled out the extent of Wilma's meddling in police business?

She took in the damp shoulders of Brian's suit jacket, the hair plastered to his forehead. 'The rain's running out of you. You'd better come in.'

'Thanks.' He took a step forward, standing up close in the narrow hallway.

Maggie jumped back, the memory of their last encounter in her home vivid in her mind.

For a few moments they stood, awkward. Then, 'Come through. Let me get you a hot drink.'

Clearly embarrassed, 'I won't,' he said. 'If you don't mind. I've to get back to the station. Bit of a flap on.'

So Chisolm did know.

Brian's voice brought her back to the here and now.

'DI Chisolm has been called down to Glasgow. Family emergency.'

Maggie's mind ran riot. Allan had told her he was estranged from his wife. That it was unlikely they'd get back together. In her head, she constructed multiple scenarios:

Clare wanted a divorce.

Clare wanted to reconcile.

Chisolm wanted a divorce.

Chisolm wanted…

'An accident involving his daughter. The DI wants it kept quiet, at least until he has all the information. But I thought in the circumstances—'

It was Maggie's turn to look embarrassed. 'Thanks for taking the trouble to come across town,' she managed to squeeze out. 'Especially on a day like today. I understand you've a lot on your plate right now.'

'Yes,' he acknowledged, eyes travelling down to the wet patch on the carpet.

Looking up, their eyes met.

Brian looked, in that moment, so lost Maggie could have wrapped her arms around him.

Instead, 'Sit down for a few minutes, catch your breath. There's something I need to tell you.'

I Want My Dad

Brian was driving back to police HQ when Douglas's call came through on his Bluetooth. 'What's the latest on Frankie Bain?'

'She's looking more alert.'

'Is she talking?'

'Not to us,' Douglas replied. 'Susan had another go not long since.'

'What about the parents?'

'Isla's with Frankie now. Susan told me the most she'd managed to get out of her was, "I want my dad".'

'How about Stuart?'

'That's the thing. We've been trying to get hold of him, but his phone keeps going to voicemail. Do you think he's taken off?'

'I'll send a patrol car to Ferryhill to try and raise him,' Brian said. 'Take it from there. What's the prognosis on Frankie?'

'Injuries are consistent with a fall. Registrar says she may be hospitalized for some weeks, so we've plenty time to get the full story.'

'You're forgetting,' snapped Brian, 'upstairs are breathing down our necks. And it's not just upstairs. The bloody press pack is baying for blood.'

'Reporters are downstairs right now,' Douglas acknowledged. 'I spotted a bunch of them in the cafe. But don't worry, Sarge, the nursing staff won't let them near.'

Brian said, 'Lucky for you. If Frankie Bain talks to the press before we get a statement, you can wave bye-bye to your career.'

Douglas ventured, 'It's maybe worth mentioning, earlier on I spotted that Mrs Laird on the concourse. Know who I mean?'

'At ARI?'

Already, Brian could feel his blood pressure rise. Maggie wouldn't cut across the investigation, would she? Not after the conversation they'd just had. There would be a perfectly innocent explanation:

meeting Big Wilma off her shift, for instance. But if so, why hadn't she mentioned it?

'She wasn't anywhere near Frankie Bain?' he asked suspiciously.

'Dunno. Susan and I were downstairs, grabbing a bite.'

'Christ almighty! Can you not be relied upon to do any damn thing?'

'Well, I...'

'Get back into that room,' Brian roared. 'Don't leave that child's side until you've taken her statement. Got it?'

'Loud and clear.'

'In the presence of an appropriate adult, goes without saying.'

'Boss,' Douglas said.

End Of

Chin on chest, Harvey Sellars slumped on the hard seat, his solicitor by his side.

Brian had moved decisively. Dispatched Duffy and Haldane to obtain a statement from the Craigiebuckler witness. Then, when he'd reviewed the evidence, put in a request that Harvey Sellars attend for interview.

Now, he said, 'On the day of your father's death, you told officers you were in Dumfries on business.'

Harvey's head came up. 'That's correct.'

'Were you there all day?'

'Not the whole day.'

'What time did you leave?'

'Can't remember, not the exact time. I had meetings all morning. Then I grabbed something to eat. Mid-afternoon, probably.'

'You arrived back in Aberdeen when?'

'About teatime. I wasn't long back when two uniformed cops came knocking. Gave me the bad news.'

'You live in Craigiebuckler, is that correct?'

Harvey nodded.

'Please answer for the tape.'

'Yes.'

'How would you react if I told you we have a witness saw you there in the middle of the afternoon?'

'Who was that?' Harvey darted a sideways look at his solicitor, who responded with a barely perceptible shake of the head.

'Please answer the question.'

'I'd say they were wrong.'

'How would you answer if I said you've been lying about your whereabouts on the afternoon of your father's alleged suicide?'

Fists balled, Harvey Sellars leaned across the table. 'What do you mean, "alleged"? My dad committed suicide. End of.'

'That's yet to be established,' Brian said calmly. 'I repeat, do you admit you lied to my officers and, again, to me?'

Slouching back in his seat, 'Not lied as much as… Look, I might have got the time wrong.'

Susan joined the conversation. 'A further check on your schedule that day by Dumfries CID revealed…'

Colour drained from his face. In a gesture of defeat, 'Okay. I hold my hands up. I had an early meeting cancelled at the last minute. Begged a favour: got the next one brought forward. Meant I could skive back up the road.'

The detectives exchanged knowing looks. Somebody's head would roll.

Susan asked, 'Did you go straight home?'

Once more, Harvey's eyes slid sideways to the solicitor. He didn't respond.

'I'll ask you again: where did you go when you reached Aberdeen?'

'Mum had asked me to unblock a drain.' Shrugging, 'Dad was always too busy. I thought since I had time in hand, I'd go there first.'

Brian said, 'Talk me through your movements.'

'I gave the doorbell a quick buzz. I've a spare set of keys, but I thought someone was in because Dad's van was in the drive.'

'Was that usual?'

'No, but he could have nipped home for something. When there was no answer, I let myself in. Checked out the job. Went round to the garage for a plunger, and…'

'Go ahead.'

'…Dad was hanging from one of the crossbeams.'

'Alive?'

'I guess. His hands were pulling at the rope around his neck.'

'What did you do?'

'Just stood there in the doorway.'

'For how long?'

'No idea. Dad kept scrabbling at the rope. Kicking his legs out, like he was trying to reach the stepladder. But it was too lightweight. He only succeeded in sliding it further away.'

'You didn't think of rushing to his side? Moving the steps to support his weight?'

'No.' With a sheepish look, 'Must have been in shock.'

Brian said, 'I put it to you, when you found your father hanging in that garage, you not only failed to go to his assistance or summon an ambulance, you kicked that stepladder away?'

Cupping his hands over his ears, Harvey Sellars shouted, 'No.'

Susan came back in. 'Turning to your relationship with your dad, you've said it was difficult, is that not so?'

Harvey spread his hands on the table. 'We had our ups and downs.'

'How much of that was attributable, would you say, to his predilection for cross-dressing?'

He snorted. 'Bugger all. I couldn't have cared less. Might have been mortified when I was younger, but not these days. If I had a bone to pick, it was nothing to do with that.'

'What was it to do with?'

'What he did to me.'

'Can you be more specific?'

'I was adopted.'

Susan said, 'Lots of children are adopted.'

'Agreed. Except I didn't find out until I was about to get married.'

'How did that come about?'

'You need your birth certificate to post the banns. I'd never seen mine before. Why would I? Mum handled school stuff, medicals, all that side of things. At the time, I faced the pair of them down. Mum said she'd wanted to tell me since my eighteenth, but Dad wouldn't hear of it. Said we were happy as we were and it was dangerous to dig up the past.'

'I can understand your disappointment,' said Susan. 'But I'm sure your dad did it for the best.'

'"Disappointment"?' Harvey echoed. 'Growing up, I always

303

wondered why I didn't look the least bit like him. We didn't have one single thing in common.' Shaking with suppressed rage, 'That bastard stole my life.'

'Can you explain to me how?'

'Took me years to track down my birth mother. By the time I did, she was dead. Breast cancer. With her death I lost all hope of finding out who my father was. My real father. Lost sight of ever authenticating who I really am.'

'Your birth name…' Susan began.

'John Bishop. They sandwiched it between their own when they adopted me. Years I've been waiting to bring him out of the shadows, and now it's never going to happen.'

'So,' said Brian. 'I'll ask you again, when you came upon your adoptive father hanging in his garage, what did you do?'

Harvey said, 'Looked him in the eye. Though I doubt he even saw me. Then turned my back and walked away.'

XIV

More Fish in the Sea

'What did he want?' Wilma demanded.

'If you're referring to Brian Burnett, he came to bring me bad news.'

'To do with Brannigan?' Then, seeing Maggie's anguished expression, 'It's about Inspector Chisolm isn't it? Where is lover-boy? I thought he'd have been here like a shot the minute you picked up that phone.'

'Gone. Called away on a family matter.'

'Well, I wouldn't get your daunder up. There's plenty more fish in the sea, thon MacSorley fella for one. You said yourself he was heart-sore.' Wilma gave her a nudge. 'Must be worth a bob or two.'

'Drop it,' Maggie said.

'So you didn't pass on the Sellars intel?'

'On the contrary. I gave the information to Brian Burnett.'

'How did he react?'

'How do you think?'

'Dis-com-bob-u-lat-ed, I'll bet,' said Wilma, drawing on her new-found vocabulary. The syllables rolled off her tongue like cars off the Orkney ferry. Then, 'He didn't waste any time. Chisolm's no sooner out the way than he comes sniffing.'

'Talk about the pot calling the kettle black? Brian's car couldn't have been past the end of the road before you come calling.'

'I'm here on business,' Wilma protested.

Maggie straightened from loading the washing machine. 'Do you never sleep?'

'Old folk.' Wilma marched through to the dining room and plonked herself down at the table. 'They're the ones with the dosh. There's plenty of them an all, near on 20% of the population. Think of the money we could bring in.'

'How, exactly?' asked Maggie, following.

Wilma's face clouded. 'Well...'

'You haven't the faintest idea.'

'At least I come up with ideas. All I ever get from you is same old, same old. If you'll let me finish, old folk are soft targets. If it's not so-called builders at their door looking to fix the roof or lay the drive, it's push-pay conmen trying to press-gang them out of their savings.'

'Push-pay fraud is mostly perpetrated on the telephone,' Maggie countered. 'Plus, the mobile phone Sim farms are often based overseas, in places like Nigeria or India. Which brings us right back to where we started.'

'You're wrong,' Wilma argued. 'There's a long list of examples on Aberdeen Council's website: bogus callers trying to get into folk's homes by pretending to be someone they're not.'

Maggie's lip curled. 'That's rich coming from you.'

'And it doesn't stop there. Old folk aren't safe in their own homes. There was that case in Edinburgh: guy murdered a seventy-nine-year-old woman, after posing as a postman.'

'You've made your point. But where do we come into the mix?'

'Set up our own dating agency. I've done the homework. Not only is Scotland's population ageing, but the average household size has decreased, with one person households now the most common. Think about it.' She pulled a tragic face. 'All those lonely old souls.'

'They can't all be lonely,' said Maggie. 'Most of them will have families.'

'Who don't have any time for them.'

'Friends. Hobbies: gardening, knitting, whatever.'

'Still makes for a long day, sitting in a house on your own.'

'They can watch television. Then there's the radio. And books. And...'

'Folk still have a need for closeness and companionship. That mannie in Cove is a prime example.'

'Don't know what you're talking about,' Maggie said irritably.

'Woman didn't turn up for a medical appointment. When the police called at the house they found skeletal remains. Husband claimed his wife was abroad. Story goes he couldn't accept she had died.'

'You've been reading too many red-tops.'

'God's honest truth,' Wilma said, hand on heart.

'He could have bought a pet.'

'You've pets on the bloody brain. Did you know there are dozens of dating sites in the UK for the over 60s?'

'All the more reason for us to stay well out. We've been down that road,' Maggie grouched. 'We should learn from it.'

'It could run side-by-side with the data match screening and our other investigation business. Think of the billing hours: one lot for running a background check on their dating match, another for...' Re-arranging her up-do, Wilma said, '...I don't know, getting a payout off some dodgy double-glazing firm.'

Maggie said, 'You haven't thought this through. It's just another crazy idea floated on a wing and a prayer. What's more, it points to a clear conflict of interest. We can't be seen to be setting folk up and then profiting from their mistakes. We've our reputation to think of.'

Wilma made to rise. 'There's no point me sticking around, if all you're going to do is shoot me down in flames.'

'I'm being practical. There aren't enough hours in the day as it is. Besides, to quote an expression of yours: "You can't ride two horses with one arse".'

The silence between them stretched.

Maggie was first to break the impasse. 'When it comes to skillsets, would it be fair to say I'm the one with the more intellectual lean-ings. You're the one with the...'

'...imagination.'

'Yes, well—' Swallowing the implied criticism, she said, 'I've been mulling over how we can differentiate ourselves from our competi-tors. It's not enough just to say we're female. When you think about it, both romance scams and fraud targeting older people play to our strengths as mature women. Between us, we've a wealth of life experience. We've experienced relationship difficulties, bereavement. Maybe we should focus on domestic cases.'

Wilma leapt on the idea. 'The field's wide open: cheating partner, pre-marital background checks, hidden children.'

Picking up the thread, Maggie added, 'Co-habitation. Child custody issues or non-compliance with court orders.'

'Nanny cams,' Wilma continued. 'Divorce, adoption and peace of mind enquiries. Domestic staff background checks.'

'Finding birth parents. Tracing adopted children.'

Wilma rubbed her hands together. 'Now we're motoring.'

'Question is, how do we reach our target audience?'

'Run ads in the press. It has a proven success rate. And old folk still read newspapers. Look at the stuff in the Sundays: ads for stairlifts and wide-fit sandals and God knows what.'

Maggie said, 'Advertising is expensive.'

'Not if you stick to local papers like The Deeside Piper, The Inverurie Herald, The Buchan Observer. Then there's The People's Friend. That has a wide readership.'

'If we spend money on advertising, we'll have to charge a premium. How do we justify that?'

'Use the right language to pull them in: "discreet", "trustworthy", "take the risk out of"', "complete peace of mind".'

'You can't make claims you can't substantiate,' Maggie countered. 'You'd have to say, "cut the risk" or "increased peace of mind."'

'You're splitting hairs. All I'm saying is, we bill them for the initial consultation, charge a premium for the background check, bill again for our report. Think about it, we'll be doing these old folk a favour. They've money to spend and no time left to spend it.'

'Well,' Maggie deliberated. 'If you put it that way.'

'Plus, we'd be using our full skillset.'

'We'd hang onto our corporate clients,' she qualified. 'Add to them as and when we can.'

'We wouldn't turn our noses up at anything interesting came our way, would we?' Wilma asked doubtfully.

Maggie shot her an old-fashioned look. 'As if I could stop you,' she said.

Death Drop

'Settle down,' Brian said, in a pale attempt at aping Chisolm.

Mel Coutts had elevated him to Acting Detective Inspector. Brian had swelled with pride when he'd reported to the DCI's office to be told the news. His buoyant mood evaporated as he retraced his steps. In the DI's absence, the buck stopped squarely with him.

Now, 'Bring me up to speed on Operation Eco-Warrior.'

Susan said, 'I spoke to the paramedics who attended at The Chanonry. When they extracted Frankie Bain from the wreckage of the tree-house, she was in a right state: filthy, hair matted, clothes stiff with dirt. Feral, almost. Looked like she'd made a groundsheet out of the tent. The sleeping bag she was in was sodden. It's a wonder she didn't die of hypothermia.'

'Tree canopy would have saved her,' said Duffy. 'Lucky she scarpered when she did. A few weeks later, the leaves would have dropped.'

Douglas came in. 'Lucky only up to a point. That tree-house collapsed so suddenly, Frankie didn't have the chance to save herself. According to the paramedics, she landed flat on her back with one leg tucked under her.'

'Death drop,' Susan piped up. 'It's a dance position. Favoured by drag queens.'

Duffy snorted. 'Try telling that to Vinnie Sellars.'

'God's honest truth. There's even a West End play by that name.'

Brian asked, 'Had Frankie been there the whole time?'

'Pretty much.'

'What did she do for food? Did she say?'

'Scavenged in bins,' Susan replied. 'That, and ate scraps left out for the birds.'

Douglas said, 'The report from Mitchell's Hospital, could it have been Frankie stealing the cat's dinner?'

'Quite possibly.'

Brian again. 'She didn't interact with anybody?'

'Said not, other than a man walking his dog. Apparently she stopped to pat it. Frankie must have looked distressed, because he asked her if she was okay.'

'This man,' said Brian. 'Did you get a description?'

'Affirmative. Didn't fit any of our suspects. That apart, Frankie said when she was on the move, she hid when she saw someone coming.'

'What I don't get,' Duffy puzzled. 'If the kid was so concerned for her mum's safety, why did she run away?'

'Thought her dad would ride to the rescue,' Brian answered. 'Response ran down Stuart Bain sleeping off a bender. Sobered up when he heard Frankie was in hospital. They gave him a lift to Foresterhill. He's just off the phone.'

Lisa had been quiet. Now, she asked, 'What's he saying?'

'Frankie told him she thought the separation was temporary. She knew her mum was mad at her dad, but thought he'd talk her round. Then she heard Isla on the phone talking about divorce, and panicked. Reckoned if she ran away, it would give her mum and dad such a fright they'd get back together.'

Susan said, 'Poor kid. You can bang on all you like about nuclear families, but children just want security: loving parents, food on the table, a warm bed at night.'

'Get you,' Lisa remarked. 'Into psychology are we?'

'You do any better?' asked Douglas.

Bristling, Lisa said, 'It's not you I'm talking to. You haven't exactly covered yourself in glory, have you, sunshine?'

'That's rich,' he sneered. 'Coming from you.' They'd all heard the rumours by now.

Brian banged a closed fist on the table. 'More pertinent, Stuart Bain also alleges his wife was repeatedly assaulted by Jason Eadie, and that a number of these assaults were witnessed by his daughter.'

Douglas whooped, 'Knew he was our man.'

'We'll see about that.'

Duffy again. 'So Frankie doesn't have gender or sexuality issues?'

'Not that she's admitting to,' Susan replied.

'What about the razor blade?'

'Said she found it on the windowsill after the painter had gone. Hid it under the bed in case Jason threatened her again.'

'And the blood?'

'Cut herself in the process and wrapped her finger in the first thing that came to hand.'

Duffy's eyebrows shot up to meet his non-existent hairline. 'And you'd believe that?'

'There's nothing says otherwise.'

'Does the kid's account tally with the forensic report, Sarge?' Then, hastily, 'Sorry, I mean boss. Assuming the effing report has materialised.'

Brian acknowledged Duffy's apology with a curt nod. 'Test results were inconclusive. What I can tell you is the blood wasn't menstrual.'

'So Frankie could have been cutting herself?'

Susan said, 'If it was significant, wouldn't the hospital have flagged that up?'

'She might have made an attempt, and given up.'

'While we're on the subject of forensics,' said Duffy. 'Anything back on the Fittie case?'

Brian sighed. 'Not a thing. Pathology said it could take long enough to get ID.'

'If they ever do.'

'On other developments, we've had intel on the Sellars case.'

'Where from?' Duffy asked.

Brian tapped the side of his nose. 'Don't get too excited. Suffice to say, I've had Harvey Sellars in. He's admitted to being present at the scene, but denied any involvement in the suicide.'

'But...' Lisa began.

'It raises as many questions as it answers. How reliable are the witnesses? What were his movements between the verifiable time he arrived back in Aberdeen and response calling at his home?'

'He could have been anywhere,' said Duffy. 'Covered his tracks.'

Brian nodded. 'We'll need to overlay Harvey's account with witness evidence. Seek out inconsistencies. We'll be pushed to build a case, so keep it under your hats for now. Getting back to the matter in hand, Bob, send a couple of uniforms to bring Eadie in.'

'Will do.'

'Douglas and Susan, head back up to ARI. Find somewhere relatively private. Take a statement from Isla Bain. And keep your eyes peeled for any injuries. See if we can put a case together.'

'Boss.'

That's all for now. Thanks, everyone. Stick with it.'

Some Women

'This is harassment,' Jason said, when Susan had read out the caution.

'Something you'd know all about.'

'Don't know what you mean.'

For some minutes they sat, eyeballing each other, Jason affecting a casual pose, Susan re-appraising her interview plan. She'd expected him to go 'no comment', having declined the offer of a duty solicitor.

Alongside, Brian's thoughts whirled. Chisolm had briefed him on Lisa's entanglement with Harry Geddes. Told him to play for time. Plus, he was expecting a summons from Mel Coutts at any moment.

Susan jotted a note. 'Are you in a relationship, Jason?'

'Off and on.'

'With Isla Bain?'

His chest swelled visibly. 'Her and the rest.'

'These relationships, would you describe them as intimate?'

Stripping her with his eyes, Jason replied, 'What do you think?'

Susan smiled. 'I'm the one asking the questions.' Glancing up at the camera, 'For the recording, can I take that as a yes?'

'Yes,' he muttered.

'These intimate relationships, would you call them confrontational?'

He raised a questioning eyebrow.

'Do you row a lot?'

'No more than most. Women,' he complained. 'They can wind you up.'

Leaning forward, Brian confided, 'And how. To the extent you could bloody kill them.'

Vigorously, Jason nodded his agreement.

'How would you react,' Susan pressed, 'if I said that's what happened last Saturday night when you were with Isla Bain?'

'Hang on,' he said, jumping to his feet. 'What are you trying to pin on me?'

Brian commanded, 'Sit down.'

With a poisonous expression look, Jason did so.

'I put it to you,' said Susan, 'that you put your hands around Isla Bain's neck, compressed her throat and did attempt to strangle her.'

His eyes widened. 'That's not true.'

'We have a witness.'

'If you mean the kid, she'd say anything to get shot of me.'

'Why is that, Jason?'

'Kid hates me.'

'Does she have good reason?'

His lip curled. 'Like what?'

'Like the play-fights that end up in punches.' Noting Jason's surprise, Susan added. 'Oh, yes, we know all about those. Just like we know about the repeated calls your ex-partner made to the emergency services alleging domestic abuse.'

With a sneer, he said, 'She never made a formal complaint.'

Brian again. 'Not then. But times have changed. You may be interested to know she has moved on from the women's refuge and is happily settled with a new partner.'

'Bully for her.'

'So happily settled she's ready to reconsider.'

'What do you mean?' Jason asked, his tone uncertain.

'Press charges.'

'Fucking bitch!'

Susan said, 'To return to Isla Bain.'

'We were having sex. Gerrit?'

She raised an eyebrow. 'And?'

'Rough sex. They like it, women.'

'Some women,' Susan qualified.

He smirked. 'There you are, then.'

'I hate to disappoint you, Jason,' she said smoothly. 'But rough sex isn't a defence, not anymore.'

Momentarily, he looked panicked. Then, recovering, 'It's her word against mine.'

'You're wrong,' Susan countered. 'The medics at ARI have examined the marks on Isla Bain's neck, and....'

'Okay,' said Jason, holding up his hands. 'But it was just sex. I wasn't trying to kill her, I swear.'

Always

'I feel such a fool,' Maggie wailed, 'I told everyone who would listen that Frankie Bain had gender issues. Even Allan Chisolm.' Her heart stuttered at the sound of his name.

Brian quirked an eyebrow. 'She hasn't?' He was sitting in the big chair in the bay window, a boyish figure in a slim-fitting grey flannel suit.

Maggie felt a sudden pang of nostalgia for the old days: happy days, when Brian would sit chatting in the kitchen with George, or the three of them would share a meal.

'I don't know. Frankie wouldn't open up to me. She might be gay. She might be trans. She may just be confused about her sexuality. Identity and sexuality issues sometimes mask underlying psychological problems, and puberty is an unsettling time for kids, whatever their sexual orientation or gender identity. Speaking for myself, it came as a huge shock: what it means to be female, with all its implications.'

Brian said, 'What's the protocol in these situations?'

'If Frankie does have gender dysphoria and chooses to seek help, she'll initially be referred – whether by the school, her parent, GP or an outside agency – to the Gender Identity Clinic at Cornhill.'

'Then what?'

'NHS advice for children is "watchful waiting". If Frankie did ultimately want to go down the path of medical intervention, it would take place at the Sandyford Gender Identity Clinic in Glasgow. Regardless, what she needs right now is support: a solid framework that will give her the confidence to open up, whether at home, at school or in a clinical setting. And with all the changes in her life recently, that support framework has been lacking.'

'Poor kid.'

'One of many, sadly.' Hesitantly, 'Did you manage to make anything of Wilma's intel on that suicide?'

Brian threw her a cautionary look. 'I'm working on it.'

'It's just, she'll have seen your car, and...'

'Better we don't go there,' he said stiffy. Then, relenting, 'Tell her it's under investigation.'

Trying to keep her voice light, Maggie asked, 'How is Allan, by the way?'

'Not in a good place,' Brian replied. 'He hasn't been in touch?'

'Other than a couple of texts.'

Maggie would never have imagined she'd have felt Allan Chisolm's absence so acutely. It wasn't as if they were partners. Lovers, granted. But even their love-making had been sporadic. Beneath her blue lambswool jumper, she trembled at the memory.

'Pretty much radio silence my end, too. Any news we do get is channelled through the DCI. I gather Allan's daughter is out of danger, but recovery is going to be a long haul. If she makes a full recovery.'

'Do you think he'll come back?' Maggie asked in a small voice.

'He has no option. Loose ends to tie up, if nothing else.' Then, seeing Maggie's stricken expression, 'I'm sure it will all work out.'

'Where does that leave you?'

'Spare prick at a wedding,' he replied with a bitter laugh.

'Come on,' Maggie said. 'I'm sure that's not true.'

'You lie with such fluency these days,' he came back. 'Must have got that from Big Wilma.'

Maggie's eyes dropped to the carpet. Brian knew her through and through.

'Seriously,' he continued. 'As the saying goes, every cloud has a silver lining. For as long as Allan Chisolm is in Glasgow, I'm Acting DI. If I keep my nose clean, the powers that be might make it permanent.'

Maggie was in two minds whether to be glad or sorry. 'You deserve it,' she said, without conviction.

Brian rose. Crossing to the sofa, he dropped on one knee and took her hands in his. 'You know I have feelings for you, Maggie.'

Her pulse raced. 'I know,' she whispered, mouth bone dry.

He offered a sad smile. 'Always have. Always will. But...'

She waited, heart thudding.

'...I've come to accept we're never going to make it. As an item, I mean.'

Her whole body relaxed.

'Can we settle for best friends?' he pleaded, looking just like a loveable puppy-dog.

Loosening her hands from his grasp, Maggie enveloped him in a tender embrace.

'Always,' she said.

A Practical Solution

Brian wasn't long gone when Maggie's phone pinged.

She checked the display: Allan Chisolm.

Swiping the screen. 'Allan?'

'Maggie.'

Her heart skipped a beat.

'Sorry I haven't been in touch. I've been at the hospital. Phone's been switched off.' His voice sounded remote, distracted. 'You'll have heard.'

'Yes. Brian came over.'

'Good man.'

Before she could help herself, 'Where are you staying?' Maggie blurted.

'At home.'

'Oh.'

'It's not what you're thinking. A practical solution. Being under the same roof helps co-ordinate visits, that sort of thing. It all happened in such a rush,' he added, by way of compensation.

'I understand,' Maggie lied.

Though she didn't.

Not one bit.

'How is...' She hesitated, not wanting to voice Clare's name. 'Everyone?'

'Alice is in a bad way, as you can imagine.'

'But she's out of intensive care?'

'She is, thank God. Hannah flew in from New York a couple of days ago. At least I think it was two days. I've lost track of time.'

'That must be a comfort.'

'I can't tell you. It's months since I saw her last. Would be wonderful to be all back together, were it not for...' His voice cracked with emotion.

'I can imagine,' said Maggie, a dull ache in the pit of her stomach. 'How is...' she steeled herself to say 'Clare', then chickened out, 'your wife holding up?'

'Magnificently, as ever. What I mean is...' This was followed by an embarrassed silence. '...Clare is a strong woman. Bit like you.'

Only not, Maggie thought sourly.

She wondered whether the new boyfriend had been given his marching orders. If Allan and Clare had slept together. The prospect made her feel physically sick.

'How long...?' she began.

'Too early to say. Look, this isn't a good time. I'm at the hospital right now. I've just nipped outside for a breath of air. And to call you. Didn't want you thinking I'd taken off without...'

...a backward glance.

In her head, Maggie finished the sentence.

'Would I do that?' she said, struggling to keep her voice light.

His tone softened. 'You're such a worrier, Maggie Laird. I'm sorry to have added to your travails. But whatever develops...'

Silence hung between them a thundercloud.

'...I'll keep you informed, I promise.'

Quines of Crime

'Good news,' Maggie beamed, from her seat in a buttoned red leather booth. 'Just took the call. We've landed another corporate client: legal firm in Golden Square. Trial period,' she cautioned. 'But if all goes to plan, it will be steady money coming in.'

Across the table, 'Call that good news?' Wilma groused.

They were in Topolobamba, a Mexican street food restaurant at the west end of Union Street. "Cheap and cheerful", Wilma said, when she'd talked Maggie into taking the night off. And cheerful it most certainly was, its vibrant turquoise fascia reflected by the frontage of the bar, where the restaurant's name was spelled out in illuminated scarlet letters.

The smile wiped from Maggie's face. 'Don't be such a killjoy.'

'It's not me that's the problem. I've bust a gut for this business, and all I get is flak.'

'Oh, Wilma,' Maggie said, crestfallen. 'All I want is for us to be the best we can be.'

'We're on the same page there. I've been knocking my pan out trying to better myself since the day I moved in next door.'

'I know.'

'You don't know the half of it. Expanding my vo-cab-u-lar-y.' This last enunciated with precision. 'Ian doesn't see the point, but I think if you speak proper, folk give you your place.'

'How is he?'

'Does nothing but moan these days. Complains I sit half the night reading up on PI stuff. Starve myself. All so I can be more like you.'

Taking both Wilma's hands in hers, Maggie said, 'And I've spent the past however long trying to be more like you. You've taught me a lot: not just updating my computer skills, but real business savvy. I'm more self-confident. When I think back to when we started out.'

'Pair of eejits.'

'I wouldn't go as far as that.'

'Jeez,' Wilma burst out, 'can we not agree on any damn thing?' Upending her bottle of Corona, 'Here's to us.'

'To us,' Maggie echoed, picking up her frozen margarita.

'While I remember, Carruthers case. How did the client react?'

Wilma had reported back on her conversation with Anne Cromar, but hadn't had a chance to sit down with Maggie and learn how her findings had been received.

'Fell about laughing,' Maggie replied. 'Caught me sideways, I must say. I thought Flo Carruthers would be disappointed we didn't find any skeletons in the subject's cupboard.'

'Not like the mannie in Cove,' Wilma joked, scooping guacamole from a turquoise pottery bowl onto a cheese-coated tortilla chip.

Lips pursed, Maggie said, 'That's in poor taste.'

Wilma doused the nacho in sour cream. 'Sorry.'

'No abandoned wives,' Maggie ran on. 'No. children, legitimate or otherwise. No trail of debt. No nasty habits.'

'And true to his profile. According to the ex-girlfriend, he's comfortably off, and his interests check out. Except for that one detail,' Wilma said, 'The adoption. Anne Cromar told me finding out so late in life the Sellars weren't his real parents damaged Harvey's self-confidence and had an impact on his mental health.'

'To the extent he'd murder his dad in cold blood?'

'I never said that,' Wilma countered, sitting up straight. 'But he sure as hell was involved.'

'That's for the police to establish.'

'What do you think they'll charge him with?'

'Assisting a suicide? Perverting the course of justice? I don't know.'

'And another thing…' Cupping a hand to her mouth, Wilma bent to whisper in Maggie's ear.

'You don't say!' she exclaimed, eyes out on stalks.

'Gospel,' said Wilma.

Maggie picked at a lamb tostada. 'Poor man. It's usually women you hear about being criticised for their physical attributes, you don't think it applies equally to men.'

'Probably explains why his marriage was so short-lived.'

'And why he doesn't have many Facebook friends.'

'Couldn't he have done something about it?'

'What?' said Wilma, taking a long swig of beer. 'Hang weights on it, like them holy men in India?'

Glancing over her shoulder, Maggie warned, 'Keep your voice down.'

'Have you heard anything back from Brian.'

'Not a dickey bird.'

'Well,' said Wilma through a mouthful of nacho, 'I hope I didn't go to all that effort for nothing.'

Taking a sudden interest in her tostada, Maggie murmured, 'Whatever.'

'I take it the client won't be going on that date?'

'Correct.'

'She will pay us?'

'Didn't turn a hair when I presented our invoice. Said she was better off knowing now than later. Not only that, she called me this afternoon: she has another match lined up she wants us to check out.'

'Magic,' said Wilma, draining her glass. Indicating Maggie's drink, 'Will I get another round in?'

'Not for me.'

'Come on. What with Carruthers and getting the ad campaign up and running, we've cause to celebrate.'

'All the same, might be sensible to wait until we've measured the response.'

'It'll be mega.'

'I hope so. Failing that, the corporate income stream is finally looking healthier.'

Wilma's mouth turned down. 'You don't say.'

She signalled to a guy in a sombrero, 'Same again.'

When the drinks arrived, 'Any news of lover boy?'

'Don't call him that,' Maggie huffed. 'Anyhow...' She glugged an icy mouthful. '...we were never that close.'

'Come off it,' said Wilma, greedily necking her beer. 'You've been acting like a lovesick schoolgirl.'

Maggie set down her drink. 'I've spent half my life spent cooking and cleaning and picking up after people. George is dead. My kids don't need me anymore. It's my time. I've decided to move on.'

'Don't make any hasty decisions.'

'Never thought I'd see the day I was the one wanting to break out and you were the one urging caution.'

Wilma reached for the menu, 'Fancy a pudding?'

Maggie shook her head. 'I'm stuffed, but don't let me stop you.'

Beaming, Wilma read, 'Chocolate chilli ice cream. Sounds just the ticket.' She motioned to a waiter. Pointing to the menu, 'I'll have that. And another two margaritas.'

'Not for me,' said Maggie. 'I've drunk quite enough. '

'Relax! They're all ice.' Then, 'What's the latest from Seaton? That wee Frankie still in hospital?'

'You don't know? I thought you'd have been over to Westburn like a bullet. But, yes, they're going to keep her in for a few days yet.'

Wilma said, 'That leg will be in plaster for a while. When it comes off, her fractures will probably need regular checks. Make sure they've healed properly.'

'The good news is, I heard from Lynsey Archibald, Stuart and Isla Bain have agreed to go for marriage guidance counselling. Plus, Frankie has been invited to a birthday party the week after next. It's not a lot, but it's something. Hopefully, she'll begin to make friends.'

'Unlike that kid they found on the beach at Fittie.'

Pushing her plate aside, Maggie said, 'On a cheerier note, how are your boys?'

'Least said soonest mended. What about your two? Kirsty's boyfriend still around?'

'Seems so. And Ellie's such a fixture in our house I think,

sometimes, she'd be quicker moving in.'

'Two frozen margaritas,' their waiter said, setting the drinks on the table. 'And one chocolate chilli ice cream.'

'Yum,' Wilma said, reaching for her spoon. Through a mouthful of ice cream, she mumbled, 'I've been thinking. What you said about the competition. We may have started small, made mistakes along the way. But we have the knowhow, the initiative, the determination to be as good as any of the big detective agencies.'

'Better,' said Maggie. 'Not despite being women. Because we're women.'

'Strong women,' Wilma added, putting her spoon down.

'Shmart women,' Maggie slurred. 'We'll blaze a trail. Confound our critics. And that includes bloody Allan Chisolm.' Reaching for her drink, 'We're gonna shmash that glass ceiling.'

'Get you,' Wilma marvelled. 'If this is what a couple of margaritas does for you, bring it on.'

Swaying in her seat, Maggie mouthed, 'Know something? You're a total star.'

Coyly, Wilma dipped her chin. 'You an' all.'

Maggie raised her glass in a toast. 'Here's to us.'

'Quines of Crime,' Wilma pronounced, gleefully slapping her thighs. 'Beat that for a strapline.'

Maggie smiled a glassy mile. 'Quines of Crime.'

Sources

Gender Recognition Reform (Scotland) Bill

Supporting Transgender Pupils in Schools: Guidance for Scottish Schools

NHS Sandyford Gender Service

Stonewall Scotland

Mermaids

Scottish Trans Alliance

LGBT Youth Scotland

LGBT Health and Wellbeing

Four Pillars

TransparenTsees

2020 Bell v Tavistock (overturned on appeal 2021)

2020 Ipsos Mori Poll: Sexual orientation and attitudes to LGBTQ+ in Britain.

Torrey Peters, *Detransition, Baby* (Serpent's Tail, 2021)